A fighter withou
Can she trust hi.   .... just another lost
cause?

Angel

By day, I do all the grunt work at my family's struggling L.A.
brewery. By night, I blow off steam at an underground fight
club. I never thought the pandemic would bring Deanna
Delgado back into my life—the woman who ghosted me three
years ago after one unforgettable night. But the brewery needs a
miracle to survive. And that miracle could cost me the only
person who's ever had faith in me.

Deanna

My family calls me an idealistic do-gooder, but I see a better,
brighter future for my community. My biggest problem? I've
just lost the job I love. To ease my pain, I've hooked up with
Angel Rosas, the filthy-sweet one-night stand who's somehow
dropped back into my life. There's so much more to Angel than
he lets on. Is he the man I can trust with my body and my heart?
Or is he just another lost cause?

PRAISE FOR THIRSTY BY MIA HOPKINS

ONE OF THE BEST ROMANCE NOVELS OF THE YEAR. "A powerful, honest look at love as both a motivation and a risk."

THE WASHINGTON POST

"Thirsty held me captivated from its first page to its last . . . A singular reading experience."

USA TODAY

"Bold and unapologetic . . . Well written with honest descriptions, vibrant characters, and an impactful narrative."

SMEXY BOOKS

"A brilliant read. There are good writers, and then there are writers that just leave you in awe. And Hopkins has definitely left me in awe."

HYPABLE

"A sizzling, emotionally intense story that is both gritty and heartwarming, an addictive page-turner that will stay with me for a long time to come."

"Sexy and soul-wrenching, with Sal's irresistible voice luring you through a living, breathing Los Angeles."

"An amazing read! I stayed up way too late to finish and haven't stopped thinking about the characters. Highly recommended!"

"Mia Hopkins keeps it sexy in *Trashed*, wrapping Eddie and Carmen's romance in a story that's ultimately about culture, community, and the happily ever after we all deserve."

THE DAILY WAFFLE

"Delightfully raunchy, yet tender and loving. Hopkins does a great job of capturing both the vulnerability and the passion of sex in her writing."

BUSTLE

TANKED

AN EASTSIDE BREWERY NOVEL

MIA HOPKINS

AUTHOR'S NOTE

Tanked is a standalone contemporary high-heat romance novel with a happily ever after. This book is for mature readers only. It mentions explicit sex, violence, homelessness, poverty, child and domestic abuse, substance abuse, postpartum depression, illness and loss of life spurred by the covid pandemic. Please exercise caution if these are sensitive topics for you.

Un brindis por aquellos que nos miran y sonríen desde el cielo.

PROLOGUE
DEANNA

NO DOUBT ABOUT IT. I am getting wing-manned.

Wing Man and his buddy, Bad Haircut, work in an office building downtown. I didn't catch what they do. I'm smiling and pretending to listen. Luckily, the loud music here in the brewery keeps me from having to pretend too hard.

Out of the corner of my eye, I keep a close watch on my coworker Ingrid. She is tipsy, and her cheerful unguardedness makes her even more attractive to men than usual.

Bad Haircut is slightly older than Wing Man. At first, he was the introverted one of the pair. After three beers, this is no longer the case. He and Ingrid are dancing even though nobody else is dancing. He says something. She laughs and flips her hair. He says something else. She laughs and flips her hair again. Ad nauseam.

On the barstool next to me, Wing Man looks bored. He pulls out his phone. There's a photo of a young woman and a baby.

"That's my girlfriend. That's our little girl. She's seven months old. I love them so much."

The line sounds canned. If it's a trick, it's a good one, if not too subtle.

I can't believe I drew my eyebrows in for this.

Carefully, I adjust my glasses, look at the phone and back up at him. "Oh, they're beautiful!" I try to appear appropriately heartbroken that he is off the market. Satisfied, he smiles to himself and returns the phone to his pocket.

I take a long drink of my beer.

After a few more songs, Ingrid and I make quick eye contact. She touches her left earring. That means, "Let's get out of here." Right earring means, "You can go home. I'll text you the address where I end up for the night."

We tell the gentlemen we have to go—no explanations besides it's late and we weren't meaning to stay out. Bad Haircut protests. I have a feeling he doesn't get out much because when we apologize, instead of being cool, he gets aggressive.

"Aw, why you gotta go?" He leans too close to Ingrid. I slip between them and hold a hand up to help him keep his distance.

"Don't touch me," he growls at me.

"Dude, I didn't," I say. I look at Wing Man. "Come get your boy."

Wing Man shrugs and stays seated. "Don't make her mad," he tells his friend. "Big girl like that? She'll take you out, bro."

Bad Haircut stands between us and the door. "One more drink," he tells Ingrid.

She's too unsteady on her feet to do much more than smile and lean on me.

"It's time for us to pay up and go," I try to move Ingrid toward the other end of the bar, but Bad Haircut is in our way.

"How about you just go," Wing Man says to me. He waves his hand in my face. "Bye-bye."

His friend laughs and reaches for Ingrid.

I see a flash of the Eastside Brewery T-shirt before I know what's going on.

"Holy shit," Ingrid says in my ear.

I turn. The crowd has parted. By the front door, I see a tall barback holding Ingrid's would-be lover by the collar. He uses the man's body to bang the door open. The patrons inside the brewery let out a collective gasp as he grabs Bad Haircut by the back of the belt, lifts him off his feet and swings him forward in a perfect arc. Then the barback lets go. We watch as Bad Haircut goes sailing and lands face-first on the sidewalk outside.

Wisely, he stays down.

The barback and the bouncer seated outside give each other a friendly little fist bump.

The crowd applauds and closes up like stage curtains.

I've never seen anything like this in real life. I am thoroughly impressed. Ingrid giggles. When I call for the check, I notice Wing Man is nowhere to be found—flown away, I guess.

Outside, the summer night is muggy and warm. There's no sign of Wing Man or Bad Haircut. Thank God. As the bouncer keeps an eye on us, I wait with Ingrid for her ride. I notice she's glowing and she stands up straighter, like a plant that needed to be watered and finally got a drink. She loves it when guys lose their shit over her, and she thrives on drama like this.

Her grumpy sister arrives at last. She's got rollers in her hair. I help Ingrid into the car, make sure she's buckled in, and shut the door.

"That was so much fun. Let's do this again?" Ingrid says through her open window. "Next Friday night?"

I don't really want to go out again, but I know she's trying to get my mind off my mess of a love life. "Sure," I say.

They drive off.

After a short walk, I reach my car. As I pull out my keys, I realize with a flash of annoyance that I've forgotten something. When I signed for the tab, I left my credit card on the tray.

"Son of a bitch," I mumble to myself.

Eastside Brewery closes earlier than regular bars. It's midnight when I arrive again. The bouncer is gone, so I let myself in through the unlocked door. The lights are on, but the place is empty and the music is off. I feel like I'm sneaking backstage after a show.

"Hello?" I shut the door behind me.

I know the owners, so I know a little of the brewery's backstory. I spot clues that this place used to be a bakery. There are marks on the polished concrete floor where display cases were once installed. I look up and see high ceilings, vents and fans. In the refrigerators that used to hold birthday cakes, wedding cakes and pasteles de tres leches, I see rows of cans and bottles filled and ready to take home.

I walk up to the bar. "Hello?" I say again.

No answer.

I creep behind the counter and through the swinging doors into the kitchen. A big, shirtless man stands by the mop sink in the corner. His Eastside Brewery T-shirt hangs on a nearby shelf. The water is running loudly into the bucket, echoing in the big space.

"Eddie?" I say.

The man shuts off the water, wipes his hands on his apron, and turns around. "Naw, Eddie went home." He has a quiet, deep voice. He steps out of the shadows. "Can I help you?"

I'm twenty-eight years old. My career as a social worker has ensured I've seen a cross section of humanity, a striated rainbow of highs and lows. I grew up in a tough neighborhood, got scholarships, navigated the bullshit and institutionalized racism of the university system, got jobs, lost jobs. I've fallen in love and had my heart broken—but let's not talk about that, not tonight. I have a big, overbearing family who taught me that if life knocks me down nine times, I had better get up ten—otherwise, I'm not fit to call myself a Delgado.

All this to say...I think I'm a tough cookie.

I guess even tough cookies crumble in the face of nuclear hotness.

"Can I help you?" Shirtless asks again. His dark eyebrows furrow.

The barback—it's him. Up close, I see he is younger than me, and he's tall, ridiculously tall, maybe a foot above my five-foot-three. He's got wavy dark hair and the very first chapter of an excellent beard. Eastside Brewery owes a small portion of its popularity to its owners, Eddie and Sal, two handsome brothers who are very much off the market but still make awesome eye candy.

In my opinion, they aren't even in the same league as this guy.

I struggle to keep my eyes on the level. This is not easy when there's a big naked chest in your face. Fit but not bulky, he is cut and carries his muscle well. Smoky gray tattoos enhance his shoulders, his chest, his abs, his—

"Miss?" He lifts one eyebrow.

I blink. "Oh, yes. Excuse me. I'm looking for my card."

"Your credit card? Did you lose it here?"

"No, I left it. On the tray, I think. After I signed my check. About half an hour ago or so," I babble. "Eddie's not here?" I know Eddie—Eddie's safe.

"He went home," Shirtless says again. "But I can help you. Come with me."

I follow him out the swinging doors and stare freely at his smooth, muscled back. There are tattoos here for me to ogle too —skulls, roses, feathers, Aztec iconography, and the word Fallen in spidery, delicate script.

For the first time in a long time, I feel it.

Desire.

I want to touch this man so badly my fingertips tingle. Instead, I keep my arms straight down my sides and walk stiffly to where he stands by the bar.

He pulls a ring of keys from his pocket and unlocks a safe under the counter. Inside there's a wallet, a silver bracelet and a small cardboard box of credit cards.

"Happens a lot here," Shirtless says. "People get drunk and forget they had a tab."

"I wasn't drunk," I say quickly. "I rarely get drunk. I think I was just in a hurry to get home after all that...stuff. Also, it's late for me. I have to work tomorrow, pretty early, in fact."

He nods. I don't think he's listening. "What's your name?"

"Deanna Delgado."

"Delgado," he mutters to himself. His long, strong fingers rifle through the cards, and I notice—with some thrill—that he doesn't wear a wedding ring. "Benítez, Cortéz, Castañeda..." He finds my card and holds it up between his index and middle fingers like a magician. "Delgado. There you go."

For the first time, I look at him directly and our gazes lock together. His eyes are big and dark with long lashes. Heat pours through me. "Have we...have we met before?" I ask.

"I don't think so," he says, but he doesn't look away. "Eddie and Sal are my older brothers. I'm Angel."

Fallen angel. Apt.

"Nice to meet you," I say, like a dork. "My name is—"

"Deanna Delgado. I got that." He wiggles the card.

I take the credit card and slip it into my wallet. When I look up, Angel's eyes are waiting to meet mine again. My body temperature goes up a thousand degrees.

"All good?" he asks.

"Yes. All good." I fight to stay cool even though this staring game is making funny things happen to me. I clear my throat. "Also, I wanted to say thanks. For helping us out with that guy tonight. He was drunk, that's all."

"Maybe, but he was also an asshole," Angel says. "That kind of bullshit doesn't happen here. Not on my watch, anyway."

My lady parts tingle. "Well, um, yeah. Good," I manage. "Thanks again. Anyway." Tingle tingle. "Good night."

I turn. My feet are heavy as they take me away from the most gorgeous man I've ever met.

"Hey, hold up," he says.

I turn around. To my dismay, he's putting his shirt back on, but the cotton strains over his shoulders in the most delightful way. How could someone getting dressed be so sexy?

"Do you have a minute?" he asks. "I need some help." He opens up a big metal refrigerator and pulls out a clear pitcher filled with bright green liquid. "I'm working on something new. I could use some feedback before I let my brothers try it tomorrow. Interested?"

I look around, and my internal alarms go off. I'm alone in an enclosed space with a stranger—albeit a very, very good-looking stranger—who is offering me what could be double-strength Rohypnol punch.

Angel sees my hesitation. He grabs two clean glasses and fills them from the same pitcher. "What if we sit at the big table?"

It's like he's read my mind. The front door is still unlocked for an easy exit if I need one. The big table is right next to the front windows where people can see directly inside.

I look at the glasses in his hands. "What is it?" I ask.

"A new agua fresca. I've been working on it for a couple weeks." He studies my face. "There's no alcohol."

My alarms stand down, but I stay alert. "Okay," I say at last. "Sure."

I have a feeling Angel is not a smiley man. He nods and says, "After you."

I sit and he takes a seat opposite me. He puts the glasses down in front of us and waits for me to choose the one I want, further suggesting that he understands my justified fear of getting drugged by a stranger.

"The ingredients are lime, fresh ginger, mint, agave nectar and spinach," he says.

I guess I make a face at the last item.

"You can't taste the spinach," he says. "It's just for color."

We clink glasses. "Salud," I say.

The drink is refreshing. Sharp and complex. I didn't realize I was thirsty until I had a taste. Now I want more. Which could be said of this entire experience with Angel.

"What do you think?"

"It's so good," I say. "Much less sweet than I expected. I like it."

"I made it for my sister-in-law. She's pregnant. She can't have beer, and she has bad morning sickness. I think the mint and ginger might make her feel better."

This is the squishiest, most adorable thing I've heard in a long time. Even though I'm sitting down, I'm in danger of swooning. I put my hand on the bench to steady myself.

He takes another sip and gives his bottom lip the tiniest of licks. "The more I drink it," he says thoughtfully, "the more I think we should sell it. As an option for people who can't or don't drink."

"That's a good idea. What would you call it?"

"I don't know. I haven't thought about that. But it should have a name—you're right."

A handsome man telling me I'm right. Catnip.

We finish our drinks together. He asks me how I know Eddie. I tell him I used to be his brother's caseworker right after prison, before Eddie got his act together. That was about three years ago. I ask Angel when he started working at the brewery—I don't remember seeing him here before. I would've remembered if I had.

"On and off since it opened," he says. "I was living in Salinas for a while. I just moved back down here for good."

For good. I like the sound of that.

My lady parts tingle even more.

"So I know you have work early tomorrow and you have to get out of here," Angel says. "I need to lock up. If you hang out for five minutes, I can walk you to your car. You shouldn't be out there alone."

I wait as he turns off the lights, locks the doors and sets the alarm. The last thing he does after we walk out of the front door is lower the security gates and padlock them.

We walk side by side toward my car. He's changed into a clean white T-shirt that smells like laundry detergent. The night air caresses my bare arms and neck. My skin feels extra sensitive. Even my hearing sharpens—I can hear his keys and coins jingling in his pocket. I can hear him breathing, slow and steady, then quick and shallow as we approach my car.

I unlock it. Angel opens the door for me.

"Listen, I don't know how to say this, so I might as well just say it." He hesitates before blowing out a breath. "You're very beautiful. I couldn't keep my eyes off you tonight. I could barely do my job."

To say my jaw drops would be an understatement. My jaw falls straight through the core of the earth and knocks out some poor woman walking on a sidewalk in China.

"Is this a joke?" I look around. "Did Ingrid set this up?"

"Can I kiss you?" Angel asks.

Definitely a joke. I roll my eyes. "Sure. Why the hell not," I say sarcastically.

Angel takes me in his big tatted arms and kisses me.

At first, I am too stunned to respond.

But then.

Dear God.

When he pulls back, I blink at him behind my glasses. "Angel's Brew," I say. My voice cracks.

"What?"

"You should call the green drink Angel's Brew."

He smiles, and of course, it's beautiful. "Angel's Brew. I like it."

He kisses me a second time. When he lets go, I realize my body temperature is so high, my good judgment, my inhibitions, my hang-ups and even my heartbreak have all been completely incinerated. They're ash.

"Come home with me," I whisper.

"Yeah," he says. "Okay."

THREE YEARS LATER

ONE
ANGEL

THE ONLY MUG left in the kitchen is chipped and says BOSS BABE in faded pink letters. Yawning, I grab it off the shelf, rinse it out and pour myself a cup of coffee.

My brother's voice breaks the peaceful quiet like a hammer.

"Hey! Get out here!"

"Yeah, hold up," I mumble. Can't drink my coffee without two packets of Sugar in the Raw. I sweep the spilled sugar into a nearby trashcan to avoid the wrath of Eddie's wife, Carmen, who keeps a kitchen more immaculate than the Virgin Mary's soul.

"Angel!" Eddie pronounces my name as most people do, in English. In my family, only my mom ever called me Ángel, the Spanish pronunciation, and that was so long ago, I can barely remember her voice.

"Angel!" Eddie calls again.

"¡Ahorita voy!" I shout. "Hang on a minute." I take a sip and burn my mouth. The big clock above the steel sink says eight a.m. It's going to be a long day—they all are, these days.

"Where are you?" Eddie reaches into the crack of the heavy

back door, which I propped open with an old brick. He pops his head inside. "Come look at this bullshit," he says.

I follow him around the building. It's late November so I put up my hoodie. Eddie's wearing our dad's old Pendleton, one of the few things our old man left behind when he passed away two years ago. We walk around the dumpster and the beat-up delivery truck, Big Bertha. We walk past the raggedy Astroturf lawn and the stack of chained-up folding chairs that serve as our outdoor seating during the pandemic. The patio tables and three canopies from Costco are safe inside the building after someone tried to steal them the first night we left them outside. My oldest brother Sal's wife caught the perpetrators in the act. I was there for closing, and I'll never forget what I saw: Vanessa roaring like a lion, phone recording in one hand, the other hand holding up an umbrella from lost and found like it was some kind of flaming sword of justice.

"You motherfuckers!" she screamed. "Come and steal from us again, I swear to God, I'll curb stomp all of you and serve your brains on tacos!"

I've never seen people run so fast. Shit, I would've run from her too.

So basically, Eastside Brewery has survived. Changing policies, shutdowns, lockdowns, supply shortages, clients and suppliers closing their doors, neighbors leaving town and never looking back, assholes trying to jack our shit, bills past due, vendors knocking down the door demanding to be paid, illnesses and worst of all, funeral after funeral after funeral. Against all odds, the business is still standing, held up by the simple stubbornness of my brothers and their wives.

Me? I'm just the little brother. The barback, the cellarperson, the brewery grunt. Whatever is needed. Three years I've been stuck here, every day just like the one before. Same, same, same. Every day the same.

As my old boxing trainer used to say, "Unless you're the lead dog, the view never changes."

Anyway.

You ever had brain tacos?

I did once, when I was drunk.

They're pretty good, if you don't think too hard about it.

Salty. A little like me.

Eddie taps my forehead. "Hey, space cadet. Wake up. Look."

We're standing in front of the taproom. The brewery had been open for just two years, growing and gaining momentum before the coronavirus fell like an axe on all our heads.

And now...what the hell?

I blink.

Red words, big and ugly, right across the security doors. A heavy, dripping spray by someone who doesn't know how to do graffiti.

FUCK THIS WHITE PEOPLE SHIT

Silent, Eddie and I stand in front of the message and let it sink in. I add a new line to my mental list of things we have to deal with: *randos who blame us for gentrification.*

After a minute Eddie says, "I mean, breweries *are* 'white people shit,' if we're being honest."

"But we're not white," I point out, helpfully.

"No," he says. "No, we are not."

"We're not welcome either."

"That's nothing new," Eddie says. The irony is thick. Our family has lived in this part of town for three generations, your favorite felons next door. Slingers, taggers, bangers. When he and Vanessa started Eastside Brewery, Sal set the Rosas family straight and made us legit. But welcome? In this neighborhood, with our history, that's much more complicated.

Eddie shakes his head. "No one would pull this shit in the old days, you know that, right?"

I shrug. I wasn't here for the old days.

"No one would touch us. No one would dare disrespect us." My brother feels the paint with a fingertip. It's dry. "Our family was feared."

He goes on and on about the unspoken code of honor between homeboys. I don't say anything. Sal and Eddie left their gang a few years ago. Technically, they're retired. But with all the pain, chaos and flux in the neighborhood, plus an endless beef with the Hillside Locos, I am positive the homies in East Side Hollenbeck are too busy holding on to their corners to even think about two of their former soldiers leaving the streets to make craft beer. "White people shit" is the least of their worries.

But I don't interrupt Eddie, mostly because he hates when I do that, but also because looking at him, I see that he, like all of us, is tired. Fucking tired—bags under his eyes, stubble, sagging shoulders. He's got a three-year-old and a newborn at home. On top of that exhaustion, his wife Carmen's parents just passed away, her father from pneumonia, her mother from covid.

Life and death, hand in hand—a double dose of each.

So I do the least I can do: I wait for Eddie to finish what he's saying.

When he's done, I say quietly, "I'll clean this up before everyone else gets here."

Eddie pats my shoulder. We both know the rest of the family doesn't need to see this. "Thanks for taking care of it, man," he says.

I take another drink of coffee and head out to the storage shed for gloves, rags, paint thinner and whatever industrial solvent looks strong enough to clean up this mess.

Four hours of miscellaneous shitwork later, I'm grumpy and hungry. At noon, Sal and Vanessa roll in, and Eddie opens the taproom, which means masks on for everybody. Boner, a line cook and Carmen's replacement while she's on maternity leave, makes me a sandwich for lunch. It's a torta ahogada, so red and saucy I have to pull up my sleeves to eat it. I wolf it down while sitting on a milk crate next to Big Bertha. I'm finishing up just as my oldest brother, Sal, pokes his head out of the back door and peeps my hiding spot. Looks like my lunch break is over, such as it is. I wipe my face with a wad of paper napkins.

How do I describe Sal? Imagine the biggest, scariest gangster you can. Then make him really nerdy and good at Excel.

"Hey," he says.

"Hey."

"It's time to clean the mash tun," he says.

A big job. I suppress a sigh. "Yeah."

His wife Vanessa appears behind him. "What? He can't do that right now," she says to Sal. She points at me and taps her watch. "Your booster shot, remember? I scheduled it for you two weeks ago. Go get it. The mobile clinic is parked by the employment agency today."

It's fun to see my serious, grumpy older brother outclassed by his tiny wife. "Fine," Sal grunts. "But do it when you get back. First thing."

"Aye-aye, captain." I'm happy to get a break whenever I can, even if it means getting stuck with a needle.

Before I can escape, Sal's eyes narrow and drop down to my hands.

Shit—I forgot to cover up.

"What's all that?" he asks, squinting. My knuckles are bruised and discolored.

"Nothing. Just sparring at the gym." Quickly, I pull down

my sleeves. "Hey, the clinic is kind of far. Can I take the van?" I ask, hoping to annoy and distract him.

"If you can afford to fill it up yourself, sure," says Vanessa. "Otherwise, that tank has to last us through the next delivery."

In addition to brewery grunt duties, I am also doing deliveries until there's enough money to hire a real delivery driver. With my luck, on our next run, Big Bertha will stall out halfway up some hill downtown whether I gas her up or not.

Vanessa pulls on Sal's forearm. "Listen, we have to plan your strategy for the beer summit. And I really have to talk to you about this mobile canning service," she says. "I've looked at the numbers. They're bleeding us dry."

Sal follows her back inside. To me, he says, "You heard the lady. Beat feet, kid."

I'm off the hook, for now. Sal lets Vanessa lead him inside, and the metal door shuts behind them with a loud bang.

"Fuck," I whisper to myself.

I zip up my hoodie, put my sore hands in my pockets and head toward the employment agency. It's not close. I pick up the pace to keep warm.

Weekday traffic is back up to pre-covid levels. Trucks and cars choke the street. An old utility pickup loaded with tools passes me, blowing soot and carbon monoxide in my face. In the distance, workers raise the arches of the new Sixth Street Bridge. Steel cables, wooden framework and concrete all glow in the early afternoon sunlight. When I squint, instead of a bridge, I see two dragons flying over the railroad tracks, racing each other into downtown.

This morning, I stole a half dozen aspirin from the medicine cabinet. I wanted to take the whole bottle, but it rattled, tattling on me. I take a couple from my pocket, pick out the lint, and swallow them dry. Aspirin, sort-of fresh air and a walk—maybe I'll feel better soon. But the ache in my skull says maybe not.

A bus passes me, riders in masks sitting every other row. The ad on the back of the bus is a man with a big mustache. He's wearing a blue suit. Behind him is the word ACCI-DENTES and a phone number that is mostly the number eight.

I want to sock myself. I can't believe I forgot to cover my knuckles.

My brothers watch everything single thing I do. After our mother and sister died in a car accident, I was sent to live with relatives in Salinas. Back in LA, my brothers and father ran wild with their gang, getting in trouble with the law and eventually ending up in prison. I didn't hear from any of them for years. I think they wanted me to be the one Rosas brother who made it out of the life, who escaped the street. But that didn't happen— not exactly.

I've been back for three years. Eastside Brewery has been a shelter when I needed one, a place to work and ride out the pandemic. But even though it is my family's place, it still doesn't feel like home. To my brothers, I'm just an employee. They've shot down every idea I've shared that I think might make the business better. Non-alcoholic drinks on the menu? Profit margins too low, Angel. A merchandise counter? No space for inventory, Angel. Karaoke night? We can't afford any equipment, Angel. No, no, no.

But everything they ask of me? I say yes. Ten toes down. Yes, yes, yes.

I try not to take it personally. They are struggling to keep the brewery afloat. There's a lot on the line, and there isn't much wiggle room to take any kind of risks right now.

Will Sal believe me about the sparring? I can guess what's going to happen. He's going to talk to Eddie about it. They're going to plan their approach, sit me down like a meeting in the principal's office. I can hear them now.

"Why are your hands like that?"

"Where do you go at night?"

"Are you keeping on the straight and narrow?"

"What are you doing with yourself?"

If I were fourteen, angry and lost, this kind of nosey, brotherly love would've been a gift from Heaven. I would have been overjoyed if anyone—literally, anyone—gave a shit about me back then. But I'm twenty-four now, and whatever they think they know about me is wrong. On top of that, I'm not interested in setting anyone straight. It's too much work, and I'm usually misunderstood whether I try to explain myself or not.

The truth is simple.

I just want to be left alone.

In exchange for doing whatever needs to be done for our family business, and for laying low, and for not giving anyone any trouble, I just want to be left alone.

Fat chance.

I pass Sal and Vanessa's house, where I've been staying since I came down from Salinas. I used to sleep in their garage, which they turned into a pretty decent little apartment with a bathroom and coffee maker and everything. But then covid hit, and cash got even tighter than before. Sal said they had to rent out the apartment. Now I'm on the couch in the living room. With my particular background, I don't mind couch surfing. I honestly don't need much. But Sal and Vanessa live with her grandmother and her ten-year-old daughter and a noisy old wiener dog named Chancla, and Eddie and Carmen and their kids are always over for food, and guess what? Now I'm Tío Angel, surrounded by family day and night.

I mean, I love them all. But it's a lot of togetherness. A lot.

The new tenant opens the door to the garage and steps out.

"¡Buenas tardes!" He waves his hand.

I wave back. For a minute, I can't decide whether to stop or keep walking. He's going to want to chat. He's a chatty old man

—a gentleman, I should say. I like him, but I don't want to be late for the appointment Vanessa made for me. I am not in the mood to get in trouble with her too.

Juan Luis walks down the driveway to greet me. He's carrying his guitar case, and he's dressed in a pressed suit and tie. We speak Spanish—polite, grammatically correct Spanish like the kind my grandmother taught me. Not the impatient, rapid-fire Spanglish the rest of my family uses.

"Good afternoon," I say. "You look sharp today. Are you on your way to a gig?"

"Yes," he says. He's a small man, neat and tidy, with gray hair cut high and tight and a trimmed mustache. I have no idea how old he is. He's a guitar player and singer, un cantante. The fingernails on his right hand are long but neatly filed. "It's another funeral. This one is for a nice family from Nayarit. Their grandfather passed away. His widow hired us to play at the memorial and during the reception at the house."

From our few conversations, I know the many funerals Juan Luis has played recently weigh down on him, even though the fees were often his only lifeline during lockdown.

"Where is the funeral?" I ask.

"Montebello. Resurrection Cemetery."

Juan Luis doesn't have a car. "Do you have a ride?" I ask. How much cash do I have right now? Not much, but I take out my wallet and offer it to him. "How about bus fare?"

"You're very kind, young man." He puts his hand on my shoulder and gives it a squeeze. It's a warm gesture. I try not to wince from my injuries.

"Are you sure?" I ask.

"I'm all set," Juan Luis says. "Ignacio and Francisco are coming to pick me up this time. They'll be here soon."

I put my wallet back in my pocket. I tell him I'm on my way to get my booster shot, and he congratulates me. He got his shot last week. He slept for a night, a day, and a night afterward. Then he felt better. I can't remember the last time I got a day off. I tell him I don't think labor laws apply if you work for your family.

"They should," he says. "What if you fall asleep and drown in the beer?"

We chat a little longer. A van that was on its last leg thirty years ago limps to a stop by the sidewalk. I put Juan Luis's guitar case into the back and shut the doors, careful not to slam them and cause the whole van to come apart. Juan Luis climbs in. I wave to his bandmates, both of them artifacts from a time when serenading your lady love under her balcony would not get you an infraction for disturbing the peace.

"Tonight, gentlemen? Chelas?" I say to them through the window. "I'll bring you some six-packs."

They applaud me as their sad van *put-put*s away.

One perk about working in a brewery—free beer really cheers people up. And these days, people need a lot of cheering up.

I check the time on my phone. I now have ten minutes to complete a thirty-minute walk. I put on my hood, secure everything in my pockets, take a deep breath and start jogging. I say a little prayer that the newer residents of the neighborhood have better things to do today than call the cops on a brown man running down the street. That's the last thing I need—the police stopping me and pulling up my record. I keep my head down and find a good pace.

In my younger days, I could run. I could *run*. Back when I thought I could outrun everything and everybody, I would run the length of Salinas, circle the fields and take the dusty trails into the hills. I'd look down on the lettuce and artichoke fields, the trains cutting through the valley on their way to somewhere far away. I'd give anything to hitch a ride.

Back then, the only place I wanted to go was here, Los Angeles, where my brothers and father lived. I wanted us to be a family again, the way we used to be. My father—before he relapsed back into drugs and gang life—working a steady job. My mother, keeping house, praying the rosary, hanging out with her comadres at church. My brothers and me, playing soccer or American football in the park after school and buying raspados from the snow cone cart. And my little sister, tiny but tough, always trying to keep up with us.

But that life is long gone. Nowadays, this city doesn't feel like home. Maybe home never really existed—at least, not for someone like me.

Breathe in, breathe out.

I haven't been training as much as I should be. A few runs here and there, regular visits to the boxing gym. My lungs start to ache a little. I can feel the impact of my feet on the pavement rattling my joints. But even just a short run like this gets my blood going. I can hear my own breathing. The ache in my head fades. I perk up, awake again.

And I'm reminded, again, how doing things with my body has always been the way I recover from pain. Whatever that pain was. A run, a fight, a fuck—these things are my therapy. My medicine.

A punch to the head—that's a kiss from God.

A reminder: I'm alive. I'm still here.

I sprint.

When I reach the parking lot of the employment office, it's five minutes past my appointment time. I'm panting, and my heart is beating loud and steady. I put my mask back on.

There's a pop-up canopy with folding chairs which I'm guessing is the waiting area for people who've just gotten their shots. I walk up to the trailer. There's a nurse sitting at a small table next to the entrance. She's wearing a mask and a face shield. I tell her my name and hand over my ID and vaccination card.

"You're a little late," she says. "We let the next appointment go in ahead of you, but she should be done in a minute."

"That's fine by me, thank you," I say, relieved there's still a slot for me.

"Here she is," the nurse says. "She's finished now. It'll be just a minute before the staff is ready for you, Mr. Rosas."

At the sound of my name, the woman stepping out of the trailer looks up. Behind those glasses, and behind that mask, I'd recognize her anywhere.

I smile at her, even though she can't see it.

And just because I like the sound of her two names together, I say them both.

"Deanna Delgado."

TWO

DEANNA

I FINISH the last drops of my donut shop coffee and pull into the driveway. When I open my car door, the heat escapes all at once. I climb out, unlock the heavy padlock at the entrance of the parking lot and heave the rusting gate open. This gate gets heavier and heavier each day. I yawn. I'm exhausted—nothing new.

There is a pile of...something on the sidewalk. Turds? A dead bird? A dead bird *and* turds? I sidestep this burning mystery and drive my car inside.

Phone, purse, glasses, water bottle, mask. I don't check my face in the rearview mirror anymore. Too depressing. Once upon a time, I did my hair and makeup for work. I wore nice office clothes and sensible heels. But those days are long gone. Today I'm dressed in a winter hat, fleece leggings, a sweatshirt and fingerless gloves. There isn't enough money to run the heater in the office, so my coworkers and I huddle in our cubicles dressed like we're ice fishing in Canada instead of sitting at desks with computers that don't work and rolling chairs that haven't rolled since 1992.

I unlock the big lock on the front door and step inside my

meat locker of an office. As soon as I step inside, the phone on my desk rings. I check the time. 7:48 a.m. This is the first of dozens of calls I'll field today. I rush over to answer it.

I'm congested and the tip of my nose is cold. I croak, "Evergreen Vocational Services Center, Deanna Delgado speaking."

"Ms. Delgado, good morning, ma'am." The voice of the man on the end of the line is crisp like the crease on a uniform. He sounds like he's been up for three hours, doing push-ups and eating high-fiber cereal. "This is Humberto Gavilan with Parole. How are you today, ma'am?"

"What can I help you with, Agent Gavilan?"

"If you don't mind, let me first verify that you are indeed the caseworker for Arturo Aguilar. Is that correct?"

I swallow down a groan. *Goddamn it, Art.* "Yes, that's correct," I say. "I am his caseworker."

"Then I'm afraid I have an update for you."

Reflexively, I brace myself for bad news. I pull out my trusty legal pad and a pen, ready to take notes. "Okay, what's going on with Arturo?"

"Last night, we received a call from Mr. Aguilar's reentry facility in Lincoln Heights. It seems he removed his GPS device and left the premises without permission around eleven p.m. The program manager at the facility told us Mr. Aguilar had good rapport with you and recommended we reach out to see if he's made contact."

"I wouldn't say we had particularly 'good rapport,'" I say. "He checked in regularly with me after I helped him enroll in a solar panel training program. That's all."

"That counts as 'good rapport' in my world, Ms. Delgado."

A desperately low bar, I think. The light on my ancient work phone is off, indicating no messages overnight. "He has not reached out to me," I say.

"All right," Agent Gavilan says. "If he does, will you please contact me immediately?" He spells out his name, gives me two phone numbers, and tells me his unit: Fugitive Apprehension Team.

My heart sinks at the word *fugitive*. Art was booked for burglary before he was released from prison as a non-violent offender to finish his sentence at a low-security facility. He was getting counseling and job training. I felt optimistic about his future, and so did he. My heart sinks even lower when I realize that he had only four months left before his release date. With additional escape charges, how much more time will he spend behind bars?

"If Mr. Aguilar makes contact," says Agent Gavilan, "I would appreciate it if you could get as much information as you can from him about his location, his contacts and his activities. Anything. He has close ties to East Side Hollenbeck, and we suspect he has gone into hiding with the help of his associates from the gang."

"I really don't think he'll call me," I say. "We didn't have anything but a professional relationship."

"If he gets desperate, he will seek out assistance wherever he can."

"All right," I say, still doubtful.

"Thank you, Ms. Delgado. I do appreciate your support. We have a few leads to follow up on this morning, and with our usual investigative techniques, we are confident Mr. Aguilar will be apprehended promptly." He emphasizes the word *confident*. He puts a slight twang on it, like a Texas Ranger.

When I hang up with Agent Confident, Ingrid walks through the door. She's wearing a fleece coat that looks like a cross between a bathrobe and a bedspread. "Why are you frowning already?" she asks. She sits down at her computer at the front desk and boots it up.

"Do you remember Arturo Aguilar?" I ask.

She shakes her head. "No."

"Really? With tattoos over his eyebrow?" I point to my left eyebrow. "Quiet? Got into the photovoltaic program at the vocational college?"

She shakes her head again. "Nope."

"What is wrong with you?" I ask. Before my phone rings again, I sneak a peek at my inbox. It's horrible, as usual.

Ingrid shrugs. "We have a lot of clients. Double what we had last year and quadruple what we had the year before that. You can't expect me to remember all of their names."

"Why not? I do."

"Well, you're weird," she says.

Before our other coworkers arrive, Ingrid and I open the blinds and review the schedule for the day. I'm giving a workshop online, followed by virtual appointments and a staff meeting. At noon, the mobile clinic will arrive and set up in the parking lot. Vaccines and boosters for the community, starting with our office.

Going through our usual routine, Ingrid and I turn on the copier, switch on all the lights, and start up the poor old coffeemaker that holds this whole operation together. Ingrid buzzes in two walk-ins just off the bus from Sylmar. Outside, our boss, Tod, parks his car and sits for a minute, gathering himself after his god-awful commute from Glendora. I take advantage of this moment of quiet to tell Ingrid all about Arturo Aguilar and my conversation with Agent Confident.

"Why do you think he took off? With so little time left?" Ingrid asks.

"I don't know," I say.

"Did he have any problems with substance abuse?"

"No, not Art."

"Gang affiliation?"

"ESHB."

"Do you think they'll find him?"

From my limited dealings with them, the Fugitive Apprehension Team are tenacious overachievers. This makes me worry about Art, and I feel sad thinking about the reasons he made this particular decision. He must have been desperate. Why?

"They'll find him," I say quietly. "They always do."

Ingrid looks at her watch. "It's almost time for your workshop. Do you need help setting up?"

"No, I'm good."

On the shelf behind me, I line up the photos of my bulldogs, Funfetti and Meatball, and water my sad little cactus with the last gulp of water in my water bottle. I dust off the social work degree hanging on the wall—despite everything, I am still proud of this little piece of paper and all I have done in the years since I earned it. Lastly, I take off my mask and turn on the camera. In the monitor, my face is tired and sad. I can hardly bear to look at myself. Instead, I look at the faces of a dozen of my clients, who, against all odds, have shown up this morning for my weekly workshop. And that's what makes me smile at last.

"Hello, everybody," I say. "Good morning. I see lots of familiar faces. Is that Jimmy I see? How are you, Jimmy? And Beto? Are you on the road? Who's that in the background? Is that your daughter? Look at you! Hi, cutie pie. How old are you? Two? Oh, your dad has his hands full, doesn't he? You are the cutest. Alana? Are you there? Hey, girl, good to see you again. We missed you last week. Is everyone ready? Shall we begin?"

The clients on my screen—on buses, in cars, on the street, in a park, in break rooms, at home with their kids—give me a thumbs-up. All of them formerly incarcerated, and they are every level of tired, distracted, worried, grieving and anxious. They look like they are carrying the weight of the world.

"Okay." I pull up my notes. "We're here today to talk about a very important topic. The job interview. I have some slides and pointers to share, of course, but I also want to reserve some of our time today for exercises and discussion about your real-life experiences with job interviews. So let's start with the basics..."

Tod rolls in and gives me a wave. Ingrid puts a mug of fresh coffee on my desk and gives me a nod as more walk-ins approach the front desk. The office cranks to life.

Around noon, Ingrid and I walk to Al & Bea's and share a green chile burrito on the patio, our weekly treat. Ingrid can eat a truck. I have no appetite today, so I eat two bites and let her have the rest. I also let her go on and on about her new boyfriend, some guy she met on an app this past summer. After messaging each other for weeks, they had a magical weekend of hooking up and decided to be exclusive. This is a bold move for Ingrid, who rarely lets any man get too close. I'm not sure what it is about this particular guy that has her changing her tune because he sounds incredibly boring to me. Basically, he sells insurance and works out. It doesn't sound like much of a life, but I shouldn't talk.

"So how's your family?" Ingrid asks. "How are your mom and dad? I saw a liquidation sign on the furniture store, and I wanted to ask you about it."

"That? Yeah, my dad put it up last week. They're not really going out of business. The sign just brings in customers."

"That seems...dishonest."

"That's what I said. He claims he's not lying, he's just preparing for a liquidation in the future. The very distant future."

"Oh my God, what a legend. And your mom?"

"My dad thinks I'm a lost cause, but my mom hasn't given up on me. She's still hoping I'll get a real job, after all this time."

"She wants you in the family business?"

I shake my head. "No, the family business is going to her eldest son, the MBA. With two more sons in med school and her youngest daughter getting a JD, the boss cannot stand that there's a black sheep in the family with the audacity to be a social worker. It messes up her matched set." I smile to myself. "I think she's considering not including me in the family news-letter at Christmas."

"You know, to be honest, I'd be ashamed of you too." Ingrid smiles. "Meet my children, Range Rover, Audi, Audi, shitty Honda, Benz."

"Shut up," I say, and I laugh, although it's taken a lot of years to get to the point where I can laugh at my parents' disap-pointment in me.

Ingrid shakes her head. "Why do we do this job? Why?" She takes off her winter hat and runs her fingers through her hair. "You know, my hair is falling out. It clogs up the shower. It's disgusting." She sighs. "It's stress. Work stress. I hate it." Ingrid studies my face. "How about you? How's your stomach stuff?"

"Better, but not great. My doctor says go easy on the caffeine, so I'm trying two cups a day instead of seventeen," I say. "But my problem is not caffeine, it's stress. I see stories in the news all the time about new legislation for reentry programs. New funding here, new funding there. When is the funding going to find its way to us? Tod was supposed to hire three people last month. We've been clocking twelve-hour days. How much longer does he expect us to sustain the center without more help?"

She shrugs. "You know, he's not looking so good himself."

"What?"

"He's burned out. I predict he'll give notice before the end of the year."

I pause mid-bite. "What do you mean?"

"What I mean, Deanna, is he's going to leave. That commute? With that pay? He's way overqualified for his position. And he got a taste of working remotely during lockdown. He's going to resign. Why keep coming to the hood if you don't have to?"

I think about what she's saying. "Tod was always the biggest champion of our program. Wrote all those grants. Got us all that money."

"Yes, but that was before the pandemic." She finishes her Diet Coke with a big slurp. "I don't know. People just want more."

"More what?"

"Freedom. Money. Opportunities. More everything. Don't you?"

Sensations flash in my brain before I can stop them: a sweet murmur in my ear. Heat rising up my spine. A hand on my throat. I blink.

"I don't know," I lie. My voice is hoarse. "I liked my job, before our caseload got out of hand."

She rolls her eyes. "Besides hiring other caseworkers at the office, isn't there anything you want? Anything just for yourself?"

"No," I lie again. "Not really."

"I don't believe you. Search your heart."

Instead of answering her, I pick up our trash and throw it in the bin. "Come on. It's almost time for our shots."

THE FIRST TWO TIMES, I looked away. The first shot felt hot and thick in my veins. The second shot felt like a tiny pinch, nothing more. Both times I looked at the ceiling, at the floor, at my hands resting in my lap, at the clock, at the red sharps container attached to the wall. I looked at everything else I could look at except the needle.

But this time, I watch it go in.

It's faster than I thought. The metal disappears into my flesh and stays there for half a second before the nurse pulls it out. She slaps a bandage on my arm, hands back my vaccine card, and directs me outside to the sitting area to make sure I have no adverse reactions.

I grab the handrail attached to the folding steps leading out of the mobile clinic. I'm feeling warm all over when I hear another nurse say, "It'll be just a minute before the staff is ready for you, Mr. Rosas."

What?

I look up. As if my dirty thoughts could conjure him like a spell, there he is.

Angel Rosas.

In the flesh.

My sin. My secret. My favorite regret.

Just the memory of him has been the jet engine behind dozens—maybe hundreds—of vibrator sessions in the three years since we slept together.

In a strange trance, I make it to the bottom step. Now we're facing each other. I want to be annoyed at him for not respecting social distancing before I realize he's been standing still this whole time. I'm the one who's made my way to him, moth to a flame.

"Deanna Delgado," he says, and his voice makes my body vibrate with heat.

What can I say to him? Words mix together in my mouth and I can't get any of them out. What's wrong with me?

That's when something very strange happens.

My head suddenly feels heavy—too heavy to hold up.

"I think I...I think I need to sit down," I say.

Angel catches me a split-second before I hit the ground.

THREE

ANGEL

ONE SECOND I'M staring at Deanna, flashing back to the greatest night of my life. The next second I'm holding her in my arms. The nurse springs into action, directing me to the folding chairs under the canopy. Another nurse appears. Then nurse number three appears, their supervisor, who starts asking lots of questions.

I grab the seat next to Deanna and concentrate on holding her upright. She's groggy. As the nurses chatter at her, she blinks once, twice, three times, slowly coming to.

One of the nurses takes off her mask. And now I am staring at Deanna's perfect, perfect pink lips. Before I can stop myself, I remember them wrapped around the base of my dick.

Angel, cut it out.

"Have you had something to eat today?" one nurse asks Deanna. "Have you had any water to drink?"

Deanna looks at the nurses and tries hard to concentrate. She answers their questions the way someone who is half-asleep would respond, trailing off or giving answers that don't match what they're asking. They suspect she might be dehydrated and bring her a cup of water with a straw. She drinks. I have to look away from her mouth for a second.

Angel, I swear to God, stop. Stop being such a perv.

The nurses ask more questions. One of them brings her a small package of cookies. She takes a small bite. Then she sits up straight and brushes the crumbs off her jacket.

"I'm making a mess," she says. "Ugh, look at this mess."

As if being horny as fuck isn't enough, I suddenly feel my heart standing at attention along with my dick. Deanna's fear of making a mess is so strong that it brings her back to consciousness. Why? And why does that make my chest ache like I've taken a punch?

One of the nurses determines Deanna works at the employment office and brings out one of her coworkers, a tall woman with long, dark hair. Arms folded, the coworker gets right in Deanna's face.

"What happened?" she asks, impatient.

"I guess I fainted." Deanna doesn't realize she's holding my hand, or that my arm is around her shoulders, keeping her from sliding to the ground.

"It's not uncommon," says one of the nurses. "Have more water."

Deanna drinks a little and tries to get up. "No, I'm fine."

"No way," the coworker says. "You need to take the afternoon off."

"No," Deanna says. "I have appointments until the staff meeting."

"Don't worry about any of that. You need to go home."

"She's in no condition to drive right now," says the nurse.

"I'll get you an Uber," says the coworker.

"That's too expensive and you know it," says Deanna.

"I can drive her home," I say.

All of them, the nurses, Deanna and her coworker, suddenly

realize I'm sitting there. They clock the tattoos, the muscle, the Ben Davis pants. Suddenly I feel like a joke—a big thug of a joke. But I don't feel like laughing at all.

I unzip my hoodie to show off my Eastside Brewery T-shirt. "I work at the brewery. My brothers are Eddie and Sal. I'm Angel—Angel Rosas."

Usually that's enough to open doors in this neighborhood, but these women are clearly more difficult to impress.

"I'll get you an Uber," says the coworker again, not even acknowledging what I said. She takes out her phone.

"Deanna and I know each other," I insist. "We're friends. Right?"

Instead of confirming this, Deanna chooses that moment to let go of my hand and rub her forehead. "Ingrid, seriously. It's too expensive. Don't call the Uber."

With a sigh, Ingrid puts the phone back in her pocket. "You need rest. If you go back inside the office, you're just going to do more work. I know you."

"I'm completely fine."

"You're completely not."

"Okay, okay," Deanna reaches into her purse and takes out her car keys. To my extreme surprise, she hands them to me. "Then Angel will take me."

"Him?" Ingrid finally looks at me. I swear ice crystals form in the air between us. "Are you...sure?" she asks Deanna.

Deanna leans on me and stands up at last. She's still a little shaky on her feet so I keep a hand on her back to give her support. "I've known Angel a long time. He's not lying." She gives Ingrid a quick rundown of her work duties and asks to do the staff meeting remotely.

"No," Ingrid says. "That camera is a pain in the ass."

Deanna sighs.

"Get some rest. I mean it." Ingrid turns to walk back to the office but stops to glance suspiciously over her shoulder at me. To Deanna she adds, "Call me when you get home."

"Go," says Deanna. "Go, we're good."

Supervised by the nurses, Deanna sits in the waiting area while I get my shot. After the required waiting time, we both get our A-okay to leave. Deanna directs me to her car, the same little Honda Fit she drove three years ago. I open the passenger door for her and make sure she's all buckled in before I shut it. On the driver's side, I have to adjust the seat all the way back to accommodate my legs. After switching up the mirrors, I start the car. I vaguely remember that she lives somewhere near Koreatown, but the directions are hazy.

Before I can ask, Deanna says, "Don't take me home." She waves her hand. "Ingrid doesn't know what she's talking about. I just need to rest for a minute and I'll be fine."

"Are you sure?"

"I don't want to go home. I have too much work to do today."

"So where do you want to go?"

She thinks for a moment. "The brewery. Take me there."

In the short drive back to the taproom, I watch Deanna out of the corner of my eye. She holds her head in her hand, hiding the rest of her face that isn't already covered by a mask. How do I make sure she doesn't pass out again? Talk to her? My brain races to come up with a subject for small talk that isn't completely cringe.

"How's Eddie?" Deanna asks, saving me from my own awkwardness.

I clear my throat. "Um, he's good, yeah," I say.

"The last time I saw him was at the wedding. What's his wife's name again? How are they doing?"

"Carmen." I think about all the hell my sister-in-law has been through lately and decide to let Eddie tell Deanna the more detailed story. "She just had a baby, like two months ago."

She makes a little happy sound. "That's their second one, right?"

"Right. Julia is two. Now there's Massimo."

"Massimo?" Deanna asks.

I nod. "Carmen named him after some chef, I guess. We call him Max."

Deanna makes that happy sound again. I get the feeling she's good with kids.

"And the business?" she asks. "How has it been, working there during covid?"

Again, I realize this is not the right time to unload the whole story on her. I don't want to tell her how much the brewery has been struggling or how worried we all are about going bankrupt. "Pretty tough," I say, "but we're getting through it." I bust out the usual joke I hear Vanessa make when she tries to cheer up Sal. "Luckily, people haven't given up drinking beer."

Like Sal, Deanna doesn't laugh.

We don't say anything for a few minutes. At a stoplight, I'm desperately trying to figure out how to ask her all the questions I want to ask her when I realize she's looking at my bruised hands on the wheel.

"What's up with that?" she asks.

"Boxing."

"What, bare-knuckle boxing or something?"

"No, regular boxing, at a gym," I lie some more. "I didn't wrap up properly. Stupid mistake."

Behind her glasses, her eyes narrow at me. Can she tell that I'm not being honest? Time to redirect.

"How about I ask you a question now?" I say.

"Um, okay." She wiggles a little in her seat, uncomfortable.

"Do you know what I'm going to ask you?" I ask.

"Is that the question?"

I smile. "No."

"I think I know what you're about to ask."

Honestly, there are a hundred questions I want to ask her, ranging from the obvious "Did it hurt when you fell from Heaven?" to "Is the reason you never called me back because you were kidnapped by government scientists trying to figure out how a woman could come six times in a row like that?" But I settle on the one question I want answered first. "Why did you ghost me?"

She's quiet.

I'm quiet, waiting.

At last, she says, "Lots of reasons."

"Like what?"

"Like, it wasn't the right time for me to start something," she says. "That was a complicated time in my life."

"It didn't seem complicated when you took me home with you," I say.

She plays with the strap on her purse. "My perspective changed when I woke up."

"Is that why you left me there in your apartment? Without a note or anything? I'm surprised you weren't afraid I'd steal your stuff," I add.

"I don't have any stuff worth stealing."

"Not true," I say. "I could've stolen your bulldogs. Sold them. They liked me."

"That's not funny. Don't joke about my babies." Her voice is impatient, but when I catch a sideways look at her, her eyes are smiling.

"Okay, no more jokes about your dogs. But what's the real reason you didn't call me back?" I ask. "Is it 'cuz of my family?"

"No."

"Some kind of bad reputation?"

"No."

"Are you embarrassed to be seen with me?"

"No." She shakes her head. "None of that."

"You wanted to go back to mediocre dick?"

"Stop." She makes a sound that is half sigh, half grunt. "For one thing, your age bothered me. Once you told me your age, I knew there couldn't be anything else between us." She shakes her head. "From your current maturity level, I see I made the right choice."

"What?" I'm genuinely surprised. The difference in our ages didn't even cross my mind. "Twenty-one?" I say. "What's wrong with twenty-one?"

"Everything!" she says. "There's a huge difference between twenty-one and twenty-eight. You were practically jailbait."

I pull into a parking space in front of the brewery. There are two other cars in the lot, a slow afternoon, as usual. "I've been called a lot of things, but this is the first time I've been called jailbait." I put the car in the park, turn off the engine and face her. "How are you feeling? Can you walk inside by yourself or do you want a minute to rest?"

"I can walk by myself." She takes a deep breath and rubs her temples with her fingers. "Just slowly."

"Of course." I take the key out of the ignition. "You're almost thirty-two now, right? That's old. You don't want to fall and break a hip."

"Shut up."

Deanna holds on to my arm as we walk inside, and I try not to enjoy the thrill of her body so close to mine again. Boner is behind the counter, stacking clean glasses for the crowd that never arrives. At the bar, there are two customers in khakis and polo shirts happy to be drinking on the clock. There's no one else in the taproom.

"Boner, this is Deanna," I say. "Say hello."

"Uh, hello," says Boner, looking up. He has round wire frame glasses that make him look like an owl. "How's it going?"

I like Boner. He's a twitchy, brainy white dude with lots of piercings and maybe even more tattoos than me. We work together a lot and I appreciate that he's both laidback and detail-oriented at the same time. When you're working shit hours, it's good to be stuck with someone decent—the hours pass quicker.

I set up Deanna at one of our booths and bring her more ice water. "Do you want something to eat?"

"Not really, but the nurse told me I should." She takes off her mask and drinks the water.

"What would you like?" I look at the chalkboard over the bar. "We have most of it right now."

She squints at the menu of tacos and tortas. After a minute she says, "I can't decide. Can you please bring me something small? Something simple?"

"I got you," I say. I leap into the kitchen like some kind of deranged frog, all excited to take care of her. There's some chicken stock on the back burner, nice and hot. I find some odds and ends in the walk-in refrigerator and make Deanna what I make for myself sometimes on my lunch breaks, a dish my grandma showed me how to cook when I was a kid.

When I'm finished, I bring out Deanna's bowl. Boner is sitting in the booth across from her. Their heads are bent together and they're laughing at some kind of secret joke. Deanna looks so relaxed and happy. The weird spike of jealousy I feel makes me want to knock Boner in the head. Instead, I put the bowl between them with a little side dish of extra cheese.

"Sopita," I say, like a proud little first-grader. "Pasta soup."

"Thank you." Deanna doesn't look at me at all. She's focusing all her attention on Boner. "Did that really happen? The head chef walked in on them?"

"Swear to God," Boner says quietly. "I can laugh about it now, but they were both sacked on the spot."

They laugh again. Neither of them invites me to join them so I take the initiative and sit down next to Boner, pushing him deeper into the booth with my fairly large ass.

"Eddie came to see me after he got fired," Deanna says. "He said the restaurant had downsized. He'd been working there for what, two months? I was so annoyed with him. He acted like the job assignments I found him grew on trees." She picks up her spoon and takes a bite. I wait for her reaction. She doesn't say anything, but she takes a second bite, followed by a third. I'll take that.

"He's a different person now," Boner says. "A manager, a dad. He even calls himself the get-shit-done guy. I guess it was always in him."

"That's good to hear," Deanna says. "I'm glad he's happy now."

I know a little bit about what my brothers have been through. Underdogs made good—who doesn't love a Cinderella story? Eddie often says that every day outside of prison is a good day, that even everyday shit like paying bills and being stuck in traffic has a special shine because there have been years when he wasn't able to participate in any of it.

But the kind of transformation Deanna and Boner are talking about is never as simple as switching on a light or opening a door. There are layers of hurt underneath it all, and I've watched both Sal and Eddie struggle in private to keep everything together.

I lean back in my seat and listen to Deanna and Boner chat. Apparently, Boner went through Deanna's employment agency back in the day, but she wasn't his caseworker. I had no idea he's also formerly incarcerated—maybe that's why we get along.

They discuss the vocational center and what Deanna's work

is like. Boner talks about how he's been to rehab twice before, but the results never lasted long. They talk about the drug court program that finally got him back on his feet. Soon they lose me with the ins and outs of reentry programs, and all of a sudden, I feel out of place again.

I'm annoyed.

Maybe it's true. She's the adult, and I'm just the kid who can't keep up, always just pretending to know what's really up.

The customers seated at the bar wave Boner over for more beer. I stand up to let him out. When I sit back down, I realize that Deanna has finished her soup. She wipes her mouth with a napkin and reaches for her wallet.

"That was good," she says. "How much do I owe you?"

"Nothing," I say. "Off menu. On me."

"Are you sure?"

"Put away your money."

She zips up her purse and places it back down on the seat. "Okay. Then thank you."

"You're welcome."

We make real eye contact for the first time today. Her eyes are dark and deep, with long lashes like velvet. I haven't seen her in three years, but everything that happened between us comes back to me in a rush.

The rest of the world falls out of focus as we stare at each other. The last time we played the staring game like this, she was pinned beneath me in her bed and I was grinding deep inside her, each of us trying hard not to come.

I have never enjoyed winning a game as much as I enjoyed losing that one.

My skin feels hot and tender, like I'm on the edge of getting sunburned.

Across the table, Deanna's facial expression doesn't change, but her cheeks turn pink, and I know she feels the temperature rising between us.

The question slips out again before I can stop myself. "Why did you ghost me?"

She says nothing. Her eyes dart over to Boner.

"He's too far away to hear us," I say. "Did you ever think about changing your mind and calling me back?"

She looks straight at me. "No."

"Never?"

"No," she says again.

"I gave up calling you." I lower my voice. "But I never gave up thinking about you."

She breaks eye contact and looks down at the empty bowl between us.

"Just be honest. I can take it," I say. "What's the real reason you never called me back?"

"We're too different," she says, avoiding my eyes. "It's that simple."

I open my mouth to argue with her.

"Angel." She closes her eyes and rubs her temples. "Don't."

"We may be different, but we were so good together," I say quickly. "Too fucking good for just one night."

She looks up at me again, but her expression is so sad and tired, I back off.

"Hey, are you...are you okay?" I ask.

"Not really," she says. "Listen, I hate to ask you this, but is there a place in the back where I can lie down, just for a minute?"

FOUR

DEANNA

MY ENTIRE LIFE is built on talking.

I talk all day long. To clients, employers, trainees, coworkers, managers, families, strangers, friends. People who are hurting. People who are getting stronger. People who are scared. People who want to make a change.

I ask, beg, cajole, trick, convince, persuade, proselytize, mesmerize, dazzle, encourage. I swim in an ocean of words and fight every day against the tide to be understood and to understand.

But in this dream—I know I'm dreaming, because real life never feels this good—I only have to use a single word to get what I want.

"Do you want this?" he asks.

"Yes," I say, and the dream begins.

I'm lying on my back in the dark. I'm naked, and the sheets are clean and cool against my skin.

At first, he's just a voice, a whisper from the deep, dark muck of my id where I hide everything I want—no, everything I covet. Here in the dark, I am not good or kind or sweet. I am not naughty or sinful or cruel. Those are public designations, labels from people who have nothing to do with this part of me. Here, I am neutral. Here, I am nothing but the pure force of my desire.

"Do you want me to touch you?" he asks.

"Yes," I say again.

He puts his warm, steady hands on my ankles. I hear the slide of skin on skin as he moves his hands slowly upward, pausing on first on my shins and then on my knees. When he reaches my thighs, he gently massages my tight muscles, and tension swirls and darkens like storm clouds in my body.

Slowly, he pushes my legs wide apart and lies down in the space I've made just for him. Warmer now, his fingertips trail up the insides of my thighs and stop. Anticipation blankets me like darkness.

There's a beat of silence, enough for me to realize that the heat of his stilled touch makes my breathing simultaneously quicken and deepen in my chest.

"Vas a matarme, Deanna," he whispers. The air of his words kisses my wet, aching pussy. "Do you want me to go down on you?"

Clear. Shameless.

"Yes," I say a third time.

He spreads my legs wider. With those same wicked fingertips, he strokes the slick folds of my sex. I force myself to stay still. The rhythm of his caresses both soothes me and arouses me, holding me like a string stretched taut between two points. When he finally puts his mouth to me, the tip of his tongue finds my clit at once, and now my body is an instrument, and he's the musician who's trained his whole life to do nothing but play me.

As he licks, he presses his broad, hard shoulders against my legs, pushing me higher up the bed. Beneath us, the sheets get hot. I am drenched, and the wicked sounds of his mouth make me even wetter. When I squirm, he slides one hand under my body, holding me close to his face.

"Stay still," he whispers.

With the other hand, he slides a long, thick finger into me. I grip him hard, desperate to ease the tension he's building in me, lick by lick. The smell of my body, familiar and sweet, fills the room. I am so hot, the air feels thick and heavy against my skin. He finds my G-spot and I have to swallow down a scream. He begins to stroke me in time with his tongue, and now I'm falling apart from the inside out.

He holds me, suspended in the air. When he lets go, I will fall.

I will shatter.

A loud bang, metal on metal, shakes me out of my dream.

I blink, caught for a moment between worlds.

I'm in some kind of small warehouse, sitting in an office chair with my feet up on a short stack of wooden pallets. There's a sweatshirt rolled up like a pillow between my head and the wall behind me. Outside a small window, the sky is black and the street lights are on. My neck is a little stiff and my arm is a little sore, but otherwise, I feel rested for the first time in ages.

I also feel turned on in a way that I know I shouldn't, napping in the vicinity of industrial equipment.

Another loud bang.

I sit up and look around. Metal tanks, kegs, hoses. On the other side of the large room, Angel is standing next to a large tank with an open hatch. The air in the brewery is hot and steamy and smells like a cross between warm sourdough bread and oatmeal.

Angel has stripped off his shirt in the heat. He's wearing black nitrile gloves. He picks up a long metal paddle and sticks it into the open door of the tank. With long, careful movements, he pulls wet grain out of the tank and into an empty barrel. He does this again and again, releasing clouds of steam with each stroke. He is focused on his work and doesn't notice me watching him.

Finally, my eyes can drink him in.

He is as beautiful as I remember. Tall, strong, lean. As I study the way his ink rides his muscles, my body drowns in desire, still fresh and sharp from my wet dream. I should feel ashamed, sitting here in the back of the brewery horny as hell, but I don't. He brings this out in me—only him, even after all this time.

I take a long, thirsty look. He's wearing an Eastside Brewery cap. He turns it backward and crouches down to look deep inside the tank. His pants ride a little bit low but instead of a plumber's crack, I see the fabric hugging his hard, round ass. Like everything about him, his ass is much nicer than it needs to be.

Angel was a gift I gave myself a long time ago. The reality of him, and the reality of me, would only damage that fantasy. We're very different people. We'd only let each other down. It's much better to keep the memory of that night in the past where the real world—this messed-up version of the world—can't destroy it.

My phone buzzes. I look around. My purse is on the desk next to me. Annoyed, I pull out my phone and check the time. It's almost eight—I've been asleep for seven hours. What? I also see my notifications: three missed calls from Ingrid and a text message:

Are you still alive or what? Call me. We have to talk about the staff meeting ASAP.

I can't think of anything that kills horniness faster than an ASAP text message from Ingrid. With a sigh, I stand up, stretch, yawn and call her.

"What's going on?" I say.

"I was this close to calling the cops, Deanna. What the fuck?"

"I'm sorry. I fell asleep. What's happening?"

"Okay, brace yourself." She turns down the music in her car. "I have bad news and worse news. Which do you want first?"

"Just talk, Ingrid."

"Remember how I told you I thought Tod would be quitting soon? I was totally right. He's leaving at the end of the month. He'll be working at a reentry program closer to home. San Bernardino."

"Shit." Tod has been a good boss, especially through the worst of the storm.

"But that's not all."

"What do you mean?"

"The board of directors is using Tod's departure as an opportunity to close the Evergreen office. Apparently, they've been planning to do it for months. They just needed a little push, apparently."

My heart sinks.

"They're taking some of us on at the mother ship beginning in December," Ingrid adds, "but not all of us."

I groan. I had heard rumors of restructuring our program based on the success of "one-stop shops" where clients receive all their services—housing, employment, substance abuse—in one place, like our main administrative office downtown. But with the flood of people released from the prisons to mitigate the spread of covid, I didn't think they'd make the change now.

"When you say, 'not all of us,' do you mean they've already decided who's staying and who's going?" I ask.

Ingrid is quiet for a moment, and now I know the answer.

"I'm sorry, Deanna," she says. "I think it was your seniority.

You earn more than the new caseworkers. They're using the restructuring as an excuse to cut you loose."

I study the spot where the sole of my shoe is starting to come apart. "Punished for earning the big bucks. Such as they are." I sigh. "What about my clients? Who's going to take them? There are barely enough caseworkers now, and we're all overloaded." I peel the sole away just a millimeter and look at the glue behind it. "People are going to fall through the cracks in the transition, and right before Christmas too."

"We have three more weeks," she says. "I've seen you work miracles before."

I let out a laugh. I sound unhinged. "Not like this."

"Tod is upset. He told me he wanted to hire you on, if you'd be willing to transfer. Apparently, he can bring on some of his own staff for his new position. Big mero mero, as usual."

"San Bernardino? The Inland Empire?" My stomach turns like a tumbleweed bouncing around in the desert. "That's too far. No, my contacts are here. My community is *here*."

Ingrid gives me the rundown on which of our coworkers are staying and which are going. I spin the office chair slowly and try to get my emotions under control. I concentrate on the shining tanks and low catwalks around me. The cement floor is gleaming clean. There are pallets stacked with sacks of I-don't-know-what up against the walls. There's some kind of control panel with lots of dials and buttons, and a rack holding a few wooden barrels like a distillery or winery.

I hear another loud noise. Angel has climbed a ladder on the other side of the tank he's cleaning. He points a hose through the top of the tank and begins rinsing it down.

I stare at his face and measure it against the image burned in my memory. His cheekbones seem more angular, his beard darker. As he concentrates on his task, I see the sharp focus in his eyes. Only his lips are exactly the same, full and made for kissing. My own lips tingle, aching.

"Hey, are you there?" Ingrid asks.

"Huh?" I sit up. "Yes, I'm listening."

"I'm home now," she says. "If you're still feeling gross after the shot, you need to stay home tomorrow, okay? They're screwing you over hard. No need to bend over and make it easier for them."

I want to laugh, but I can't. "See you tomorrow."

"I'm serious. Call in sick. Don't be a hero, Deanna."

She hangs up without saying goodbye, as usual. Ingrid is an acquired taste, but over the years I've come to appreciate her. I wouldn't say she has a heart of gold. Maybe gold-plated, like a grill. I try and fail to dodge the sadness that comes with realizing I won't be working with her much longer.

My stomach cramps up.

Laid off.

What am I going to do? About bills? About my apartment? About my dogs' astronomically expensive ear medication?

I've never been unemployed, and I haven't looked for a job for ten years. What if I just don't have the skills to compete with other applicants? How does collecting unemployment work? What about my insurance? I have two, maybe three months of expenses saved, tops. What if I can't find work before it all runs out?

Before I spiral into full-blown panic, a familiar-looking woman in jeans and a pretty blouse comes in from the taproom. She is wearing suede boots with sky-high heels. I haven't worn heels like that in three years.

"Are you feeling better?" she asks with a warm smile. I recognize her—she's Angel's sister-in-law, the business manager and the brains behind the brewery. I struggle with her name for a second—Valerie? Vivian?—until I land on it in my giant mental database: Vanessa.

"I am. Thank you for letting me stay back here. I had no idea I'd sleep so long." I smooth down my hair with my hands. I must look like hell.

"Not a problem at all. We were worried about you. Angel in particular," she says, tipping her head toward the back wall. "Pardon my reach."

She powers off the computer next to me and grabs the jacket and bag hanging on the hook on the wall. I realize with some embarrassment that I've fallen asleep at her desk, right in the middle of her workspace. I'm about to apologize when she holds up her hand. As if she can read my mind, she says, "I didn't need this desk at all today. You're good." She puts on her jacket. "We're short-staffed these days so I worked the taproom this afternoon. Everyone is wearing a lot of hats right now."

"Short-staffed?" My sleepy brain snaps to professional attention. "Are you in the position to hire anyone? Because I can help you with that. What are you looking for?"

She pulls her long ponytail from inside the collar of her jacket. "A full-time delivery driver is our biggest need right now, but we can't hire one because we can't afford the wages."

"Who takes care of your deliveries now?"

"Sometimes Eddie, but mostly that guy." She points at Angel. "He's been doing a lot lately. We're lucky to have him, but with barback and maintenance work, he's stretched pretty thin."

I run a couple calculations quickly in my head. "Have you ever considered taking on brewery apprentices for the maintenance work?"

Her eyes light up. "Like unpaid internships?"

"No, these would be paid positions. Minimum wage," I add, "but paid. Our population is formerly incarcerated, as you know. It's difficult to find them permanent positions. Our program screens candidates for their suitability, matches them with employers and provides them support as they transition to the workplace."

She nods slowly, thoughtful. "I remember how hard it was for Sal when he first got out. I don't disagree that this would be a good environment for your clients, and we'd be happy to provide them with on-the-job training here at the brewery."

But.

"But I can't see how to make those numbers work right now," she says.

"There are some government incentives to help you with costs—not many, but some," I say quickly.

"If we were in the position to take on apprentices and pay them what they deserve, I would do it in an instant." Vanessa zips up her jacket. "But it will be a long time before our sales are back on track to support anything like that. I keep hoping the heavens will open and drop a giant infusion of cash on us, but so far, no luck. Apparently, miracles are hard to come by right now."

With her words, I picture all the clients I need to place in the next month. So many people. So few businesses are willing to take a chance on convicted felons, no matter how much rehabilitation, education, or training they've had. Eastside Brewery would be the perfect training ground for them.

My emotions must be written on my face because Vanessa stands still for a moment and throws me a bone.

"Can you email me with some details?" she says quietly. "I'll look over them with Sal and we'll have a talk. God knows we could use the help."

I nod. "Okay. I'll do that."

"Good. I'm heading out now. Can you please tell Angel I'll see him at home?"

"I will. Thank you."

"Good night, Deanna."

I watch as she walks away, a small, tough woman in *fuck-you* boots. She's got a business, a husband and a family. We look like we're about the same age, but I don't have any of those things. In a few weeks, I won't even have a job.

I drop my head in my hands. The first tears tingle behind my eyelids, and I take a deep breath, willing them to stay where they are.

"Hey."

I jump. Angel sits down on the stack of pallets next to me. He's shirtless and a little sweaty, and my body whips from sad to horny like I'm riding an emotional Tilt-A-Whirl. He takes off his baseball cap and runs a hand through his thick, damp hair.

"You sacked out hard," he says, putting the cap back on. "How are you feeling?"

For a moment, I can't talk. He smells so fucking good. Like toasted corn and fresh bread, like some kind of ancient harvest god people held weeklong orgies for. Instead of answering him, I take a deep breath, lean back in the office chair and stare.

He looks back at me, suspicious. "What?"

I could drive home now, eat a single-serving container of yogurt and spend an hour looking for something to stream before sobbing myself to sleep. But this day has kicked my ass. I don't want to let it have the last word.

So I ask, "What time are you done today?"

He takes his phone out of his back pocket and checks the time. "When the taproom server gets here to help Boner. In twenty minutes or so." He puts his phone away. "Why?"

"Because I really, really need a drink."

Angel gives me a crooked smile that could easily burn my clothes off if I let it. "Luckily for you, I know the perfect place you could get one," he says. "And I even know a party we could go to."

"Really?" I say. "I haven't been to a party in ages."

"This one is going to be a real rager."

"Perfect," I say.

FIVE

DEANNA

"YOU WEREN'T KIDDING," I say. "I haven't partied this hard since freshman year."

Angel hands me another beer. "Told you."

We're parked on an old couch in a converted garage. Hanging on hooks on the wall are two black garment bags and a beautiful dove-gray charro suit in a plastic dry-cleaning bag. There's an ancient electric fan, a card table with a colorful oilcloth cover and a few guitar cases. Three old guys in jeans and sweatshirts are sitting in the driveway on plastic folding chairs, talking and laughing quietly with each other in Spanish. They're gathered around a small space heater like it's a camp-fire. An elderly wiener dog named Chancla is asleep at my feet.

That's it. That's the party.

Angel pops open his can and takes a drink. He turns to the men.

"Por favor, señores. ¿Una canción para mi amiga?"

The three raise their drinks at him before setting their cans down on the cement. They pick up their guitars from nearby stands and tune up.

"For the lady," says Juan Luis in Spanish, and he and his

bandmates, Nacho and Pancho, give me warm smiles. "We played this one last week at the procession of Santa Cecilia."

"What's that?" I ask.

"It's a celebration the mariachis hold for the patron saint of music," says Angel. "You should see it next year. It's beautiful."

The men make eye contact with each other. There's a beat of silence. Then they play a quick, trilling intro, and the vibrating guitar strings fill my head with impossibly beautiful sound. The wiener dog raises her head.

"Como un rayito de luna..."

Their harmonized voices are gentle and worn. They sound like old-fashioned movie stars, professing sincerity from a time when everything—even love—was black and white.

I watch them and listen.

My heart aches more and more with each note.

What would it be like to have someone feel this way about me? To have someone to go home to, both on good days and on very bad days, like today? Someone who would know what to say to make me feel better, to make me believe that everything was going to be okay even though it probably wasn't? Someone bright and true, a ray of moonlight in the dark.

For a moment, I let my heart get swept up with longing—for what? A person?

No, a fairytale.

Angel places his hand over mine. I jump back a little bit, surprised. To avoid looking at him, I keep my eyes on Juan Luis's guitar, on his long fingers gliding effortlessly up and down the neck. Angel's hand is firm and slightly rough. I stay completely still as the music washes over me, peeling the cover off my battered heart.

"Are you warm enough?" Angel asks softly.

"I'm fine," I say, and give him a fake smile. I am not fine.

We sit together, unmoving. Where our arms touch, Angel's

heat passes through into my body. Suddenly I feel like I am not here. How could I be here, in some stranger's garage, listening to music so beautiful it feels like a magic spell, holding hands with a one-night stand I thought I'd never see again?

As soon as they strum the final note, I'm stepping over Chancla and heading out the door. I turn my head so no one can see the tears spilling out of my eyes.

"What's wrong?" Angel asks.

"Excuse me," I tell the musicians. "Thank you, that was beautiful."

Angel stands up to follow me. "Deanna?"

"I'm fine," I say again, quickly. "Sit down. I just...I just need to make a call. I'll be back."

Before he can reply, I walk into the dark yard next to the garage. Away from Angel's heat, the cold air is sharp. I wipe my tears away with the sleeve of my sweatshirt. My phone is in my hand before any big, swirling emotions can hit me and knock me off my feet. I make the call. It rings once, twice, three times. A generic voicemail message plays. I clear my throat before the beep.

"Hey, it's me. I'm...working late again," I lie. "Can you keep the dogs overnight? I put extra food in their backpack, and their ear medication is in the little pocket. I really appreciate it. I'm sorry. Call me if you need anything." I sound strange and needy, so I take a quick breath and add, "Um, I'll come say hi first thing in the morning. Love you."

I hang up and stare at the lighted screen. Brainlessly, I scroll through my texts and emails. There's nothing there that I can take care of right now, but it feels better to distract myself from my sadness and stress than to actually feel anything.

Angel comes out to join me. He studies my face for a moment before holding up my beer.

"We charge eight dollars for this one at the taproom. You

should drink it." He brings the can up to his ear and shakes it a little. "There's five dollars left in there. Five-fifty, maybe."

I'm almost shivering, but I take the cold can and drink.

"It's good," I say. "Which one is this?" I hold up the can and read the label aloud by the light of my phone. "Let Your Conchas Be Your Guide." I take another drink. "Cute."

"Pan dulce and coffee imperial stout. Limited run," Angel says. "During lockdown, that's how we stayed alive. Making funky beers in small batches and getting beer fans excited enough to drive down to the brewery to stock up." He watches me as I drink again. He looks thoughtful. I brace myself for conversation. I brainstorm some boring things to say, statements I can use to brick a wall around myself against his curiosity. I can't talk about how I lost my job—I don't want to think about it at all, but Angel looks like he's about to ask some concerned questions. I take another drink to stall.

Instead, he surprises me. "I'm hungry," he says. "Are you hungry? I know a place we can go that's open right now."

I study him. I'm not stupid. The chemistry is there—the same chemistry that set us both on fire three years ago. The more time I spend with him, the more likely I will end up doing something irresponsible tonight. But I check in with my body anyway. I'm buzzed and melancholic—a bad combination. I know I'll make better decisions after some food.

"You have to drive," I say. I finish off the can. Twelve percent ABV is no joke, and I've just had two of these on an empty stomach.

Angel takes my can and puts it in the nearby recycling bin. He zips up his sweatshirt and puts up the hood. "Okay. Let's do it."

I reach into my pocket and hand over the keys.

⚑

AFTER A SHORT DRIVE, we pull into a small parking lot and park next to a minivan. I check out my face in the visor mirror, fix my hair quickly and put on a fresh mask from my purse. Angel hops out of the car as if he's impatient. At first, I'm annoyed by his rudeness, but he quickly walks around to the passenger side and opens my car door like a chauffeur. He is wearing a small goofy smile, and I am again surprised by him, as if every now and then he wants me to catch a glimpse of the eager-to-please boy playing hide-and-go-seek behind his tough exterior. But then he puts his mask back on.

"Mademoiselle," he says.

I climb out of the car, and he shuts the door behind me. He takes my hand, puts it in the crook of his elbow, and escorts me across the lot. I haven't walked next to anyone like this since my little sister's quince. In my slightly drunken state, Angel's quiet playfulness is contagious, and I give him a little curtsy as he opens the door of the restaurant for me.

But is this a restaurant? The inside of it is stuck in time, maybe 1983, with worn Formica tables, tile floors and walls, and an old wooden trashcan with a flap carved with the word PUSH. A neon sign flashes in the window facing the street— Open 24 Hours. Everything is spotlessly clean, and there's a beautiful white orchid in a turquoise pot sitting on the glass display case. A few shiny donuts sit inside the case. Next to the case is a steam table of Chinese food—the usual suspects, fried rice, noodles, vaguely orange chicken. By the cash register, there's a display of a dozen different international phone cards and a lotto machine.

"Hey, Mom, where are you?" Angel calls, and for a moment I'm confused. Eddie told me their mom and sister died a long time ago in a car accident. Do I have that wrong?

"One moment!" a voice calls. A small, plump woman in jeans, a fleece sweatshirt, a white apron, and a hairnet exits the back kitchen to meet us. She's Asian, about fifty. Her hair is hidden in the hairnet and her mouth is obscured by a disposable mask, but her eyebrows, eyeliner and fake eyelashes dazzle me with impeccable glam.

"Angel! Where you been?" she sings, throwing up her hands. "You forgot about me?"

"Never, Mom," Angel says. He leans over the counter and gives her an elbow bump. "I missed you. How's it going? How's the fam?"

"Everyone's coming home for winter break!"

"Your daughter too?"

"Yes, even Quinn. The new semester doesn't start at Dartmouth until January 18. I'm so happy to have all my kids home again. And you know what? I will make them work. They will come work at the shop, just like old times." Even behind the mask, her smile is vibrant. She turns to me. "Who is this friend? She is so pretty."

"This is Deanna," Angel says.

"Deanna, a pretty name too. You call me Mom, honey. This is my place. You hungry?" She turns to Angel. "The usual?"

Angel says something in what I think is Vietnamese, and Mom claps her hands. "You got it." She looks at me and points to the menu board above our heads. "It's not up there. This is something I make for myself and my family when we're working. Angel saw me eating it on my break and he wanted to try it. So now I make it for him. And now for you." She points to the tables and chairs. "Go. Sit. I will bring it out when it's ready."

Angel lets me choose a table in the middle of the small shop and sits down across from me. Mom brings us Styrofoam cups of cold water. We take off our masks and drink.

"I sometimes come here after we close up the brewery," Angel says. "It's a good spot late at night. Friendly, not sketchy."

"Mom works here by herself?"

"Sometimes," Angel says.

"Is she safe?"

"The graveyard shift cops keep an eye on her." He smiles to himself. "My first job was night shift cashier at a twenty-four-hour liquor store. The owner—this mean old Cambodian man, smart as hell—chose the location because it was at the intersection of three different patrol areas. He made me keep the bathroom clean and stocked with soap and paper towels. All the cops used our restroom. Code Brown."

I make a face. "Gross."

"What? It's true. That was our free security. And a side benefit to me, personally, was that they never hassled me the way they hassled all the other fools on the street who looked like me."

"What do you mean?"

"Every Latino kid with tattoos got an immediate label. 'Gang affiliated.' It didn't matter if they had nothing to do with a gang. But me? They saw me as that kid who unlocked the restroom for them. A good kid. Hard worker. They left me alone." Angel nods to himself. "Perception is everything. People will tell themselves a story about you whether it's true or not."

I look at him sideways. I know he is a hard worker because I've seen it with my own eyes. But he's right—anyone who didn't know him would think he's just a thug. A gangster.

"But were you in a gang?" I ask point-blank. He knows I know his family history, but not all of it.

"What do you know about Salas?" he asks.

"Salas? What's that?"

"Salinas."

"Not much. I'm familiar with the prisons, but that's it."

"Salinas sits on the border between the northern and southern gangs in California." He looks down at the Styrofoam cup in his big hands. "If anyone learned I had brothers who were Sureños, I wouldn't be here right now. I'd be in a field somewhere. Helping the artichokes grow." He looks up at me. "And not the way farmers do."

That takes me a second to understand. Then I hate what happened to him, what he had to endure. He was just a kid. It must have been hell.

Before I can ask him how he ended up in Salinas in the first place, Mom appears carrying a plastic tray. She balances the tray on the edge of our table and places two giant steaming bowls of soup on the table. She places a plastic container of cut limes and fresh herbs between our bowls. "These are all from my garden back home," she says. Last, she places a plastic bottle of something red and wicked on the table. "I make this," she says with a wink. "It will knock your mind—is that the right saying? No, no. It will blow your socks off. Blow? Knock? Whatever. You get it."

"Thank you so much, Mom," Angel says.

"You got all you need? More water?"

"All good."

She puts two sets of plastic chopsticks and soup spoons on the table next to us along with two forks before returning to the counter. Without hesitating, Angel plucks leaves from the herbs and drops them into his soup. He dresses it with lime and two spoons of chili sauce. I copy everything he does. He picks up his chopsticks and digs in immediately with a loud slurp. I try to do the same but my fingers fumble the long plastic sticks.

Angel hands me a fork.

"Thanks," I say sheepishly. "How are you so good at chopsticks?"

"I grew up with a lot of Asian cats," he says. "When I ran away, I lived with my friend's family for a while. They took me in. They were Chinese Vietnamese, like Mom here. They taught me how to use chopsticks. I was so bad at it at first. Even the little kids in the family used to make fun of me. Funny stuff."

I twirl some noodles around my fork and take a bite. They're light and fresh. I take a spoonful of hot broth. I taste beef, heat from the chili sauce, even a hint of sweetness. The herbs are bright, alive. I feel myself getting healthier with each bite.

"Is this your first time eating pho?" Angel asks.

"My friends in college used to talk about it, but I haven't had it until now."

"You're lucky. This is Mom's family recipe."

From behind the counter, Mom asks, "Is it good?" Her smiling eyes tell me she already knows the answer.

"You should put this on the menu," Angel says. "You'd make a fortune."

Mom shakes her head. "Your happy face is my fortune, m'ijo."

Angel smiles warmly at the endearment. And as I take another bite, I think to myself, this city. This wild city with its infinite mess and infinite stories. Just as you think you know all the secrets, a hundred more reveal themselves.

Mom returns to the back kitchen, leaving us to eat in silence. The food is too good to interrupt with conversation. When we reach the bottom of our bowls, Angel takes a drink of water and leans back in his chair.

"So," he says, "what's going on with you?"

"What do you mean?"

"What happened to you today? Besides the shot."

"What?"

"You seem upset. Something is definitely wrong."

He has caught me off guard, relaxed and soothed by hot soup. There's kindness in his eyes, and I feel safe enough to tell him, even though I haven't come to terms with the truth myself.

"I got laid off today," I say slowly, "while I was asleep at the brewery."

"What? They fired you for that?"

"No, no," I say, waving my hand. "I didn't get fired, and definitely not for that. They're closing our office and combining it with the big one downtown. I didn't make the cut, so I won't be moving there with them."

"They laid you off by phone call? That is cold as hell."

"My coworker called me to tell me beforehand. I'll go in to have the real conversation with my boss tomorrow."

"I'm sorry," he says. "That sucks."

"Thanks. It does suck."

"What will you do now?"

"I don't know." I pluck one more leaf of basil from the container and pop it into my mouth. It's grassy and sweet. "My manager is starting over in San Bernardino. I think he may offer to take me on there."

"Oh, that's good."

"What?"

"You're going to do it, right? Take that offer?" He copies my actions and picks the last leaf of basil between us before taking a bite. "You're not really laid off if you have another job waiting for you once this one ends."

"No, they are really laying me off. I will be laid off."

"I mean, you will have another job right away. A good one." He pauses. "Why don't you want it?"

"Because I live here, not San Bernardino. My contacts are here. My family is here."

"But you don't live here. You live somewhere"—he gestures vaguely west—"over there. Koreatown or something, right?"

"That's not what I mean. Los Angeles. This is my home."

"San Bernardino is not that far," he says. "An hour's drive, maybe?"

"It's too far if the population I want to work with is here." I'm annoyed. He's not hearing me. "I've worked in this community all my life. I don't want to start again."

"It's not so bad, starting over. Home can be anywhere."

Now I feel it—the differences between us. "Maybe for you," I say. "You go wherever you want. Up and down the state, no roots at all."

He frowns.

Mom appears suddenly to clear our plates. A couple of customers enter the shop, ogling the Chinese food on the steam table.

"You want anything else?" Mom asks us.

"That was perfect," I say. "Thank you so much."

"Good, honey. I'm so happy. Now you come up here and pay me," she tells us as she walks behind the counter. I admire her hospitality almost as much as her bluntness.

We do as we're told. I pay for my bowl and Angel pays for his. Angel buys an extra dozen doughnuts in a pink box and thanks Mom, who tells him not to be a stranger before she moves on to help her other customers.

Angel and I walk out together to my car. The night air is cold but the real chill is the one that's suddenly formed between us. Now that I'm sober, he hands me the keys. I start up the engine and the heater and get ready to drive him back to his brother and sister-in-law's house.

I suppress a sigh of disappointment. This is why a one-night stand needs to stay a one-night stand. There's nothing real between Angel and me. I should've left the past in the past.

We don't talk until we reach the freeway. There's a homeless encampment in the shadow of the underpass—more and more encampments appear in the city every week. Next to the makeshift tents, one man is smoking a cigarette stub under a street light. He's dressed in two coats and everything about him looks sketchy.

"Hey, pull over, will you?" Angel says to me.

"What? Why?" I ask.

My law-abiding middle-class brain immediately goes into panic mode. Like most Angelenos, my car is my safe place. Why are we stopping here? Is Angel going to buy drugs? We'll get robbed. Carjacked. Stabbed, right here in a tent village under a bridge.

"Just pull over next to this guy," Angel says. "Please."

Something in his calm voice puts a pin in my anxiety. I pull over, still wary.

"Hey, brother," Angel calls out to the lone man on the sidewalk. Angel rolls down the car window and holds out the pink box. "Take this." The man looks just as wary as I feel, but he shuffles forward, perplexed, to receive the donuts. Angel pulls a five-dollar bill from his wallet and hands it to the man. "Stay safe out here tonight."

"All right. You too." The man's voice is rough and ragged. "Thank you kindly."

As we drive away, I ask, "Do you know him?"

"No," Angel says, "but I know a little bit about what he's going through."

I thought I wanted to be sad.

I thought I wanted to mope under the covers and feel sorry for myself for the rest of the night. But with a single sentence, Angel has calmed those impulses and put my problems in sharper perspective. Perhaps my day hasn't been the tragedy I want to make it. I have advantages—a car, a place to live, some savings—that others don't. They give me safety that many people in this city don't have.

After a long time, I say, "I apologize for what I said." I think about the people he's introduced me to tonight—Juan Luis,

Nacho, Pancho, Mom—and their obvious affection for him. "I shouldn't have called you rootless. I don't really know your circumstances. That wasn't fair."

Angel says nothing. Outside, the city streets are empty. The asphalt is slick with dew and the wet reflections of the street lamps glow like ghosts. It's been a long, long time since I've been out this late.

"To be honest, I feel that way a lot," Angel says. "Rootless. Nowhere really feels like home."

"Salinas?"

He thinks for a moment. Then he shakes his head. "No, not anymore."

"How about here?"

"Sometimes. But not really." He takes a deep breath. "And I'm sorry too. I should've listened before jumping in and assuming you wanted to leave LA." He pauses. "I guess for me, work is just work. I always said yes to everything. It never mattered to me what the job was because it was work and I was lucky to have it at all. But you're different from me. You have an education and actual skills, so it makes sense that you would also have a choice. You should make the choice that's right for you."

I stop at the next light and take a good long look at him.

"What?" he says.

I want to tell him how strange I feel, resolving a disagreement so easily that all the annoyance and disappointment I felt a moment ago are gone, dissipated into the cold night air.

This kind of communication does not really exist in my romantic relationships.

This kind of communication does not really exist in my life in general.

Here's how arguing usually goes in my world: the actual disagreement chased by a few hours—at least—of resentful quiet treatment, followed by bickering about inconsequential things.

This finally ends with an explosion of pent-up anger and sloppy, inaccurate insults, mostly below the belt. Someone usually storms off in a dramatic way. Then the chisme, perpetuated by everyone's gossipy family, friends and frenemies, gleeful as toddlers blowing dandelions in the wind.

Instead of actually repairing the relationship, people in my life cut each other off completely or pretend nothing ever happened at all—until the next blowout, of course. Lather, rinse, repeat, ad nauseam.

"What?" Angel says again.

"Nothing," I say.

"Tell me."

"You just surprise me, that's all," I say.

"In a good way?"

"Yes, in a good way."

We smile shyly at each other.

"So. Back to your brother's house?" I ask quietly.

My hand is resting on the gear shift. Angel reaches down and with the barest touch, grazes the back of my hand with the bruised knuckle of his middle finger.

My breath catches at the contact, and he knows it.

I almost can't get the words out. "That's where you're staying, right?"

He looks me in the eye, and I fight to meet his gaze just as boldly. But his voice is as soft as his touch when he says, "I'll stay where you want me to, Deanna."

SIX

ANGEL

"IT'S REALLY LATE," Deanna says. "I should take you home."

"You should," I say.

Without another word, we drive the half-mile toward Sal and Vanessa's house, but when we reach their street, she doesn't make the turn. Instead, she gets on the freeway.

Every nerve in my body flickers on. Like a hundred strings of Christmas lights, all at once.

Yes.

Fuck yes.

The freeway is almost empty. We pass downtown. New buildings stand between the old ones. I count four cranes, waiting to add more beams, more floors, reaching up to the sky, higher than Heaven.

Deanna's hands are at two and ten. Her face is calm and still, but she grips the steering wheel like she's a teenager taking her driving test. Like she's afraid she is about to lose control of the car.

I reach out and put my hand on her wrist. She jumps slightly, but she doesn't look away from the road. I slip just the tip of my thumb under the cuff of her sweatshirt. Her skin is smooth and warm, and her pulse is strong, an echo of the heart-beat going wild in my chest. I draw a small circle with my thumb on the inside of her wrist. She inhales, just a little, and I imagine—no, I remember—how she did that the first time I entered her body, way back when. She breathed me in, like smoke. First in small gasps, bit by bit, then in a long, deep drag. And I disappeared into her, into her bloodstream like a narcotic.

I feel high. Loopy. A little philosophical.

She changes lanes and, like a gentleman, I put my hand back on my knee.

I have to wonder, what is it like? For a woman? For her?

To live in a world full of men who want to take something from you, who want a piece of you, who want either to keep you or throw you away, who can hurt you? What leap of faith do you have to take to let one of those men in? To show a bit of yourself and your vulnerabilities, and hope for—what, in return?

Pleasure?

Kindness?

In exchange for another night, another shot, with Deanna, I promise myself that I will give her both. As much pleasure and kindness as I can, as much as she will let me.

But—as my pants remind me—there is a problem. A big one.

My whole life I have been a physical person. Training, sparring, fighting, running, working out. Working menial jobs required me to use my body, to be strong. Here in LA, I have found ways to stay physical, but sex has been a challenge.

After Deanna, there was no one else for a long time. When I was in the apartment, I had a couple booty calls with a regular at the brewery, but she moved back to Texas to be with her family when the pandemic started. She was nice, but we were basically workout partners, nothing more. Then I had to give up the apartment for the couch in Sal and Vanessa's living room. That's when my sex life tanked completely. There's no privacy in that house at all. Even the lock on the bathroom I share with Vanessa's grandmother is broken. Abuelita has walked in on me showering a few times. After the sixth or seventh time, I began to wonder if she ever really did it by accident.

"Don't mind me, m'ijo. I'm just getting the Tiger Balm."

"Ay, sorry, Angelito. I left my glasses in here and I want to finish the Jumble."

No privacy. Zero. Not even to take the self-guided tour, if you know what I mean.

And that's the problem. It's been months since I jacked off. I'm on a hair trigger. As soon as Deanna touches me, I'm going to come. I know it. It's going to be fucking embarrassing.

What am I going to do? What?

As I panic in silence, we exit the freeway and make the drive up Western Avenue into K-town. Doing deliveries has helped me understand the layout of Los Angeles, but some neighborhoods, like this one, are still a mystery to me. We pass rundown storefronts locked tight behind security gates, closed Salvadoran restaurants and bakeries, and a few all-night Korean barbecue spots with full parking lots. She turns left at a shiny Korean shopping mall lit with neon, and circles the block a couple times until she finds a parking space in front of a Korean Baptist church next to her building. I remember it—a big white apartment building with bars on all the first-floor windows. It's old, U-shaped with a narrow courtyard, five stories tall.

She does an expert parallel parking job into the tiny space. I watch her face. She bites her lip to concentrate on the task. This makes my dick so hard my head aches from blood loss.

"Ready?" She looks at me and gives me a tiny smile.

"Yeah," I croak.

We get out of the car and she locks it. I follow her up the steps to the heavy gate to the courtyard of her building. All of the security bars and fences have been painted bright white, but the old metal is rusting through, insisting on being seen. Refusing to be whitewashed.

She unlocks gate after gate after gate until we're finally in the lobby of her building. There's a wall of ancient brass mailboxes and bins from the post office filled with junk mail. I follow her down a dim hallway over cheap institutional tile and carpet. The smell of new paint competes with disinfectant, old wood polish and a dozen different home-cooked dinners.

We walk up worn-out steps to the third floor. At her apartment, she unlocks three more locks. I'm glad she is secure, but I'm annoyed that she has to protect herself against the world. I'm annoyed that all these locks are necessary to make her feel safe.

I follow her inside as she turns on a small lamp and locks the locks again. One, two, three.

And now I'm locked in with her.

My brain and body are buzzing with anticipation. I am barely able to register what her apartment looks like. I remember that it's a studio. Small, with one of those beds that fold down from the wall like in old cartoons.

She puts her things down and takes off her shoes. Then she walks around the apartment, picking up half-chewed dog toys and tossing them into a bin by the front door.

"Sorry my place is such a mess," she says. "I wasn't expecting—"

I grab her wrist, the same one I touched in the car. I pull her close, pinning her arms between us. I look deep into her dark, astonished eyes, blinking behind her glasses. It's too much—too much beauty, too much vulnerability, too much everything. She is too much.

I kiss her. Thirsty, I drink in the sensation of her soft, pillowy lips, her surprised breaths against my skin.

I force myself to go slowly, to savor that first wave of exhilaration. I haven't been close to anyone like this in so long that every cell in my body hums. My brain's proximity alert is howling like a car alarm.

Deanna grips the front of my sweatshirt in both hands as if she is about to fight me. Still locked in our kiss, I cup my hand gently behind her head and lean her back, exposing her throat.

The ghost of a memory lingers in my mind—does she like this? As a test, I rest my other hand on her soft, warm neck, my fingers barely grazing her skin. She gasps into my mouth and when her lips part, I dive in, stroking the tip of her tongue with mine. She tastes sweet and fresh, like the herbs we had for dinner.

Slowly, I tell myself again. Slow down. I want her to know that I'm making these decisions, one by one. That she can trust me in bed. That I'm not some immature kid who doesn't know what he's doing. She needs to know I can be in control.

When I stroke her neck with my fingertips, she groans, lets go of my sweatshirt and slides one hand down my abs.

If she touches my dick, I'm going to come. Panicking, I jump back so fast my entire body cramps up with frustration.

She opens her eyes. Before she can register any kind of rejection, I spin her around and hold her, pinning her forearms to her sides. "I have wanted a taste of you for three fucking years, you know that?" I growl in her ear. I tighten my grip, trying to keep her still. But she arches her back, and her round, firm ass presses up against my hard-on. Agony.

"Before you get that taste," she says, "I need to know. Do you have a girlfriend? A wife?"

"No. Neither." I smile to myself. She did this the first time we slept together too—a little interview. Maybe some guys would find it a turn-off. I find it hot. She protects herself.

"Good. I'm single too. Are you sleeping with anyone else? Do you have casual sex?"

"No," I say, "not for almost a year. How about you?"

"Nope." She sways her hips back and forth, and I'm so turned on I am having trouble seeing straight. "Not since you."

That surprises me.

"Any STDs?" she asks. "When's the last time you were tested?"

"No, I've never had any." I take a breath and try to give her a clear-headed answer. "I changed primary care doctors this past summer. The new one recommended I have a shit-ton of tests and bloodwork done, so I did. Everything came back fine."

She looks over her shoulder at me. "Hmm."

"What?"

"And your last covid test? Mine was negative. I took it Saturday before I went to visit my family."

That's a new addition to her questionnaire. "Negative. Vanessa makes us take them every week." I rest my forehead against the back of her head. She smells so good—like peaches, ripe and ready to eat. "Now I have a question for you," I say.

"Go ahead."

She rubs her big ass against me again. Nalgona. Fuck, she's so hot. I swallow down a groan and grab on to her hips to keep them still. "Will you let me take care of you tonight?" I ask.

"What do you mean?"

I lean in and whisper in her ear. "I want to make you come. Hard."

She laughs quietly. "I want that too."

I give her ass a little slap. "Be good and listen."

"Ouch! Fine."

She is smiling a little. I spin her around and kiss her again, one soft kiss on her bottom lip. "What I mean is, I want you to relax and let me do everything. You don't have to touch me. You don't have to do anything. Just lie back and let me make you feel good."

"Are you serious?"

"Yes," I say.

"But why?"

I think for a moment. How can I say this? "Because...it's been a long time for me." I look into her eyes and hope she gets what I'm saying.

She reaches up and rests her hand on my cheek. The gesture is so gentle and kind, my fucking heart kicks in my chest like a horse. I haven't been touched like this in—I don't know. Forever. If ever.

"Okay," she says. "Tell me what to do."

I take her in my arms. Her apartment, the dim light, the building, the block, the city itself—everything melts together to form a protective dome around us. We're in our own little world. I take a deep breath and finally let myself enjoy the pleasure in this moment.

"Ready?" I whisper.

"Yes."

I take off her sweatshirt, and she takes off mine. It's cold, but as we drop each article of clothing, I feel myself getting warmer. Our layers disappear, one by one, and my picture of Deanna becomes clearer. The scent of her, the shape of her, the feel of her body against mine. One element, then another, then another, until she gives me the full symphony of her beauty, all at once.

Now we're naked.

Completely unmasked.

I stare. Golden brown skin, dark wavy hair, curves like a wild mountain road I want to take at two hundred miles per hour. She's glorious. But when I look into her eyes, I see she's not happy.

"Are you okay?" I ask.

"I'm fine," she says. But she's struggling with something
—what?

"Tell me what's wrong," I say.

She folds her arms in front of her. "I haven't been taking
care of myself," she says quietly. "I haven't been working out or
sleeping well. I haven't been eating right either."

"Deanna," I say, "it's a pandemic."

"Right, I know, but…" She doesn't finish the sentence.

I echo her movements and touch her cheek as gently as I
can. Behind her glasses, her eyes widen and look sadly into
mine. "I'm sorry," she says. "I have some…body stuff I need to
work through."

"Never apologize for that." I stroke her soft skin with my
fingertips. "Listen to me. I don't know what you're feeling, but I
can talk about what I see. To me, your body is beautiful. More
beautiful than I can imagine. You're what I like. What your
body looks like, and who you are inside—that's what I like." I
glance down between us at what I like to think is the elephant in
the room. "I hope it's obvious I like you. Um, a lot."

She raises one eyebrow at me.

"You're fucking sexy," I say. "Will you let me make you feel
good?"

When she reaches for me, I grab her and pull her into another
deep kiss. She closes her eyes and moans against my lips. I sit on her
bed and pull her down with me. She's straddling me and stroking
my chest in a slow, hypnotic rhythm, but when the palms of her
hands brush my nipples, I break our kiss and flip her onto her back. I
hold her wrists and pin her to the mattress with my hips. I press my
cock against the inside of her thigh. This feels so good I want to cry.

"Angel," she whispers breathlessly.

I hold her. She can't move. I kiss her until her lips are
swollen. I kiss her neck and throat until she is squirming in my

grip. Her skin is feverish. I shift my weight on her and press a thigh between hers, easing her legs apart. She arches against me again, and the tip of my cock brushes her pussy. She's wet and hot, and I gasp, jerking back like I've put my hand in a fire.

"Oh, God," she says. "I want to touch you so much."

"Not yet." My voice is wrecked like I've been shouting. Still holding her wrists, I pull her arms up over her head and place her hands on the iron bars of her headboard. "Grip that. Keep those hands there, Deanna. Don't move them."

"Okay." When she smiles at me her glasses catch the lamp-light, and I feel it—the birth of my glasses fetish. Right here. Right now.

I kiss her again. Her tongue tangles with mine. With my hands free, I stroke her face and her collarbone. When I rest my hand on her neck again, she gasps. I tighten my grip, slightly, and she whimpers. I catch her whimper in my mouth.

I pull away. "You like that, don't you?" I whisper.

"Yes," she says.

I squeeze a little harder, on either side of her throat so as not to mess with her breathing. She whimpers again and my balls ache in response, heavy with come. Apparently what turns me on is turning her on.

I change my grip and cradle the back of her neck with my hand, grazing her throat with my thumb. With my free hand, I reach down and finally—fucking finally—get hold of one perfect breast.

"Jesus Christ," I murmur.

She is stacked as fuck. My rough hands look extra beat-up as I reach out to stroke her. Her skin is smooth and her nipples are dark brown. I brush them lightly with my fingers and they harden immediately. I lower my lips to her, suck one nipple into my mouth, and gently strum her back and forth.

When she moans, I glance up at her face. Her eyes are shut

TANKED   79

tight. Her hands are white-knuckled on the metal bed frame. Sucking harder, I roll her other nipple gently in my fingers until both are hard as cherry pits. When I let go, the very tips of them are dark pink.

I sit back. A drop of pre-come forms on the tip of my cock. We look at it together. Deanna purses her lips and asks, "Are you sure you don't want me to touch you?"

"I'm sure," I say, swiping the drop away with my thumb. "Open your legs."

Eyes on mine, she takes a deep breath. She bends her knees and slowly spreads her gorgeous legs wide for me. A blade of light from the lamp falls across her lap. In the shadows, I see a triangle of dark hair, natural, like mine. The sheets are damp underneath her, and the scent of her arousal hits the pleasure center in my brain like a lightning bolt.

I lean over her body and kiss her mouth once more. I kiss her for a long time. When her eyes flutter closed, I reach between her legs and gently run the pad of my finger down one delicate lip of her pussy.

"Angel," she whispers.

I stroke her, up and down, still kissing her, mirroring the movements of my fingers with my tongue. When she is slick and swollen, I dip my finger into her like holy water. When I find her tight, hard clit, I circle it with the barest touch. A moan comes from deep inside her chest.

I whisper in her ear, "Tell me. How do you make yourself come?"

SEVEN

ANGEL

DEANNA OPENS HER EYES. "WHAT?"

"How do you make yourself come?" I ask again. "Do you touch yourself?"

She blinks. "Not really."

"You don't?"

"I do, but...I don't."

"What do you mean?"

"Are you serious right now?" Frustration gives her voice a little edge. "Do you really want to know?"

"Yes."

She stares at me for a few seconds, trying to decide whether or not to tell me. "Okay. Look in the drawer."

"This one?" I point to the nightstand.

"Yeah."

I open the small drawer. There's a box of condoms, still sealed, some lube and this little vibrator thing. It's a weird shape and I have no idea how it works. Next to that, there's something else—a glass dildo. I pick it up. It's attached to a base. It's heavy, smooth and perfectly clear, like water. I've never seen anything like it.

"This?"

"Yes." Deanna frowns. "Are you judging me?"

"I'm judging you to be awesome." I smile. "Can I use it on you?"

She opens her mouth to say something but nothing comes out.

"What are you thinking?" I ask.

"I've never used a toy with a partner before. So this would be a first for me." She considers this. "It's been a while since I've had any kind of first, so...that's exciting, I guess."

With the toy in one hand, I lean down and kiss her softly.

"I find it exciting too."

I drop kisses in a slow line from her lips, down her neck, to the center of her chest. I kiss each of her hardened little nipples. I kiss down her stomach, and when she takes a sharp breath, I put a hand on her chest and pin her, gently but firmly, to the mattress. Her heartbeat flutters against the palm of my hand as I lower my head down between her legs. I rest my forehead just below her belly button and take a deep breath of her—sweet and rich. She smells like peaches hanging ripe on the tree, ready to burst.

I look up at her face. "I'm going to go down on you now, Deanna. Is that okay?"

"Yes. Yes, that's good—that's okay." Her cheeks are flushed. She's still holding on to the iron headboard. I'm impressed at how good she is at following the rules.

I prop myself up on my forearms. She is so wet that when I run my thumb along her dark seam, the obscene sound makes my cock jerk against the bedsheets. I do it again and again. Her lips part just a little—inside, she is hot pink and wet, like a flower filled with rainwater. I can't wait any longer. I dip my tongue deep inside her and get my taste at last—she's as delicious as I remember, and my body roars for more.

I spread her thighs wider with my hands. I want to see—I want to taste—all of her. As I explore her, her pussy gets hotter and sweeter in my mouth. I take my time. Her pussy swells and changes color to a deeper, sensual pink. I lick and suck and tease her, my tongue clicking wetly against her hard little clit. I could do this forever. But when she gasps, I stop.

She lets out a frustrated groan. I smile to myself as I grab the dildo and show it to her.

"Okay?" I ask. My voice is ragged. Hungry.

Wide-eyed, she purses her lips and nods.

The glass is cold. When I rub it gently against her hot pussy I swear it sizzles on contact. The clear glass catches the lamplight and magnifies like a lens. I'm mesmerized as I run it up and down her pussy, stopping to tease her clit with the smooth tip. She gets even wetter. A drop of arousal runs out of her like a teardrop.

"Angel," she whispers. "Please. I'm so turned on."

"Good."

I ease the head of the toy inside her. Her tight pussy resists it. My aching cock throbs as I imagine how delicious that pushback would feel. Gently, I pull back, then find another angle and push forward slowly. She takes a deep breath. Then her body seems to grab the heavy glass toy and pull it inward.

This is the sexiest thing I've ever seen in my entire life. I pull it out, just half an inch, and seat it deeper inside her. Deanna closes her eyes and drops her head back.

"Fuck. That is so good."

As I hold the base of the dildo, I can feel her pussy gripping it, adjusting around it. Gently, I move it back and forth. The heat of her body heats up the glass, and now it feels like a living object connecting us.

I close my eyes. Time stops. I hold the toy in place and find her hard candy clit with my tongue. I concentrate on her breathing, her tiny movements, her quiet moans. Tension hums through her like electricity. I build it up, adjusting my angle by tiny degrees. When she bucks hard against me, I freeze, staying on that one spot and keeping my rhythm as steady as a drumbeat.

"Oh my God," she whispers. "Angel, I'm going to come."

My body is on fire. Through the strange conduit of the glass cock, I feel the first tremors of her orgasm. I pin her down with my free arm and lick and lick and lick her until she finally lets go of the headboard and grabs onto my shoulders. Her orgasm shakes her hard. She's silent as she comes, but her fingernails dig into my skin and her body contracts around her toy so fiercely I have to hold it there to keep it in place.

And, like a lightning flash, I remember it all.

Our one wild night together.

She was a stranger to me then, but I recognized her in myself. In this moment, I remember how clearly she mirrored my hunger and my loneliness. As if neither would ever be too ferocious for her to confront.

When her orgasm passes, she lets go of me, throwing me off like blankets in a too-hot room. The sudden motion makes me laugh a little. As I stand up from the bed to stretch, she lies back, panting. Her cheeks are red as cocktail cherries, and she's a little out of it, drunk on coming.

"Are you okay?" I say.

Instead of answering, she locks eyes with me. She reaches down and slowly eases the glass dildo out of her pussy. Halfway, she lets go and pushes it out with the muscles of her pussy before catching the base with her cupped hand.

Before I realize it, my dick is in my hand. It's hard as fuck. My balls ache, heavy with come and ready to explode from the wonders I have seen tonight.

"Are you sure you don't want me to touch you?" she says quietly, eyeing my dick.

I shake my head. I can't seem to manage words right now. If she touches me, I will explode.

"Do you want me to go down on you?" she asks.

"One hundred percent," I gasp, "but not right now."

"Okay."

Then she does something that I know I will never forget until the day I die. I will be an old man on my deathbed. I will close my eyes for the last time and the light at the end of the tunnel will be this—Deanna Delgado, wide-eyed and golden, pulling a glass cock from her body and bringing it to her lips. She locks eyes with me, pops the shiny tip of it into her mouth, and gives it a long, slow suck. And I swear, as if by magic, electrical pulses tell my brain to feel her warm, soft mouth on my cock, as if she were doing it to me instead.

"Fuck." The word fights its way out of my throat, rough and needy.

I tighten my fist. One stroke. Two.

That's all it takes.

My body locks up. My thighs flex. Like a prayer, I fall on my knees on the mattress in front of her. I look down at the purple head of my cock appearing and disappearing in the ring of my thumb and forefinger. I speed up my strokes and squeeze harder, imagining Deanna's mouth, Deanna's pussy, Deanna's ass, all of her. A feast of pleasure. I will never be full.

The first shot is furious. It comes out of me, hot and thick, and lands on her beautiful collarbone. It runs down the top of her left breast before it stops, forming a white teardrop on the end of her hardened nipple. I give one surprised shout as the spasms overtake me. I splash her with more come, and this feels —and looks—so fucking delicious, I think I might cry. Deanna watches me and smiles around the glass cock. With her free hand, she runs her fingertips slowly through the hot come, painting a line from her belly button to her throat.

And I can't stop staring at her.

A goddess. Beautiful.

And filthy, just like me.

Perfect.

I collapse on the bed next to her, gasping for breath. My entire body is raw. I slowly release my grip on myself. I feel the aftershocks of my orgasm at the base of my dick. My blood runs hot, and I can feel my own heartbeat from the top of my head to the bottoms of my feet.

I take a deep breath and watch, dazed, as Deanna gets up from the bed. She takes her toy to the bathroom. I hear the shower. I must doze off because when I wake up again, she's lying next to me in a fluffy bathrobe. There's a lazy, satisfied expression on her face.

"Fallen." She touches the wing tattoos on my back and reads the script between them. "When did you get all of these?"

"When I was extra young and extra stupid," I murmur. "I studied Catholic symbolism. Mesoamerican religions. I wanted to look tougher. More intimidating." I look sideways at her. "Do they work? Are you intimidated?

Deanna smiles. "No."

She kisses my forehead, turns off the light and pulls the blankets over us. I wrap my arms around her, and she melts against me with a little sigh.

A minute passes. Two.

Now she's asleep.

I take another deep breath of her and hold the air in my lungs for as long as I can before exhaling slowly. Tension drains from my body, drop by drop.

Drowsy, I think if I never get to do this again, I will

remember this moment. I will remember how I held her against me as she slept. How warm we were. How safe.

⸎

NOW I HAVE a dream I haven't had in a long, long time.

I'm following my grandmother into a dark building. I'm nine, maybe ten years old.

"Stay close," she says in Spanish.

She holds a white keycard up to a black pad by the door. A light turns green, and I hear a beep. When we walk through, I realize I'm carrying a backpack and a small blanket.

We ride the silver elevator to the top floor. I follow her through a dim hallway into an unmarked utility room. She flips a switch. The clock on the wall says 11:00. Without talking, I go to the corner and grab the standup vacuum cleaner. She puts on a checkered mandil from home and ties it carefully. She puts a broom, a dustpan, a couple spray bottles and some plastic bags in the giant wheeled trash can. The word BRUTE is printed across the side of it, which I looked up in the dictionary: "An animal. One who lacks intelligence, sensitivity or compassion. A brutal person."

At school, I like reading and spelling, which seems to surprise my teachers. They make a point to praise me in class whenever I raise my hand whether I give the right answer or not. They don't do this for the other students. I'm annoyed by this but I can't explain why.

Whenever I show my report card to my grandmother, she examines it carefully while nodding. I don't think she understands it, but she always says the same thing, "Very good. Keep studying, m'ijo. Don't be like me."

The whole top floor of the building is a law firm. Abuela's key card opens the glass doors at the front of the office and we wheel past the receptionist's desk. There's a maze of filing cabinets and cubicles and ten offices along one wall. We start in the back and work our way forward. My job is to sweep big pieces of trash off the carpet and empty the trash cans. My grandmother follows me with the vacuum cleaner and pauses to dust all the surfaces, putting everything back in exactly the same spot.

As we clean around each desk, I try to imagine the people who work here during the day. Some of them have framed photos of their families and kids' artwork tacked to the cubicle walls. Some have photos of their pets and a plant or two. One desk has a big jar of candy. Once I took one and my grandmother smacked my hand so hard she knocked the pink Starburst back into the jar with a loud *plink*.

"No," she said. "That's not for you."

At last, we open up the largest office and clean it up. Abuela waters the big plant in the corner and wipes off its leaves that look like elephant ears. She turns on a small desk lamp and turns off the overhead light.

I lie down on the leather sofa and take off my sneakers. She puts my blanket over me.

She sits down on the edge of the coffee table and opens my backpack. "Which story did you bring for us today? The one about Stanley?"

I yawn. The clock on the desk says 12:00. "Yes."

She hands me *Holes* by Louis Sachar, a book the school librarian recommended to me. I begin reading out loud where we left off. My grandmother folds her arms and listens carefully to everything I say. We read a lot of books together. Her English is not great, but she seems to enjoy this. She likes this book a lot. She likes any story about journeys, like *Walk Two Moons*. She didn't like any of the Goosebumps books I brought, so I don't bring those anymore, even though I really like them. For some reason, she really liked *Hatchet*. After we finished that one she told me a story about how she once killed a snake with a machete back on her parents' ranch.

"Is that what a 'hatchet' is? A machete?" she asked.

I read a few pages from *Holes*. Then she takes the book from me and puts it back in my backpack. I yawn again.

"It's strange," she says, looking at me. "When you lie down to go to sleep, you look like your mother. But during the day, you look like your father. An angel during the night. A devil during the day."

I blink at her, confused.

"I talked to your uncle today."

I don't say anything.

"Fighting? Again?" She clicks her tongue in disgust. "Your uncle said he has to go to the school on Thursday afternoon to meet with your teachers and your principal. He said he has to take time off work to do this. That's no good, Angel."

My uncle—and his belt—have already informed me of his feelings about this meeting. I will have to wear sweat pants instead of shorts in gym class for the next couple weeks until the bruises go away.

"God has a plan for you, m'ijo. I don't know what it is. Only He knows." My grandmother touches my forehead gently with her rough hand. "No more fighting. No more. Do you understand?"

I understand what she wants from me. But I don't understand how I will survive here. I'm not welcome, not at school, not in the neighborhood, not even in her house with Tío Rick and his bottomless anger. I'm the new kid, lonely and strange. And everyone can feel the cloud of death around me. They don't know the full story, but they know enough to either make me suffer or stay away from me completely.

I miss my father. I miss my brothers.

But most of all, I miss my mom and my little sister. My grandmother wailed—wailed like a wild animal—at the funeral. One coffin for my mother. A much smaller one for Esperanza.

"Okay, m'ijo," Abuela says. "Time to sleep."

Before sadness can crush me again in its jaws, I close my eyes. For the rest of the night, my grandmother will clean the building by herself. In the morning, I will brush my teeth and change my shirt in the employee restroom. We'll leave and lock up the building before anyone else arrives to see us. My uncle will pick us up and drop me off at school just in time for the free breakfast.

But before all that, my grandmother and I recite the nightly prayer she taught me when I first arrived in Salinas. In my dream, I recite it perfectly. "Ángel de mi guarda, dulce compañía, no me desampares, ni de noche ni de día..."

EIGHT

DEANNA

IS THAT…RAIN?

First, slow drops ping the gutters, the dusty window panes, the sunbaked fire escape. They pelt the bone-dry streets and sidewalks, bringing up the smell of crushed rock and old tar. Then the sky cracks open and rain—real rain—falls in heavy lashes across a parched city that hasn't been doused like this in months.

I'm in bed, buried in a nest of covers. I open my eyes. I pick up my phone and hold it close enough to see the time. It's 5:30. The room is still dark, illuminated only by pale gray light leaking in from behind my cheap blinds. I put down my phone, yawn and stretch. For the first time in a long time, I feel good. Rested. Peaceful.

The old bed squeaks as Angel sits down next to me. With some regret, I realize he's already dressed.

I start to sit up. "Just give me a few minutes to get ready," I say. "I'll drop you off at the brewery on my way into work."

"No," he says quietly. With his rough hand, he gently strokes my cheek. My whole body aches to reach out for him, but I lay back, waiting to see what he will say next.

"I want you to stay here," he says. "Take the day off, like your coworker said. I have a ride."

"You do?"

"Yeah." In the dark, I can still make out his smirk. "I drive an SS."

An old joke. "Socks and shoes?"

"Exactly."

"Let me drive you," I say.

"Absolutely not." He kisses my forehead. "It's an express bus. One shot. I'll be at work in time if I leave now."

Thunder cracks softly in the distance. I must be looking at him skeptically because he says, "I'm serious, Deanna. I'm fine. Stay here."

I reach for his hand and give it a squeeze. He's cold. "Take my umbrella, at least. It's hanging by the door," I say.

"No, I'm good. You keep it. Thank you, though."

I feel it creeping back—my self-doubt. I'm offering small pieces of myself to him, and he's turning them down. A sure sign to stop offering. I sound so needy—of course he's backing away.

"Okay." I let his hand go. "I'll see you when I see you, I guess."

Angel looks at me for a moment without saying anything. Then he gets up. Instead of walking out the door, he picks up some pillows that have fallen on the floor and places them back on the bed. He straightens the covers and tucks me in carefully. When he notices my phone is unplugged, he reattaches the charger before putting it back on my nightstand where I can reach it. Carefully, he arranges my glasses next to my phone.

He drops another kiss on my forehead and looks into my eyes. Up close, his eyes are beautiful—deep, dark and full of watchful intelligence. I'm guessing there isn't much that gets past him.

"Just to warn you," he says, "I'm going to text you a lot. Probably too much. Please don't judge me. I like you and I'm very awkward."

I can't help it. I laugh a little bit.

"Obviously it's up to you whether you text back." He stares at my mouth for a second, then rests a fingertip softly on my bottom lip. I gasp. With a single touch, he's turned me on like a switch. My body ignites from that single point of contact. Heat radiates in waves down my spine.

"But I hope you text back," he whispers, "because I want to see you again. Badly."

He presses down lightly with his fingertip, parting my lips just enough to see a flash of my teeth. Echoes of last night's orgasm run through me. My pussy clenches up, ravenous for more.

As if he knows exactly the effect his touch has on me, Angel lets go and smiles his ridiculously handsome smile. He arranges the covers one more time. "Okay. I have to go. Get some more sleep, princesa."

I watch through the blurry wall of my nearsightedness as he stands up. He puts on his hoodie and zips it up. He unlocks the bolts on my door. The old hinges squeak as he opens the door, steps outside and pulls it closed.

Silently, I jump out of bed and tiptoe across my apartment. I press my ear to the gap between the front door and the door-frame. My heart thumping like a bass drum, I listen to Angel's heavy footfalls fading down the stairs as he heads out into the rain.

When the hallway is silent, I twirl back to my bed and flop backward into the blankets and pillows. The feeling is so unreal I can't name it.

What is this?

Giddiness?

Joy?

My apartment is the place where I hide out and cry. The place where I sleep alone—correction, not alone, with two slightly asthmatic bulldogs—eat boring food and doomscroll. It is not a place to bring a man. It is definitely not a place to have the kind of fun I had last night with Angel.

The last man in my bed before Angel was Angel. This thought makes me slightly lightheaded. A lightning flash illuminates the building across the alley. A few seconds later, thunder rattles every window in my apartment building. A cacophony of neighborhood dogs joins in, praising the might of the thunder god.

There is no explanation for what happened last night except that this tiny apartment is holy ground—a place where lightning strikes twice.

I grab a pillow, bury my face in it and scream. I kick my legs. I laugh like I'm possessed. Because what the fuck?

Seriously.

What. The. Fuck.

In the last three years, Angel has gotten hotter. How can people be so genetically blessed? When we first slept together, he was fit but still boyish. Now? No one would accuse him of boyishness. Muscular. Lean. With those ridiculously hot hip lines that only ridiculously hot men have. I have admired pictures of men who look like this. But it's a different experience when 6'3" of the real thing is kneeling at the foot of your bed, naked and jacking off all over you.

Yes, that is something else entirely.

I hug the pillow to my chest. I suppress the urge to text him right now and ask him to come back for a repeat performance.

Instead, I do the responsible thing. I get up and make some coffee. I open the window in my tiny kitchen. Cold air rushes in along with the smell and sound of a rainstorm so long in coming

I'm not sure if I'm awake or dreaming it. I stare outside with my coffee mug. Instead of gulping it down while battling traffic on the freeway, I sip it like a human being. I enjoy it.

I pick up my phone and stare at it for a moment.

Should I?

Sure, why not?

I tap out a text.

You were right. Please tell Tod I'm taking a sick day. See you all tomorrow.

I send the message to Ingrid and put my phone back down to keep myself from checking my work emails. I have a massive accumulation of sick days since I never take any days off. A pang of guilt hits me, but I fight it off with the thought that if they are laying me off forever, they can certainly live without me for one day.

Taking my time, I enjoy a long, hot shower and get dressed. Instead of the sweatshirts and leggings I've been wearing in heavy rotation during the pandemic, I put on a pair of nice jeans that still fit, a cashmere sweater I haven't worn in ages and my Doc Martens. I leave my hair down. I wipe the steam off my mirror with a towel. My hand is shaky and out of practice, but I manage some eyeliner, mascara and lip gloss. For fun, I put on my gold hoops, the ones Ingrid convinced me to buy years ago while drunk shopping after a boozy brunch. "Big enough to put a fist through," said Ingrid. "Buy them." So I did.

There. Done.

I look in the mirror.

Who is that person looking back at me?

I kind of recognize her. Changing the world—that was her spark, her fire. It still is. But there was more to that young woman than just work. There was a desire to find real solutions to problems—real light in the darkness—instead of just slapping Band-Aids on everything and calling it a day. Community growth and transformation, not just filling out paperwork and punching a clock. And there was longing for...what?

Adventure.

Excitement.

Love, even.

Efren. That was the name of my first real boyfriend. I saw him play at a small club downtown, just him, his guitar and a few songs he had written himself. After his show, we started talking about life, art, purpose. He never made fun of me for wanting more for myself and for my community. We fell in love fast, and I moved right in. Our first four years together were bliss. He wrote love songs for me. We adopted two dogs. But over time, his career stalled. He played fewer gigs and refused to find a day job to help pay the bills. He'd stay home, drinking and ostensibly working on his music. I was worried about him. One evening, I misjudged how much he'd had to drink and asked him about some overdraft fees from the bank. Like flipping a switch, our discussion became a heated argument. He threw books and dishes. He broke the neck of his guitar. And then he took a swing at me.

I'll never forget the sound of his knuckles cracking against my skull. My glasses skittered across the floor. I didn't register pain, only complete surprise. At work, I had spoken to enough survivors of domestic violence to know that was it. In a moment, I was done with this relationship.

"I'm going to Ro's," I said slowly. "In the morning, you need to be gone." I picked up my broken glasses, leashed up the dogs and walked out the door, my eyes full of angry tears. Efren had the good sense not to push back. That was the last time I ever saw him. He took all his shit and left me with a swollen face, a tall stack of bills, a rent-controlled K-town apartment and two wheezing bulldogs.

So that's Efren. But here's the important part.

Efren left me a month before I first slept with Angel.

After all of that bullshit, I was in no position to start anything with Angel. Even one night was so irresponsible, like I was playing with him and exposing him to all of my heartbreak, all of my mess. It felt wrong. So I ghosted him.

I'm not proud of this.

Instead of getting to know the real Angel, I kept the memory of him safely in my Inner Spanktum. I deleted all the dating apps on my phone. I stopped going out to bars with Ingrid. I retreated from any possibility of sex or a love life. And I dedicated myself to my one true love—my work.

But now? Even my work is breaking up with me.

I frown at the woman in the mirror. She frowns back.

Yup.

It's time to visit Aphrodite.

I grab my keys and my umbrella and head out the door.

I HEAR the panting even before I reach the top of the stairs. Eight paws do a happy tap dance on the wood floor just inside the door.

I knock. They sniff and snuff.

"Ro?" I say. "You there?"

The door swings open. Meatball and Funfetti waddle toward me, wagging their butts and snorting happily. I give them both a cuddle. They each give me a kiss.

Aphrodite Papadimitriou, my friend and neighbor, smiles warmly. "Don't you look nice," she says, a little surprised. When it comes to clothes, Ro sees all. She remembers everybody's outfits from any given occasion. It's her superhero power. Right now she's wearing a pale blue silk nightgown and matching robe with a hot pink satin sleeping mask pulled up and parked on her forehead.

"You look nice too," I say.

"Thank you. I was channeling Blanche Deveraux from *The Golden Girls*. Come in, Deedee. Your boys missed you so much."

As I follow her inside and close the door behind me, another clap of thunder shakes the windows. My dogs bark exuberantly.

"Do you hear this rainstorm?" Ro says. "Isn't it beautiful?" She points out a red plastic bucket and a pile of wet towels sitting in the middle of her floor. "Watch out for that mess," she says. "I called Larry first thing. He's coming as soon as he can. Between you and me, I think Larry is a little in love with me."

"Let's be real," I say. "Who isn't?"

"Good point." Ro disappears into her kitchen. "Do you have time for an açaí bowl? I'm working on one right now."

"Sure. That sounds yummy," I say, sitting down in her papasan chair as both dogs press their big heads against my shins.

"Coming right up."

From experience, I know that Ro will take a long time preparing that bowl. She's an artist. Every piece of fruit will be just so.

I lean back in the chair. The layout of Ro's apartment is a mirror image of mine one floor above, but this is a different world. Her walls are dark turquoise, and bamboo roller shades cover the windows. Her bed is made up with eclectic blue and white sheets and pillows. Every wall is covered with either mirrors or paintings—her own or her friends'. Her tables and shelves are full of curiosities and found objects—there's a bug specimen case, an old-fashioned microphone, an antique Mardi

Gras mask. Her closet is bursting with clothes, shoes and a queen's ransom of accessories and baubles.

Meatball's and Funfetti's kennels take up one corner, along with their bowls and some toys—Ro watches my dogs during the workweek in exchange for my covering a portion of her rent. She likes that my dogs are lazy and sweet-natured. They adore her, just like I do. We've been friends since Efren introduced us, years and years ago. The pandemic has brought us closer—some days we are each other's only in-person contact. We have each other's backs.

I stand up to look at the canvas set up on an easel by the brightest window in her apartment. There's a palette, paints and a computer screen on a table next to the easel.

"What's this you're working on?" I ask.

"Just another commission," she calls from the kitchen.

On the canvas, Ro has sketched out a seashore. I move the mouse on her computer to look at the image her client has sent her. It's some kind of bay, dark blue and full of kelp, under a blue sky full of puffy clouds. The clouds cast shadows on the shore, desert hills covered with scrubby grass.

"One of the Channel Islands," Ro says, popping her head past the doorway to take a peek at me. "This is my third piece for this client. A sushi restaurant in Santa Barbara."

"I love sushi," I say. My stomach growls.

"I don't," Ro says. "Except for spicy tuna. And that crispy rice stuff. Which I'm sure is just trash sushi, but whatever. I'm trashy."

When she's finished, she brings over two photoshoot-worthy açaí bowls. She slips off her sleeping mask and flips her long, dark hair. We sit in her papasan chairs to eat and chat. Meatball takes over her couch and is promptly snoring. Funfetti plops down near the front door, watching us.

When we finish, Ro puts her bowl down and glances at the clock. "Do you have a late start or something?"

"No, I took a day off."

"What?" She puts her hand on her chest and pretends to be shocked. "Deanna Delgado taking a day off?"

"Yeah, so..." I clear my throat. "I'm going through some stuff."

Ro leans forward. "Tell me."

I lay it all out. Getting my booster, fainting, falling asleep at the brewery, losing my job, spending the night with a former one-night stand. I can't believe how much has happened in one day. As if my world flipped on a pivot, spun by some diabolical hand.

When I'm finished I let out an exasperated sigh. "So that's it. That's what's up with me today."

"Oh, my poor Deedee. This must be a major transition time for you." Ro touches her chin lightly. "I know about those."

Ro had facial feminization surgery last month. I went with her to the hospital and brought her home when it was over. I've been checking on her often to make sure she has all the food and medication she needs. She's still recovering, but she is happier than I've seen her in months.

"What will you do about your job?" she asks. "Are you okay for money? Health insurance?"

"I'll apply for unemployment once it's all official. I have some savings. I'll be all right. But I'm not looking forward to the job search. It's been so long since I did interviews or anything like that. I was so bad at it."

"Don't you work in an employment agency? Don't you teach people how to ace their job interviews?"

"Have you ever seen Tommy Lasorda pitch? He was awful."

"Stop it," Ro says, waving her hand. "Listen, you did those job interviews years and years ago. You're a different person now. You're not a kid, begging someone for a chance. You have experience. You know exactly what you bring to the table."

I concede. She's right—I have to remember that.

She smiles slyly. "And what about your new gentleman caller? Your new fella? Your new swain? What's his name?"

I look at her sheepishly. "Angel."

"Ooooh," she sings. "Nice. So what do you think you'll do about the whole Angel situation?"

"He says he wants to see me again."

"And you? Do you want to see him again?"

In my head, I say, "Hell yes." But out loud I say a noncommittal, "Sure, I guess so."

She cocks an eyebrow at me. "But?"

"But am I really in the right headspace to start seeing someone? To start something? I have a lot to think about right now." I gather my worries and say them aloud. "What if I can't find a new position? I inherited a rent-controlled apartment. What if I can't even make that? Where will I live? I can't afford the deposit on a new place. I would have to move back home."

Ro hisses like an offended cat. Startled, Funfetti raises his head before putting it back down. Meatball keeps snoring. Ro has met my family. She's not a fan. "No," Ro says sternly. "No moving back home. None of that talk." Her own family is in New Jersey. She hasn't spoken to them in ten years.

"So should I focus on myself right now?"

Ro leans back in her chair and gathers her long legs under her. Her toenails are painted a dark sparkly blue. "Well, you know how I feel. I don't want a spouse. I don't want a partner. I don't want kids. I decided these things a long time ago. But I'm not you, and you're not me. And you've been focusing on yourself since you broke up with fuckface, what, three years ago?"

I nod.

"Consider this," she says. "Maybe it's time to focus on yourself by treating yourself well. And from the look on your face this morning, I believe Angel treated you very well last night." She reaches out and taps my nose with a fingertip. "Believe it or not, you deserve nice things, Deedee."

There's a knock at the door. Funfetti gets to his feet and gives his fiercest war bark. True to form, Meatball keeps snoring. Ro hands me a paper mask and slips one over her face before flitting across the room to open the door. It's Larry, our elderly building manager.

"Good morning, Miss Aphrodite." Behind his mask, he's wearing a big smile.

"Larry!" Ro singsongs, winking at me. "Thank God you're here! Larry, this leak is out of control! The ship is going down! We'll need buckets to bail ourselves out, sweetheart!"

NINE
DEANNA

I HALF-DRAG, half-herd Meatball and Funfetti downstairs. After that workout, they only need a walk around the block, which they do even more reluctantly in the rain. I manage both leashes and my umbrella. There's no one else out walking their dogs. A passing truck hits a big puddle in the gutter. I dodge the splash but Meatball gets the worst of it. He yelps and shakes off the cold water, then looks at me with his forlorn eyes, as if he's upset that I've forced him to participate in something so undignified.

We go upstairs, another daunting task. Back in the apartment, I towel them off and annoy them further by using special pads to clean all their facial folds. After a long drink of water, they both collapse in their kennels in my kitchen. The snoring commences at once.

I take off my earrings and shoes. I look around my apartment. It's eleven o'clock. What should I do with my day? I could get some chores and errands done, maybe send out some emails feeling out possible openings. With a random weekday off, I could do a hundred productive things.

But you know what?

Fuck it.

Time for a nap.

I lie down. My bed feels extra soft and extra comfortable, with the added bonus of smelling like the man who slept in it last night. I take a deep breath.

My phone buzzes.

Hello, this is the first of many awkward texts from Angel.

I look at the screen, and my heart does a ridiculous little flip. I stare at his message. I try to think of a witty reply, but I can't come up with anything so I decide no reply is the best reply, at least for now. Instead, I use my creative energy to daydream of the next time I'll see him. Will it be romantic? Will it be like two friends hanging out? Or will it just be the no-pants dance from start to finish?

I take off my glasses, curl up on my side and allow myself the luxury of imagining the possibilities. Outside, rain falls steadily on a thirsty Los Angeles. I close my eyes and let my mind drift. I dream of raindrops landing on my bare skin.

IT'S MORNING—NO, it's not morning.

It's afternoon, and the rain has stopped.

My phone is ringing. Drowsy, I find it buried in the covers and answer without looking at the screen.

"Hello?"

"Deanna?"

Shit, I should have looked at the screen. "Hi, Mom."

"Are you okay? You sound strange. Are you sick?"

"No, I'm fine. Just sleeping."

"Sleeping? At two p.m.? Why aren't you at work?"

"I took a day off."

She pauses. "Is something wrong?"

"No," I say. "Nothing is wrong. I got my booster shot yesterday. I just wanted to rest today."

This innocuous statement launches my mother into a ten-minute monologue about her own booster shot experience and how it didn't affect her because she drank a lot of water and stays hydrated all the time. "Do you have a water bottle you can take to work? Glass is best. I got mine at Walmart."

Like an actress receiving an Academy Award, she also takes the time to credit her many, many supplements and faithful exercise routine. As she goes on and on, I think to myself that she's done this since I was a teenager—talked up her fitness activities in hopes of enticing me to join her or start up my own spiritual journey in Zumba. Before I was a teenager, she was much less diplomatic. "You're eating too much!" "You're getting too heavy!" "Isn't there any sport that interests you at school?" "What is your BMI? What? That's not healthy, Deanna." When I started high school, even my father got tired of her nagging and told her to stop. That's when she came up with more passive-aggressive ways to make her position known.

"I sleep so much better when I work out during the day. You should try it, Deanna. You'll sleep like a baby."

"Your sister Marisa uses the smaller plates to help her with portion control. Isn't that a great idea? How big are your plates, Deanna?"

My mom goes on about how other women in her church group reacted to the booster shot, and how she was the only one who had no symptoms. When she starts talking shit about the sweet church organist, Mrs. Fernandez, who got diagnosed with diabetes last year, I interrupt her.

"Mom, is there a reason you're calling me?"

"Oh, are you in a hurry?" she says. "You must be very busy on your *day off*."

"What. Do. You. Need."

"Such attitude, Deanna. I'm surprised you picked up. To be honest, all I wanted to do was leave a message. I talk to your voicemail more than I talk to you anyway."

Now my poor voicemail probably needs therapy too. "Pretend I didn't pick up and leave me the message you were going to leave."

"Fine." She huffs. "Next week. Don't forget that Thanksgiving Mass starts at ten a.m. It's online, so we'll meet at the house. Then we'll have lunch together out on the patio. Your brothers are bringing their girlfriends, and Marisa is bringing Enzo, that boy she's been seeing since summer. He's verrrry nice, pre-law, just like her. So"—she takes a moment to count —"that's ten of us. Oh, wait. Plus you, by yourself of course. Eleven."

Is it annoyance? Pent-up anger? Or is it the cocktail of bitterness and disbelief inspired by the events of the last twenty-four hours? I don't know what possesses me in that moment to say the thing I say next.

"Make it twelve, Mom."

"Are you bringing a friend? That charming coworker of yours, what was her name, Ingrid?"

"No, not Ingrid," I say. "A guy. I'm bringing a guy."

"A...guy?" I've caught my mother completely off guard. "Who?"

"You'll meet him on Thursday." I mimic the way she described Marisa's date. "He's verrrry nice."

She's quiet for a second, no doubt planning her next blow. "That's fine," she says, deceptively calm. "Twelve place settings, it is. Like the Last Supper."

"Minus Jesus." I joke. Then I brace myself.

"We're all taking rapid tests beforehand, so make sure to schedule yours to get the results on Wednesday afternoon. Can't be too safe, right?"

"Right." I continue to brace myself.

"And honey, please, will you wear something nice? Something presentable? I'd like to include a photo of the family in our Christmas newsletter. We haven't been together in so long. And don't forget to tell your...date. No T-shirts or sweatshirts. No ripped clothing or anything dirty. You know. Presentable."

Bam. There it is. One last jab, just to make sure I know who's the jefa.

I have to hand it to her. She's good.

"Okay. Got it."

"That's all I wanted to tell you. You can hurry off to do whatever important thing it is you have to do now. Bye-bye, Deanna."

"Bye, Mom. Love you."

When she hangs up, I sit up and put on my glasses. I make a mental note to never, ever again answer my phone without checking to see who is calling. I know, one hundred percent, that if my mom hadn't caught me in a sleepy, vulnerable moment, I wouldn't have gotten emotional, and I wouldn't have made the bananas decision to tell her I'm bringing someone to Thanksgiving to meet everyone.

Oh, God.

What have I done?

I'm about to commence the emotional self-flagellation when I glance down at the notifications on my phone. That's strange.

Three missed calls from an unknown number, all in quick

succession, while I was asleep. The caller didn't leave a message. I save everyone's number in my phone, even Angel's. Who could this be? Maybe someone got a new phone. But why call three times and not leave a message? Or why not text?

My phone buzzes, startling me.

Another text from Angel.

Are you free to talk? I'm on break.

My stomach flips, but not in a good way. I go to my bathroom and chew some Tums from the medicine cabinet before I text him back.

Hmm. How do I do this?

Angel and I had two one-night stands with three years in between. I have to work up the courage to ask him to come to Thanksgiving with my family. I run through the different possible outcomes.

He could say yes, in which case he would meet my family and decide I was not worth the drama and never call me again.

He could say no, in which case I would go to Thanksgiving dinner alone and sit opposite an empty chair with my family making endless fun of me about my imaginary date.

He could say nothing and ghost me, which, I have to admit, would be the appropriate response to someone pulling shenanigans like this.

I chew more Tums, close the medicine cabinet and take a deep breath. I text him back.

Yes, I can talk.

My phone rings instantaneously. I jump. I answer on the second ring.

"Hey," I say.

"Hey."

He's quiet for a moment. I wonder if he's smiling. I'm smiling, despite my anxiety.

"It's nice to hear your voice," he says.

"I haven't really said anything except hey."

"That's true." Another pause. "Tell me some more things, then."

"Like what?"

"Hmm," he says. "Tell me about how you're spending your day off."

I give him a rundown of my very lazy day. He's probably working his ass off at the brewery so I try not to dwell on the long nap I just took. I tell him I talked to my mom, but I don't ask him if he's free on Thanksgiving to escort me onto the battlefield. I haven't gotten up my courage yet.

"I don't know anything about your family," he says, "just that you grew up in the neighborhood. Why here? Has your family been here long?"

"Um, no, not long." I hold the phone up to my ear with one hand and mess with the hem of my sweater with the other. "My father's family moved here from Sinaloa to work in the factories. After high school, my dad started working at a furniture store and eventually became the owner. He met my mom at church. She was born here, but her family is from Mexico City. Chilangos."

"Do you have any brothers or sisters?"

"Too many. Three older brothers and one younger sister. We get along, more or less." I tap the edge of my sink with my fingernail. I try to sound casual, but my heart's beating like a hummingbird. Time to go for it. "Would you like to meet them all?" I ask. "We're having a Thanksgiving lunch at my parents' house next week. If you're not busy, it might be nice."

He's silent.

Shit. What have I done? I clamp my mouth shut.

"Are you sure?" he says.

"Yes?" My voice wavers, far from sure.

After what feels like a long time, he says, "I'd like to meet your family." He pauses. "Are you sure it's okay?"

I relax a little. "I would like you to come."

"Okay. Then, yes, I'll go—wait, hang on." Someone calls out to Angel. Something rustles against the phone and muffles his reply. He returns to me. "Sorry. Vanessa is leaving to pick up her daughter from school."

"Do you have to go?"

"No, not yet."

I walk into my main room and sit back down on the bed. "So how about you? What has your day been like?"

"Long, but good," he says. "I'm on my break now."

"How's the brewery?"

"A little slow, as usual. But we've been working on a few things. Sal and Vanessa are attending this beer summit in January in San Diego. It's like a convention, I guess? They've been talking to different investors to help with the business. Sal says he and Vanessa have built up a relationship with a possible buyer. A big one, apparently. So we've been preparing special beers just for the trip. Our greatest hits, I guess."

A car honks. I can hear the faint sound of passing cars and trucks in the background, the constant, quiet whoosh of traffic. The brewery is not far from the freeway.

"Where are you?" I ask.

"I'm sitting out back on a milk crate next to the delivery van. We call her Big Bertha."

I let out a little squeak. "Like Selena's tour bus?"

"Vanessa named her," he says. "I haven't seen the movie."

I gasp. "What? We have to change that as soon as humanly possible. Especially since you're from Salinas."

"Was Selena from Salinas?"

"No, she was from Lake Jackson, Texas, duh. But Salinas plays a key role in the movie."

"So you're a big Selena fan?"

"The biggest."

"Okay. Then I will be honored to watch this movie with you." More car honks. A distant siren. "So, have you been thinking about me?" he asks.

"Maybe," I say, smiling.

"I've been thinking about you. I wish we could have hung out this morning. But I mean, in some ways, this is better."

His voice is doing funny things to me. "Better how?" I ask.

"Now I get to impress you with, you know. My brain, I guess." He laughs softly to himself. "Hey, can I send you a picture?"

"Depends. What is this a picture of?"

"You'll see."

I watch the three dots on my phone. Is it a dick pic? No camera could capture the spirit of the real thing.

The photo appears. At first, I can't make out what I'm looking at. I turn up the brightness on my phone. I make out a chain-link fence next to a dumpster and some parked cars. The rusty fence is heavy with green leaves and vines that snake out in every direction, creeping onto a nearby cinderblock wall and up a diagonal cable attached to a utility pole. This plant—whatever it is—is covered in flowers so vividly red that they glow like flames on my screen.

"Did you get the picture?" Angel asks.

"Yes." I put the phone back up to my ear.

"That's growing wild behind the building. My brother's

friend is a gardener, and he said it's called scarlet trumpet vine. I like to look at it while I kick back out here."

I'm baffled. This photo is far from what I expected.

When I still don't say anything, Angel adds, "I just wanted to share that with you. Something pretty. For you." He pauses. "Um, because you're pretty."

I stifle a giggle. "Awkward."

"Like I warned you. Are you falling for my brain yet?"

"What?"

"Do you like it?"

"Your photo or your brain?"

"Either one."

"I like the photo. I'm beginning to like the brain too."

"Good. My plan is working," he says. "Listen, my break is almost over. I have to go relieve Boner."

I cover my mouth with my hand so he doesn't hear the giggle.

"What?"

"Nothing," I say. "Never mind."

"Deanna." His voice drops. Sultry and stern. "I want to ask you something."

I stop laughing immediately. Goosebumps rise on my skin.

"I want to see you," he says. "Can I come over again? Tonight?"

I remind myself not to sound needy. I literally count in my head before I answer. One, two, three. "Yes."

"Okay. My shift ends at six. I'll be there around seven. Is that all right?"

One, two, three. "Yes."

"I'll bring you dinner from the brewery. Is that okay?"

One, two, three. "That would be nice."

"How about some beer?"

One, two, three. "Sure, why not?"

"I can't wait to see you," he says.

This time I forget to count. "I can't wait to see you too."

He hangs up. I bask in the giddy afterglow of our first phone conversation.

Two seconds later, my phone buzzes. I jump again.

This is a third awkward text from Angel. See you tonight.

TEN

DEANNA

APHRODITE OPENS HER DOOR. Meatball and Funfetti waddle contentedly past her and settle down next to her easel.

She appraises my outfit. I'm wearing a flowery slip dress, another soft sweater and my Docs.

"Very nice, Deedee. I like." She winks. "Enjoy yourself."

Back in my apartment, I put fresh sheets on the bed and declutter the bathroom using a method I like to call "shoving everything in the cabinet." I unbury a candle one of my coworkers gave me for my birthday last year. It doesn't smell too bad. I bust that sucker open and light it.

It's been so long since I've lit a candle. I stare at the flame. The soft glow makes everything prettier.

"You deserve nice things." That's what Ro told me this morning.

You know what? I do. I do deserve nice things. But life has taught me that what we deserve and what the world dishes out for us are rarely the same thing.

Take Efren, for example. I loved him with my whole ridiculous heart. When we first started dating, he played lots of cool venues. He went on tour with different bands. Like a fool, I thought my unwavering support was the secret ingredient in his success as an artist. In the end, instead of sharing his best self with me, he gave me his worst self.

And my work? I gave it my all, every day, even when resources were scarce and clients refused to meet me halfway and no one supported any of us to do the colossal workload that was required. In the end, none of that matters. Laid off. I'm out.

I respect my family so much. My father built a successful business. My mother, a true matriarch, raised five kids who all finished college. Four out of the five are high-flyers. But for all the respect and acceptance I've given my family my whole life, I don't get any back. I'm a joke to them. A broke, loveless do-gooder. And I've come to accept that too—that's just the way it is. Ni modo, as my father says.

As I gaze at it, the candle flame flickers slightly in a draft from my ancient windows.

"You deserve nice things," Ro says. But maybe the "nice things" I deserve are all things I will have to give myself instead of expecting anyone to reciprocate.

My phone buzzes. A text.

I'm here.

I meet Angel downstairs. He's dressed in his usual work pants and boots, but he's wearing a black Dickies jacket, a backpack, a Dodgers ball cap and a mask. He's also carrying a brown shopping bag.

"Hey," I say.

"Hey."

He follows me inside the building back to my apartment.

"Am I going to see your dogs again today?" he asks.

"That's a sweet question," I say. "No, they're having a sleep-over at my neighbor's."

I can feel Angel watching me as I walk up the stairs. It's blustery and cold outside, but heat radiates from my skin. I'm warm all over, as if it's July instead of the end of a cold, dreary November.

My hallway is empty. We stop at my front door. Angel stands directly behind me, his chest barely grazing my back. He doesn't say a word, but my brain goes to mush. I can't seem to find the right key on my keychain. When I do, I can't get it into the lock. While I fumble around, he gently sweeps my hair off my neck. He lifts his mask. His kiss on my bare skin is pure fire. I shove the key into the lock and bust through the door like a firefighter breaking into a burning building.

Angel follows me in and kicks the door closed. He takes off his hat and his mask. He drops the bag, his backpack and his jacket. I grab the front of his shirt. And now we're on the floor, kissing as if the end of the world is coming tonight.

When Angel kisses me, I'm not here. I'm lost in the sensation of his soft, full lips. I'm floating above the earth where gravity has no hold on me and there are no silly designations as up or down. He puts his hands on my jaw and strokes my cheeks with the barest touch. When I let out a deep, inadvertent moan, he dives in and French-kisses me like he did last night, driving me out of my goddamn mind.

This tongue—this fucking wicked, miraculous tongue.

How does he know how to turn me on so hard? How does he know how to wreck me?

I mean, for sure—someone as hot as him has probably had lots and lots of sex.

Yes, that's the explanation. Practice.

But let's not forget, I've had practice too. Let's see—practice giving fake praise in bed. Practice making fake sounds of enjoyment. Practice pretending to come just so I could get some sleep. But those skills are useless with Angel. I am not faking a single one of the ridiculous sounds coming out of my mouth right now. Those are authentic.

I catch a breath and bury my face against his chest. He's wearing a clean white shirt, and he smells so good, like fabric softener and toasted grain, soap and sweat. On the other side of the cotton, his body is warm, just like mine. I yank at his shirt and slip my hands underneath. I slide them up his broad back, feeling the slightly raised outlines of his tattoos against my fingertips. He lifts himself up a little and stares like a hypnotist into my eyes. He's not smiling. He's not frowning. He's simply studying me—concentrating, learning, absorbing.

This feels more intensely intimate than the sex we had last night.

But why?

I struggle to grab on to a clear thought from the swirling wildness inside my head. And the thought I find is this—after years of being alone, after long months without anything but the most fleeting human touch, I am overwhelmed by this closeness. He's half an inch away from me. We are exchanging the same breath back and forth in a world where that could be illness. That could be death.

"What's wrong?" he asks quietly.

"I can't believe you're real," I say.

He smirks. "Do you want to check?"

He sits up and straddles me. I lean back on an elbow and reach under the front of his T-shirt. His skin is feverishly hot, but goosebumps rise wherever I touch him. His underwear rides low. Above the waistband, I run my hand as slowly as I can over his abs. I map him with my fingertips—the hard hills and valleys of muscle, the deep ridge dividing the two halves of his cut torso. The place along his curving pectoral muscle where my hand fits perfectly nestled against his heart.

"What do you feel?" His voice is soft.

"Shallow," I say, smiling.

"What do you mean?"

"Like I shouldn't like how you look as much as I do."

"Then I'm shallow too. Because I really, really like the way you look."

He leans back and takes off his T-shirt the way only sexy men do, pulling it over his head.

My mind wanders again: in the deep ocean, there are fish that have developed the ability to generate light with their bodies in order to lure other animals close. Angel is from the deepest trench of my subconscious, a man of such off-the-charts hotness that I don't mind swimming toward him and getting fucking devoured. Oh well. Goodbye, world.

Smooth brown skin. Dark brown nipples. Dozens of tattoos, detailed and simple, faded and fresh, the work of many needles and many artists. I explore him by touch. He watches my face as I do it, his eyes warm and patient. He knows he's pretty. But he looks at me like I am too, and that's something that confuses and fascinates me—that I could, maybe, be to him as beautiful as he is to me. Is that possible?

The pad of my ring finger brushes over his left nipple. He inhales sharply, and the nipple hardens.

"Just like yours do," he whispers.

He leans down and kisses me again. I close my eyes and let myself get high. We kiss for so long, when I open my eyes again, the sky outside has gone from gray to black. The candle burns down, turning to a pool of glowing golden wax. With his hand, Angel cradles the back of my head against the hardwood floor. I hold on to his shoulders and run my fingers through his thick, messy hair. With my fingertips, I stroke his face, his beard, the ridges of his eyebrows, the very tips of his long eyelashes when he closes his eyes. That makes him smile and murmur against my lips, "That tickles." Lips still touching, we laugh a little, a funny little huff of air between us. This makes my heart so joyous that I wrap a leg around him and flip him playfully to the floor.

Now I'm straddling him.

I break our kiss at last. "So, you like kissing?"

"You. I like kissing *you*." He brushes a lock of hair behind my ear. "I like doing other things to you too."

My dress is hiked up over the tops of my thighs. Still staring at my face, he reaches under my skirt and rests his big hand against my panties. I can feel the heat from his hand against my pussy. Hungrily, I push against him, and the pressure feels so good I let out a little moan.

"I like that sound," he says.

We lock eyes. He begins rubbing me through my underwear, a slow and gentle circle. When I am in a breathless trance, he reaches forward with his other hand and moves my panties aside. I rest my hands on the tops of his thighs and lean back to give him a better view. He groans, his eyes dark and hungry.

"Fucking gorgeous," he whispers. "Vas a matarme, Deanna." Echoes rise up from our shared history. I search his face and realize why. He said this to me our first night together, the moment I fell apart around him the very first time.

When he caresses me at last, the exquisite pleasure makes me shudder. He finds my clit and strokes me, slowly increasing his pressure until he hits the perfect point of pressure and rhythm. Then, like last night, he stays on it, building me up higher and higher until I can barely breathe and my nails are digging into the hard muscles of his quads.

I shut my eyes tight like I always do at the top of a roller coaster drop.

"No," he growls. "Open them. Watch me make you come."

We lock eyes again. With his other hand, he slides a long finger into my slick and dripping pussy. I grip it hard. He smiles and slides in a second one. I grip that one hard too. He teases me with a third. The wave of my orgasm breaks over me at last.

I arch against him. He keeps going, dragging me out into the deep. I drown in pleasure, hot and rich. Still, he keeps going. I have no idea what he is doing to me, but he makes my orgasm last so long I let out a desperate, amazed gasp.

"You like that, princesa?" he says.

It rolls on and on. I'm helpless, lost in his touch.

When I'm finished at last, he lets me go. I collapse against his chest, panting. He embraces me so tightly to him that as my body relaxes, we fall into breath the same way two people might fall into step on the sidewalk. I concentrate on his calm, slow breaths. Soon I come down from the upper atmosphere and land on the ground.

I slide up and give him a long, slow kiss. I kiss his cheeks and each of his closed eyes. I kiss the tendons of his neck, his Adam's apple and the hollow at his throat. As his breaths grow quicker and deeper, I kiss down his chest and give each of his nipples a tiny lick. His hands curl in my hair.

"Angel," I whisper against his skin.

"Sí, princesa."

I put my hand on his fly. Through the fabric, he is hard as stone. "Can I?" I ask.

He looks down at me with a devilish grin. "Can you what?"

I massage him through his pants.

"Fuck," he murmurs. He pulls lightly at my hair. "Say it." His voice is deep and rough. "Say what you want."

The words are strange. Naughty. "I want to suck your cock." I look up at him.

He stares down at me. Sternly he says, "Ask my permission."

How does he do this? Turn me on with just his words? "Angel," I say, looking into his eyes, "can I please suck your cock?"

"Yes, Deanna."

Together we unbuckle his belt and undo his fly. Last night, I couldn't get a good look at him. But tonight, I let my eyes feast.

Carefully, I pull his pants and underwear down over his thighs. His cock springs free. He gives it two pumps with his hand and it stands straight up, thick and rigid. When he lets go, it springs back and slaps heavily against his abs. I run my hand down his happy trail and grip the broad base of his cock. One pump. Two. Just like he did. With my other hand, I cup his cool, heavy balls.

I kneel between his legs and hold him firmly. When I squeeze, he groans and lets go of my hair. He props himself up on his arms so that he can watch me. His abs flex. He's so beautiful, I can't breathe.

I keep my eyes on his as I pop the smooth, rose-colored head of his cock between my lips. Slowly, rhythmically, I stroke him with my hand. With the edge of my tongue, I trace the line that separates the head of his cock from his shaft. Then I tease the very tip, back and forth, with licks as light as a feather. His precome is clear and slick.

He leans his head back and closes his eyes. He's breathing hard now. I tighten my fist and massage his balls. His dick flexes in my grip. That's when I take him all, sliding him down the length of my tongue and dragging him back, again and again, deeper and deeper each time. I close my eyes and concentrate on his pleasure, how he responds to each touch. I take my time. I learn him. When I lick up and down the underside of his shaft, he lets out a soft hiss.

"If you do that again, I'll come," he says softly. "Is that what you want?"

I can't say yes, so I say, "Mmm-hmm."

I lick him up and down again. Then I go deep, sucking him hard. I hit the back of my throat with the head of his cock like

I'm beating a drum. I grip his shaft. I massage his balls. I give him everything I can, all at once.

I want him to long for me the way I long for him.

His whole body flexes as if he's been punched.

"Deanna," he gasps. "Oh, fuck. I'm going to come."

There's one beat of silence, then he explodes. Breathless, he comes hard and long, shooting straight down my throat. I get a fleeting taste of him, and my body vibrates with pleasure. He's salty and honey-sweet—addictive.

When he's finished, he collapses back on the floor, arms outstretched, breathing hard. Gently, I let go and lie down next to him, resting my head on his shoulder.

After a long time, he grunts. "We made it one foot inside your door."

"One and a half feet. Maybe two." I lift my head and look. "We're still wearing our shoes."

"We're still wearing most of our clothes," he says.

"I think the date is going well," I whisper.

He laughs softly and kisses my forehead.

ELEVEN

DEANNA

SO WE WATCH Selena on my laptop. I heat up the food Angel brought from the brewery. He has stripped down to his underwear, and I take a moment to thank his ancestors for the specific combination of genes that led to the man sitting cross-legged and eating a bowl of cochinita pibil on my bed. I'm still wearing my slip dress, but I've taken off the sweater and boots. I keep catching him checking out my cleavage. He pretends he's not. It's cute, considering what horny people we both are.

We split a beer. It's called Trouble IPA.

"It's named after my brother Eddie," Angel explains. "His gang name was Trouble."

"It's crisp," I say.

"I think it's cold, with an annoying aftertaste," says Angel. "It's our bestseller, which Eddie likes to bring up constantly."

I take another sip. "Do you remember the night we met, you had me taste this drink you invented? The green agua fresca? It was so good. Why didn't they start selling it?"

He shrugs. "Sal said the ingredients were too expensive for the drink to be profitable. How did he explain it? 'The cost of production' was too high."

"That's too bad. I would've bought it."

He shrugs again. "I'm just the barback. It's their business, not mine."

I think about the way he says this. Casually, as if he says it a lot.

"Have you ever tried to take a more active role at Eastside Brewery? Asked your brothers for more responsibility beyond your everyday tasks?"

"Like what?"

"I don't know, like including you in decisions about how the business is run?"

He shrugs. "Maybe later, when things get better. They have a lot on their minds right now. Showing me the ropes would take them away from their responsibilities."

I don't agree with him, but I don't want to argue. "I guess so," I say.

When we're done eating, Angel sits up against the headboard and I sit in his lap, wrapped up in his arms. We keep watching the movie. Half of me is paying attention, but the other half of me is busy soaking in the delicious closeness of his body. Warm and drowsy, I eventually close my eyes. The next thing I know, he's gently sliding me off his lap and the credits are rolling.

"What did you think?" I murmur, curling up under my blankets.

"It was good," he says, closing the laptop, "but I felt really stressed out."

"Stressed out?"

"I knew how it was all going to end, but I was still surprised when it did. All of a sudden, the end. It was really abrupt."

"I think they wanted us to feel what they felt. Confused. Like the rug had been pulled out from under them when she died."

"That makes sense."

He puts the laptop carefully on my nightstand and, just like he did with my phone, plugs it in to charge. Nice. Then he sits down in the middle of the floor and does something completely mesmerizing—he stretches. He pulls each arm across his body, then lifts and bends it behind his head. He stretches his torso and his long, muscular legs. He does down-ward dog and ends in what is possibly the sexiest expression of the cobra pose in the history of time. His ass looks fucking amazing.

"You do yoga?" I ask.

"Sometimes. It's good for flexibility. Good for meditation." He sits up. "My brothers are all about lifting weights. But that's boring to me."

"What do you like to do?"

"Boxing. I've done mixed martial arts in the past, jiujitsu, kickboxing, Muay Thai. But Western-style boxing is my thing."

I make a face. "I've watched boxing on TV with my brothers. A Canelo Alvarez match. It was hard to see. Brutal."

"It can be. But both fighters are in the ring because they want to be." He stands up, cleans up our dishes and puts them in the sink. He puts the empty beer can in my recycling bin. "Boxing saved me."

"What do you mean?"

He sits down on the bed. "After my mom died, I was sent to Salinas to live with my grandmother and my uncle. They fostered me. But after my grandmother died, I started fighting. A lot. I got kicked out of different schools. I did continuation school, probation camps. All of that bullshit. It was hell." He rubs my legs through the blankets. "At that time, I lived with my tío Rick. He was my mother's older brother. Mean mother-fucker. He hated me. Hated that he had to look after me. I never raised a hand to him. I never disrespected him. But none of that mattered. He beat the shit out of me on the regular. One night, I got fed up. I just left."

"How old were you?"

"Seventeen."

"Did you come back to LA?"

He shakes his head. "My dad was AWOL. My brothers were both in prison on five-year bids. I hadn't seen them in years. Where could I have gone? So I stayed in Salas. If I was lucky, I crashed with friends and their families for a while. If not, I slept wherever I could. In doorways. Under the freeway. One night I slept in a recycling bin behind Walmart where they put all the cardboard boxes."

"Jesus."

"It was cleaner than you think. Warm too. It was winter then, just like now." For a moment, Angel gets a faraway look in his eyes, and my heart breaks for the kid he was. He continues the story. "I used to hang out outside this liquor store on Sanborn Road with my shithead friends. Eastside Salinas. I started talking to the owner, that old Cambodian cat I told you about. And you know what? When I turned eighteen, that motherfucker hired me. I worked in the liquor store all night and slept in the park during the day. Because I had made friends with the cops at the liquor store, law enforcement never messed with me."

"Code Brown?" I ask.

"Exactly." He smiles. "It seemed like every single shady person in Salinas went to that liquor store. But I made friends with everybody. Every meth head, crack head, slinger, banger, shot-caller, prostitute, pimp—you name it. I knew all the promoters, all the underground parties. I knew the college kids who liked to slum it on the east side. I knew which wealthy, upstanding citizens showed up drunk and high with underaged girls for another bottle of Mad Dog 20/20 at two a.m."

"Gross."

"It was. But I learned a lot about people. And it helped that I wasn't afraid to get into it if I had to."

"Did you ever get robbed?"

"Couple times."

"Was it scary?"

"Fuck, yeah, it was scary. But the owner told me to let them take whatever they wanted. He used to say to me, 'Do you know what I went through to get to this country, Angel? Let them take the money. What do I care? That's what insurance is for.'"

Angel picks up a throw pillow and absently plays with the yarn tassels. "My favorite part of the job was talking to everyday people. The delivery drivers, the distributors. There was this one dude who used to come in right when I was about to leave. Bought a banana and a small cup of coffee. Every morning, like clockwork."

"Who was he?"

"He had a boxing gym nearby. He invited me to visit. And when I did, he invited me to train."

"You make a lot of friends."

He nods slowly. "I guess I do."

"And then what happened?"

"I trained. Regularly. I kept working at the liquor store. My trainer made me get my GED. Eventually, I rented a room in a house with some of the other guys at the gym. I even fought in some amateur matches around the state. Nothing big, but for the first time I got to travel. Oakland, Stockton, San Francisco, San Diego. Even Mexico, once. Good times."

"What is it about boxing that you like?"

He reflects on this for a moment. When he answers, he speaks slowly, as if he's considering each word. "I have always wanted to know about myself. To know who I was inside, you know? Am I a coward? Or am I someone who can step up to a challenge? In boxing, you can find out. Your opponent is there of his own free will, just like you. There are clear rules. There's nowhere to hide. Either you're the better fighter or you're not."

He's quiet for a long time, thinking about his answer. He seems so content that I don't ask the question I'm really curious about—if he was able to find a good, stable life in Salinas, why is he here? But he's told me so much about himself tonight, I decide to reserve that conversation for later.

"Come lie down with me," I say instead. I take my glasses off and place them on the nightstand in their usual trinket dish.

With a smile, he stretches out next to me and tucks the blankets over us. He spoons me close. His hard-on is impressive against my lower back, but he makes no move beyond cuddling, which is not what I expect.

"Are you...okay?" I say.

"Yeah." He tightens his hold around my waist. "It just feels so good to hold you."

Maybe, after all these months, he's starving for contact, just like I am, and now we're drinking our fill.

I rest my toes on the tops of his feet.

"Híjole," he whispers. "You're cold."

He throws a big, hot leg over me and pulls me even closer. I've always wanted a weighted blanket. I didn't know they came in this model.

"Angel?" I say.

"Hmm?"

"Thanks for telling me about you."

"You're welcome." He kisses my temple. "Good night, princesa."

THE RAIN HAS STARTED AGAIN.

I open my eyes. My blankets and pillows have been kicked to the floor. Angel is tangled around me, all arms and legs and warm, smooth skin. He's sound asleep. I listen to his deep, soft breaths blending with the rain falling gently outside. In my kitchen window, the dark sky lightens. It's morning.

My heartbeat is slow and even against Angel's chest. He grips me like an octopus, takes up almost all of my full-size bed and gives off heat like a radiator, but I sleep so deeply at his side. Melatonin and calming apps have absolutely nothing on Angel Rosas.

Enjoying this moment, I stay as still as I can. But thunder cracks softly in the distance and Angel stirs. He snuggles his face against my hair like a small child with a teddy bear. He takes a deep breath and slowly opens his eyes.

We're lying on our sides, facing each other. Instead of talking, I lean forward. I kiss the corner of his mouth, his jaw, and the side of his neck. He leans his head back, looking at me through sleepy, narrow eyes. When I kiss his neck again, he shifts his hips forward and presses them against mine. I press him back, rubbing myself against the hard, thick ridge of his cock.

"Angel," I whisper in his ear, "I need your permission. Again."

"For what?" And there's that crooked smile.

He is making me say the word. He is making me want to say the word. It feels filthy and delicious in my mouth. "I need permission to fuck you."

Angel stares at me, and anticipation runs through me like electricity. He takes his time, unmoving, leaving me to twist in my desire. Finally, he says, "Yes, Deanna. You may fuck me."

I kiss his throat, licking and nipping at his Adam's apple like the devil himself is offering it to me. I kiss down his chest. In the faint gray light, I find his nipples and stroke them. Every part of him is rigid muscle, hard and tight, except for these tiny, tender points. I suckle him, and his breath quickens.

When I let go, he slips off his boxer briefs and lies down on his back. I take off all my clothes and straddle him again, my pussy hot and hungry for his touch. Like an animal in heat, I rub myself against him, wetting his dick with my slickness, grinding against him until we're both spellbound. Angel is staring up at me, his pupils large and black in the darkness. He reaches up and massages my tits, rubbing them with his big hands and pinching my nipples lightly between his thumbs and fingers.

We don't talk. I am so turned on that when he puts his hands on my hips and pulls me toward his face, my body doesn't register any kind of shame or embarrassment. I straddle his head. He tucks his shoulders behind my knees, rests his hands on my ass and pulls me down onto his open mouth. His hot tongue finds my clit immediately. At first, the sensation is so strange, I make a sound like an astonished meow. But Angel works his magic, and soon I'm holding on to my iron headboard with a death grip, out of my mind with lust. He licks and sucks me like a man dying of thirst. He reminds me that the tongue is a muscle. With it, he brings me to the edge of orgasm again and again until my whole body is spun up like a ticking bomb that he refuses to detonate.

I open my nightstand and rip open the box of condoms with my teeth. I pull one out.

"Are you going to fuck me now?" His voice is lazy and deep. He has one hand behind his head like he's a prince in his castle. He looks maddeningly, ridiculously hot.

I roll a condom on his thick, swollen cock. The thin rubber strains around his shaft. It can barely contain him.

"Yes," I say. "Yes, I am."

I straddle his hips and put a hand flat on his chest. With my other hand, I guide him deep, slowly impaling myself on his beautiful dick. The stretch is exquisite. When I let go and circle my hips slowly, Angel lets out a quiet, jagged moan. Then he grabs me and thrusts, pushing up into me even deeper.

Holding him tightly inside me, I lower myself and touch my forehead to his. "You are bigger than I remember," I say.

"Y eres más hermosa de lo que recuerdo," he replies.

I spread my legs wider and balance myself on the bed. I rest my body across his broad chest and begin to move, rocking against him and using my pussy to slowly, rhythmically jack him off. Every time I squeeze him, I feel the tension building inside me, rising and rising. It feels so good, our fucking gets louder as I get even wetter. The obscene sound turns me on even more.

Angel throws his head back and gasps for air. "Deanna," he whispers. "You're amazing."

I arch my back and speed up my movements but he grabs me and holds me still.

"My turn," he says through gritted teeth.

Lightning fast, he flips me onto my back, raises himself on his arms, draws back, and slams into me so hard that he knocks the breath out of me. He does it again and again, staring at my tits as they bounce with each hard thrust. I grab on to his forearms. I close my eyes and focus on the sensation of his cock grinding deep inside me, luscious and overwhelming.

"Te extrañé, Deanna," he says.

"I missed you too," I say, breathless.

He reaches down between us and strokes my clit with the very tip of his thumb.

At once, my body collapses around him, imploding like a star. The contractions are so strong I can feel my whole body flooded with endorphins, the pleasure almost too much to bear. I'm trembling.

"Yes, princesa," he whispers. "Yes, like that."

While I'm still coming, he lifts his hips and begins to fuck me fast and deep. As he moves, he prolongs the aftershocks of my orgasm and starts building another one inside me.

With a groan, he braces one hand on the headboard and one hand on my hip. I'm not wearing my glasses. Silhouetted in the gray light of morning, he looks otherworldly, a man so frighteningly beautiful he might actually be an angel sent from God.

All of my senses are heightened. Suddenly, he shifts his angle, and his cock digs against my G-spot. This feels so good, a wild sob escapes from my throat just as more thunder, much closer this time, shakes the building and rattles the windows.

And I come again, screaming like I'm falling out of the sky.

Angel catches me. I drag him with me into the flames. His face twisted in divine agony, he arches his back, closes his eyes and comes so hard that every muscle in his body flexes. His mouth opens but he doesn't make a sound. He pumps himself into me, every last drop, until there is nothing left.

When he opens his eyes again, he's dazed and panting.

Still shaking, I reach up to touch his face.

"Are you okay?" I ask.

"Yeah." He smiles. "Much more than okay," he gasps.

At that exact moment, the morning alarm on my phone goes off. As I turn it off, Angel gets to his feet and walks to the bathroom. He cleans up and comes back to bed where I'm still lying naked in the sheets. He kisses my face and my neck and whispers in my ear, "You're a goddess. You know that?"

Together, we climb into my big old clawfoot bathtub and take a long, hot shower. In the steam, we soap each other up and rinse each other off. When we're done, I kneel down in the tub and give him one more present. When he comes yet again, he loses his balance and almost takes the shower curtain down. Laughing, we hold each other close and make out under the showerhead, pretending it's a waterfall on a tropical island instead of my teeny-tiny bathroom in my teeny-tiny apartment in Koreatown.

We get dressed. As he brushes his teeth, I squint at his sparkly pink toothbrush.

"What's that about?" I ask.

"I needed a new toothbrush but I accidentally opened one of Vanessa's daughter's." He takes it out of his mouth and shows me. "Look. There's a little unicorn on the handle."

We stop at my regular donut shop for coffee and weave through the already-heavy traffic on the freeway. Angel plays with my old radio presets and the bulldog bobbleheads on my dashboard. He points out funny license plates. At stoplights, he leans over and kisses me, prompting honks from angry drivers when we get carried away.

I haven't been this silly over a man in a long time. But having Angel in my car makes my morning commute much, much less shitty. And I feel, if not completely bulletproof, at least in good enough spirits to finally face my boss and get laid off for real.

We arrive at the brewery just as the rain stops. In the parking lot, Angel kisses me again, hard and long. I melt against him, ignoring the gear shift and hand brake between us. We're so distracted we don't see Angel's brother Eddie until he pulls into the space next to us. We try to play it off, but it's too late—Eddie's spotted us. He jumps out of his pickup truck and stands next to my car, squinting inside.

Angel sighs. "Here we go," he says to me. "I apologize in advance for whatever embarrassing shit my brother's about to say to you." He kisses my cheek and climbs out of the car.

I lower the driver's side window. "Hi, Eddie," I say as casually as I can, given the circumstances.

Eddie looks at Angel. Then he looks at me. Then he looks at Angel again.

"Well," he says, rubbing his beard and nodding slowly, "this"—he points back and forth between us—"is not a combination I would have predicted, but okay."

"Don't be weird," Angel says to Eddie. He puts on his Eastside Brewery cap.

"When am I ever weird? I'm totally normal. A totally normal person." Grinning, Eddie bends down to talk to me through my window. He lowers his voice conspiratorially. "You know, if he ever gets out of line, you have my number, Deanna. I'll take care of him. Give him a little tune-up. I got you."

"See, that is an example of being weird," Angel says to Eddie. He looks at me and gives me a little wink. "Thanks for the ride."

The way he says it, it's dirty as hell. But I keep my face neutral and say, "You're welcome. Enjoy your day, guys."

I pull out of the parking lot. In my rearview mirror, I see Eddie and Angel both staring at me as I drive away.

TWELVE

DEANNA

AFTER A DAY and a half of hyping it up in my head, my meeting with Tod is refreshingly anticlimactic. We discuss consolidation, downsizing, reference letters, blah, blah, blah—everything I anticipated we would discuss. We both know I'm getting the shaft. He thanks me for always being professional and unshakably dedicated to our clients. I will stay at my position until the end of the year unless I find a new job before then.

When Tod invites me to join the staff at his new office in San Bernardino, I reply, "That would be a big change! Thank you so much for this awesome opportunity. May I take a few days to consider all of my options before I give you an answer?" But what I really want to do is yell, "EASTSIDE 'TIL I DIE!" at the top of my lungs, jump on his desk and spray-paint FUCK BERDOO on the water-stained acoustic ceiling tiles.

After our meeting, I do my work as I've always done it, thoroughly and well. I only daydream about Angel when I'm on the phone and put on hold. And when I'm walking to pick up my lunch at the taco truck. And on my break when I'm at Ingrid's desk listening to her go on and on about her boyfriend's favorite disaster movies.

"Have you seen *San Andreas*?" she asks. "It was better than I thought it would be. But I could watch a movie about The Rock making a peanut butter and jelly sandwich, to be honest."

I think she asks me a question.

"What?" I ask.

"I said, 'What's up with you today?'" She narrows her eyes at me. "You're cheesing."

"I am not." I'm offended, not that she's accusing me of daydreaming, but that she's probably right. I am cheesing. Smiling foolishly into space, showing the entire world I'm not the jaded celibate wolf I pretend to be.

Ingrid stares hard at me.

"What?" I ask again.

"You slept with him," she declares.

"Jesus, keep your voice down." I look around the office. No one is paying attention.

She unscrews the top of her sparkling water and takes a sip. "I can always tell," she says, smugly. "You're not hunched over like a ghost. Your skin looks better. I knew it."

Now I'm annoyed. This morning, I was paranoid about broadcasting that I'd gotten laid, so I actually put effort into *not* looking nice. I chose my rattiest leggings and an ancient sweatshirt from Venice Beach.

"Let's go out after work," she says. "Not to celebrate you getting *laid off*. But to celebrate you getting *laid*. And just in the nick of time too. I was starting to worry it had closed up down there for good." She raises her eyebrows and caps her bottle.

"You're so mean to me," I say.

"That's true."

After work, I get into her Honda that's equally as shitty as mine, and we drive down to some Irish pub with a decent happy hour. It's near USC, where Ingrid went. I try not to hold that against her.

"So where's lover boy?" I put on my usual tinted Chapstick, slip on a fresh mask and floof up my hair a little.

Ingrid pulls into a space and turns off the engine. "He's in San Diego. We'll be spending Thanksgiving at my family's so he's visiting his family this weekend. I asked him if he wanted me to go. He told me it was up to me, but that he thought I wouldn't enjoy it because my politics are so different."

I frown at her, confused. "You're not that political. And if you are, you're not outspoken about it."

She rolls her eyes at me and applies some mascara in her rearview mirror. "Brown, Deanna. He means I am very brown and his family is not ready for that."

"How do you feel about that?" I'm indignant on her behalf.

"I'm *heartbroken.*" Smiling, she puts a hand where her heart should be. "Totally *heartbroken* that I won't be spending Thanksgiving with Biff and Miffy at their beautiful farmhouse home on Coronado Island. Totally *heartbroken* that instead I'll be drinking micheladas all day on my grandparents' front porch in El Sereno with my cousins, egging the neighbors' houses and rolling into the Black Friday sales at the Glendale Galleria completely cruda."

As we walk into the bar, she explains her Black Friday offensive strategy.

"At four a.m., I'm going to be first in line at the doors of Louis Vuitton with my dad's old football helmet on, like, 'Get out of my way—that Neverfull is mine, you whores.'"

We laugh, fully aware that social workers can't fuck with Louis Vuitton.

After showing our vaccination cards at the door, we get two comfy seats at the bar and proceed to order a grip of skanky drinks and snacks. Wings. Espresso martinis. Fried pickles.

"So tell me about your cholo." Ingrid douses her food in ranch dressing.

"He's not a cholo."

"Sure, he's not."

I tell her a little bit about Angel. How he grew up in Salinas with his grandmother and uncle. How he works at the brewery with his brothers. How he's a boxer.

"He seems like a good guy," I say, "but there's a piece of the story that's missing."

"What?"

"I don't know why he moved back to Los Angeles. Why did he come down here?"

"Maybe just to help his brothers with the brewery?"

"He seemed to really like his life in Salinas. And he and his brothers weren't close. They were practically strangers by then."

"You're right. Could be shady." Ingrid pulls out her phone. "Do you want me to stalk him? What's his full name?"

"No, I don't want you to stalk him," I say. "The right moment will come up, and I'll ask him in person."

She puts her phone down, looking a little disappointed. "Well, if you change your mind, let me know. I love stalking people."

I stare at her. She stares back.

"He was good in bed, wasn't he?" she says.

"No comment."

"He was." She takes a sip of her pink slushy drink. "You're sitting different."

I cross my legs. "I am not. Cut it out."

Ingrid and I drink and talk as the bar fills up with college students. I'm getting tipsy. As I look around, I can't get over how young the young women look. They're dressed well, most likely at their first stop on a long Friday night of barhopping and clubbing. Hair, makeup, nails, the whole bit. They're with their dates or their girlfriends, doing their best to send out cool, relaxed vibes.

The bar is getting crowded. I'm anxious around all these maskless strangers, but we're sitting outside and I tell myself to calm the hell down. A group of young men stands around us, trying and failing to get the sole bartender's attention.

One of the guys, a tall Asian kid in a black and red flowered shirt, leans over to me. He's handsome, with sharp cheekbones and colorful tatted arms. He smells very lightly of weed.

"That looks good," he says. "What's that?"

"Irish nachos," I say.

"I didn't know the Irish made nachos."

"Little known fact, Irish people make great nachos," I say. "Here, try one."

I let a stranger put his fingers in my nachos, fish one out and eat it. His friends watch him as he nods and thoughtfully declares, "Yes, that is very tasty. Thank you."

Soon we're sitting and chatting with a dozen Gen Z boys talking about this bar and that bar and where they're going after this and where they're going after that. Chester—the Asian kid's name is Chester, and he's informed me that he's Filipino—is the point man in the group and apparently knows every single person in the bar.

"Chester, my man!"

"Yo, Chester!"

The boys start buying us drinks, which is weird because they're babies. A Justin Bieber song comes on, and two of the boys pull Ingrid off her chair to dance with her. She starts singing along to the song. Something about peaches? I'm laughing even though nothing funny has happened.

I believe I'm drunk.

Yes. I am drunk.

An hour later, we're sitting in a booth all together, having a passionate argument about what a shithole Hollywood is, as if I ever go anywhere besides my apartment and work. They are all looking for new things to do besides the bars and clubs. Even the underground parties are boring, apparently—not that I've ever been to any.

The booth is packed with people. Chester has his arm draped around my shoulders. I've learned he's studying business, but he's also a promoter.

"A promoter of what?" I ask. He says something, but the music is louder now. He's calling me Diana. I'm so entertained that I don't correct him.

Pretty young women walk back and forth, looking at us with curiosity. If I'd spent an hour getting ready and two old bitches in sweats and leggings rolled into the bar and got all the guys, I guess I'd be pretty curious too.

I wiggle out of the booth to go to the restroom. I wait in line, swaying a little on my feet. When I finally get a seat, I squint in the light and take stock of how drunk I am right now. Hmm. 5/10. Not bad. As I do my business, I quickly check my phone. There's one text from Angel.

I'm sparring tonight. What's your weekend like?

I text him back.

Wide open.

That sounds dirty. I hit send, smiling to myself. Then I check my notifications. Two missed calls, again from an unknown number. Still no messages. Spam? Annoying.

For now, I shrug off the mystery, flush and wash my hands for twenty seconds like a good girl. I check the drunkenness level again. 3/10. When I go outside to the booth, Ingrid is sitting in the lap of one of the boys, telling him not to cut his hair. He's got a curly brown mop.

"Are you kidding?" she runs her hands through his hair. He's mesmerized by her attention. "Do not cut this hair. This is so cute, Marco. You look like a Muppet. I swear to God, if you cut this, I will be very, very angry with you."

When she sees me, she stands up. "They all want to go to a club."

"I don't want to go to a club."

She checks her phone. "What time is it? Ten? It feels later." She frowns and announces to them, "Hey, everyone. We're gonna bounce."

A hundred hugs. Chester holds me closer than the others and says in my ear, "You're gorgeous. So gorgeous. Come out with us. Please."

I try to ignore the upside-down logic of this situation. Apparently, the way to have fun at a college bar is to be too old to go to a college bar. The way to have everyone look at you while you're out is to not want to be looked at, at all. And the way to get the attention of a cute boy is to have the attention of another cute boy in hand.

Got it.

Wish I'd known all this in my twenties.

Chester takes my phone out of my hand and puts his number in. It takes him a long time to type out his last name, which involves a lot of Ks, Ps and Ns. He hands the phone back to me and smiles. Dimples—very cute.

"Call me," he says.

Ingrid drives me back to my car at work. We roll down the windows, letting the cold wind blow. She turns up the music and we sing along, yell-screaming lyrics to songs we barely know.

I hate to admit how much fun I've had tonight. The world has been so heavy that I forgot what it feels like to let it all go, even if just for a few hours.

"The flowery shirt guy was cute," Ingrid says. "Little on the young side, but cool."

"You have to be cool with a name like Chester."

"Are you going to call him?"

I snort. "No, I am not going to call him."

She laughs at me. "Oh, that's right. I forgot. You like the homeboys." She puffs out her chest and lifts her jaw. She does a cartoony impression of a gangster. "Hey. Hey. ¡Chale! Don't call that fucker. I'm your puppet."

"Oh my God. Shut up, Ingrid."

Back at the office, the gate to the parking lot is closed and my car is locked inside. Ingrid drops me off on the sidewalk and watches as I unlock the padlock.

"Let me drive you inside," she says.

"No, I'm good. You can go." I give her the thumbs-up.

The small parking lot at Evergreen is empty but lit by two bright streetlights. I walk toward my car and hit the button on my keychain fob. My car beeps and its lights flash. I'm about to reach for the car door handle when I see someone standing directly behind my car. I jump.

A man, wide and tall.

He's dressed in dark clothes, but I can't see his face.

I panic, frozen for a second.

Then my mouth takes over.

"No!" I yell. "Get away from me!"

Instead of backing off, he takes a step closer.

Fuck.

I turn and run. That's when Ingrid pulls into the parking lot. Her headlights illuminate the man, but he raises an arm, hiding his face. When I make it to Ingrid's car, I whirl around. The man is gone.

"What the hell?" Ingrid says, getting out of the car. "I heard you scream. Who was that?"

"I don't know." I struggle to catch my breath. "He was standing behind my car. I told him to get away, but he came closer. Then I ran."

"Are you okay?"

"I'm okay. Just scared."

Ingrid looks around the parking lot. I follow her line of sight. The lot is walled in, but there's a section of chain-link fence by the building that looks like it can be bent back.

"Do you want me to call the cops?" she asks.

"The cops?" My heart is still racing. "What? No. What was the crime? 'Man standing behind car steps forward'?"

"But why was he there in the first place? This lot is private property. He could've hurt you. Shouldn't we make a report or something?"

"No, I don't want to call the cops. That makes everything really complicated. And anyway, I'm okay," I say again. "Nothing happened."

Doubtful, Ingrid looks at me for a long time. "Okay, if that's what you want. But I'll stay here and watch you while you check your car and get in."

I open my car and inspect it for anything out of the ordinary. Everything looks the same. Nothing's broken. Nothing is missing—not that anyone would want a half-empty bottle of tropical fruit Tums and a five-dollar pair of heart-shaped sunglasses from Santee Alley.

I wave at Ingrid, get in and start up the engine. Fine.

"I'm good," I say to her through the open window. "Come on. Let's go home."

I drive out of the lot and Ingrid follows me. She stays close while I pull the gate closed and replace the heavy padlock, clicking it into place.

"Are you sure you're okay?" she asks.

"I'm okay. Thank you. See you Monday," I call out.

She waves and heads toward Montebello. I get on the freeway, still a little shaken, and make my way to Koreatown.

I'M in the kitchen giving Meatball and Funfetti belly rubs when my phone buzzes. It's past midnight.

Are you awake? Want to talk?

It's a cold night again. I put my dogs in their kennels, turn on their little space heater and close the kitchen door to help keep them warm. I climb into bed and curl up under the covers. I put in my old earbuds and call Angel's number.

"Hey."

"Hey," I say.

I hear the squeak of hinges and the soft click of a door. "Everyone is asleep. I'm going to sit outside on the back porch. Whew. Jesus, it's cold out here." He blows out some breaths. "How did the meeting at work go?"

"Exactly like I thought it would. Nothing dramatic. But Ingrid and I went to happy hour to celebrate. Some bar out by USC. It was fun." I take off my glasses and put them on the nightstand. "How about you? How did your sparring go?" I pause. "I have no idea what it means to spar. I imagine two dudes and a lot of punching."

"More or less," he replies. "It's practice fighting, that's all. You wear headgear and gloves. Then you just whale on each other."

"Are there rounds?"

"Yeah. We do three-minute rounds with thirty-second breaks."

"So, did you get whaled on?"

"Not tonight," he says. "My sparring partner was a no-show, so I just worked out and watched other people go at it."

"Where is your gym?"

"Hollenbeck Athletic Club. A couple blocks from the brewery. It's been around forever. A lot of good boxers have come up from there—wait, hold up. Ghetto bird." I hear a siren and a helicopter flyover. It's loud. "They're looking for somebody tonight."

The guy in the parking lot—are they looking for him? Should I tell Angel what happened? Before I can say anything about it, he asks, "Hey, can I ask you a question? It's kind of personal."

"What?"

I hear the crack of his smile. "What are you wearing?"

I am wearing snowman pajamas my tía Marisol gave me for Christmas five years ago. They're faded light blue flannel. "Um, nothing special. Just a bra and panties," I say. "Purple lace," I add, for fun.

He blows out another breath. "Nice. Are you in bed?"

"Yes."

His voice deepens. "I wish I was there with you right now."

I think about how warm his hard, bare chest felt against the palm of my hand. If my hand were there while he talked, would I feel the vibrations of his words?

"I wish you were too," I say.

We're quiet for a moment. I'm still wound tight over the events of the evening, but talking to him is making all my tension gather in a new place in my body. I reach over and turn off my lamp.

"Angel?"

"Yes, princesa?"

"Could you...say more?" I whisper.

THIRTEEN
ANGEL

I LOOK AROUND. The police helicopter has made a couple passes tonight, so someone inside the house might still be awake. I'm sitting under a bright porch light.

No, this is not a good spot.

Quickly, I size up my surroundings. I stand, pick up the folding chair I've been sitting on and bring it to the end of the yard opposite the garage where Juan Luis sleeps. I place the chair in the dark shadow of a big avocado tree. There's an enormous overgrown aloe vera plant between me and the house. Even if Vanessa's grandmother comes outside to smoke a cigarette, there's no way she'd see me here. I'm invisible.

I sit down. I'm wearing gray sweatpants and a jacket. The cold air bites at the insides of my lungs whenever I take a breath. But the rest of my body is on fire.

"Are you there?" Deanna asks.

"I'm here."

"Oh, good. I was worried you wouldn't...be into it."

How do I remove all doubt and vulnerability from her voice? How can I tell her how much it turns me on to think she wants phone sex right now?

"I'm very into it, Deanna." I lean back in the chair and rub my hard-on with the heel of my hand. I am dying for another taste of her, but for now, this is a good substitute. "You like questions. It's my turn to ask you some. Will you be honest with me?"

"Okay."

"Promise?"

"I promise." Her breathy voice makes my dick jerk against my hand.

"Do you want me to talk about things we've done together?" I ask.

"Yes."

"Do you want me to talk about things I want to do with you when we're together again?"

"Yes."

"Do you want me to use dirty words?"

"Yes."

"Which ones?"

"All of them."

"Good girl. Do you have any fantasies? Or do you want me to make one up for you?"

She inhales sharply and lets out a soft sigh. Jesus Christ, is she already touching herself?

"Make one up for me, Angel," she says. "Please."

It's the *please* that ignites my imagination. I lean back in the chair and stare up into the tree. Between the black shadows of the leaves, I can see patches of dark, starless sky. I think of Deanna. Her deep eyes. The flavor of her in my mouth like ripe peaches. Her bright, fiery lust.

"I was there tonight," I say at last, "at the bar. Did you know that? I was there, in the shadows, watching you the whole time. You didn't see me."

She makes a quiet sound, a tiny moan that you make when

you have a small taste of something delicious.

"You were so friendly and polite. On your best behavior. I watched you as they watched you—all those men. I watched when they went back and forth to the bar like trained dogs, getting you drinks, trying to show off to you what good men they are when they are nothing but dirty, horny assholes. Just like me, right, Deanna? Dirt. Because that's what I am."

The police helicopter does another pass in the distance. The night goes quiet again.

"You smiled and said such sweet things to them, didn't you." My voice is rough. "You were polite. You listened to their bull-shit. You made them feel good. But at the end of the night, what did you do?"

"I left," she says. Something rustles quietly against the phone.

"Did you go home with any of them?"

"No."

"No, that's right. You left them in the bar with their dicks hard, wanting you. You drove home, came upstairs, and went into your apartment like the good girl you are. Because you are, Deanna. A very good girl. The kind of girl a lowlife like me dreams about getting into bed and corrupting, again and again, until morning." I smile. "Ask me what happens next."

"What happens next, Angel?"

"You come into the apartment, lock the door and take off your coat. And that's when I push you against your front door."

She moans.

"I hold your hands above your head and pin you against the door with my body. I kiss your lips and neck. Do you feel how much I want you? Do you feel my cock against you? I'm rubbing it against you through our clothes. And you're already wet, aren't you? Wet from teasing all those strangers in the bar. Wet from all that attention. You love it."

I adjust my hard-on in my pants. The tip of my dick is slick and hot. I swipe my thumb over the head.

"I undress you," I say softly. "You step out of your shoes. Now you're wearing your pretty little bra and panties. It's cold in your apartment. Your nipples are so fucking hard. I can see them through your bra. I push down the cups and look at your big, round, beautiful tits with your bra twisted around them. I bury my face in your tits. I suck on your nipples. Fuck, you're so delicious."

I imagine Deanna naked in her bed, eyes closed, holding her big, round breasts in her hands and stroking her brown nipples with her fingertips.

"I put my hand on your pussy." My voice has an edge to it now. "Your panties are so wet. You start to rub yourself against my hand. Back and forth."

On the other end of the line, I hear something whirring very softly. Jesus Christ. I saw what she has in her nightstand. That stuff is not cheap. I think about how she takes care of herself in secret, how she knows how to make herself feel good. And I realize what I want—I want to be the new toy she uses to make herself come. I want her to use me hard. I want her to fucking break me.

"I get on my knees in front of you. Look down at me. Can you see how much I want you? I lean you back against the door. With my fingers, I pull your panties to the side. Open your legs, princesa."

"Yes."

"Fuck, your pussy is so pretty. It's the color of your lips, did you know that? Dark pink. I run my tongue over you. I suck you into my mouth and sink my tongue into you like a melting ice cream cone. Inside, you taste even sweeter.

"I close my eyes and find your hard clit with my tongue. I lick you there, tiny licks, back and forth, again and again. Can you feel me breathing against your skin as I go down on you? You're panting now, softly.

"You're getting wetter. It's dripping out of you, Deanna. I drink you in. You put your hands on my head and run your fingers through my hair. You ride my face like the beautiful goddess you are. And when you're about to come, on the edge of falling off the cliff, do you know what I do?"

"No," she says, breathlessly.

"I stop. I stop, princesa."

She groans.

"You're using your vibrator, aren't you?"

"Yes."

"Turn it off. Now."

She makes a small complaining sound, but I hear the whirring stop.

"Good girl," I say. "Now take your middle finger. I want you to touch it very, very softly to your clit." I swallow. "Are you doing it?"

"Yes."

"What does it feel like?"

"Wet. Slippery."

"That's my tongue right now. The very tip. Tasting you. Licking you." I smile to myself, remembering the feeling. "Now put your finger in your mouth."

It's quiet.

"That's what I'm tasting in my mouth now. That flavor. What does your pussy taste like, princesa?"

She whispers, "Sweet."

"That's you." It's so dark under this tree. I pull down the waistband of my sweatpants. I'm not wearing underwear. The cold air licks the sweat off my skin and nips at the head of my cock. I give myself one stroke.

"You want to come, don't you?" I say to her, even though I'm saying it to myself.

"Yes."

I take a moment to wonder what she will think of what I'm going to say next. Will she be into it? Or will she hang up on me? Time to find out.

"Did you talk to a lot of guys in the bar tonight?" I ask.

She doesn't say anything for a second. I hold my breath.

"Yes," she whispers.

"You know they wanted to fuck you, right?"

She doesn't answer.

"They wanted to, Deanna. Badly." I start to stroke myself slowly, with the lightest touch. "And you know what? I think you can handle more than one dick. I think you'd like that."

Silence.

"So now I reach behind you and unlock the door," I say softly. "Tell me. Will someone else come in to join us?"

I wait. The tree, the plants and the overgrown grass all around me muffle the sound of the freeway traffic just a few blocks over. No crickets, no owls, no creatures rustling or hiding. No sounds at all here in the dark. Only silence.

Still, her voice is so soft, I can barely hear it.

"Yes," she says.

Blood surges in my body. My pulse ticks like a timer in my head and in my dick. "Get your toy out of the nightstand now," I say. "The glass one."

I hear the slide of her bedside drawer.

"Now lie down on the bed." I close my eyes and picture her. "Your tits are still pushed up by your bra and your panties twisted to the side. Your pussy is pink and swollen. You are ready for fucking, aren't you, princesa? But not yet. Not yet."

She takes a deep breath. "Angel?"

"What, princesa?"

"What are you wearing?"

Fuck it, it's a fantasy. "I'm wearing a suit." I never wear suits. I don't own a suit. "But I'm about to take it off. I take off the jacket and tie. The shoes and socks. And now I'm standing next to your bed, looking down at you. I take off my belt. I take off my pants."

She moans.

"Don't play with yourself yet, Deanna," I warn. "Don't you dare touch yourself until I say so. Yes?"

"Yes."

"Yes, *sir*," I add, because I'm kind of an asshole.

"Yes, sir."

"Good girl. I sit on the bed next to you. I stroke your hair. I tell you how beautiful you are. How precious you are. How I want to be with you all the time, not just in bed but out of it, talking to you, learning what you think, seeing how you see the world."

I pause. Why did I say that out loud?

Concentrate, Angel.

I clear my throat.

"I lean down to kiss you again, softly. Do you like that?"

"Yes, sir."

"Good. Now put your toy in your mouth and suck my dick while I tell you what happens next."

I strain my ears to listen. I hear the sound of her mouth on something, like she's licking a popsicle. I imagine it—a cherry one. It stains the insides of her lips bright pink. When she wraps her mouth around my dick, it is ice-cold. I gasp, as if the image could make the sensation real. I tighten my grip.

"You're so good at sucking dick, Deanna. See how much I want you? See how hard I am for you? Keep going."

I let a few seconds unroll in silence. I'm jacking myself off as slowly as I can, listening to her suck on the glass toy I used to make her come the first night we were together.

When I speak again, my voice is deep and rough.

"The door opens. Someone walks inside. But you keep your eyes on me, don't you, princesa. I'm the only one you see. The only one you taste. Now keep going, baby. Don't stop hasta que te lo diga."

I'm stroking steadily now. In the near distance, the police helicopter makes another pass, then disappears.

It's a struggle to speak. "He's here. Can you picture him? Handsome motherfucker. I'm surprised you didn't go home with him."

She moans.

"You thought about it, though," I say. "As he was talking to you. You thought, I'm not with Angel. We're not exclusive. I could bring this guy home. Ride some good dick all night. Then never call him again." I pause. "I've heard you do that sometimes. Litter the streets of Los Angeles with broken hearts like mine."

She removes the dildo from her mouth with a soft pop. "You're ruining my fantasy, Angel," she says. "I might ask you to leave so I can be alone with this other guy."

"Oh, snap." I laugh softly. "Fine. He kneels down behind you. The mattress can't take it. You ever have two guys in bed with you before?"

"No, sir."

"We're gonna destroy this bed right now, aren't we?" I smile to myself. "Now reach down, grab his dick and guide him into your little pussy, princesa. Help my friend out."

I strain my ears, trying to listen to the sound of her sliding her toy inside her body, but it's silent except for the sound of our soft, deep breathing. "He's not long, but he's wide," I say softly. "He stretches you out for me. He holds on to your hips and starts fucking you. My cock is still in your mouth. It hits the back of your throat when he thrusts. How does that feel, Deanna?"

"Dirty," she says, breathlessly. "But so good."

I try to regulate my breathing. I'm overheating. "You're too sexy, Deanna. He has no control. He has to stop and pull out. Look at him. His dick is all wet from you."

I adjust my feet on the ground and thrust once into my hand. The pleasure shoots straight to the base of my skull and ricochets back down to my balls. An orgasm twitches in my aching balls, but I beat it back.

She gasps softly. If I try hard, I can hear her working her glass dildo back and forth in her sweet pussy.

"You are a beauty, aren't you? Tangled up in your own panties and bra. Letting two men enjoy your beautiful body." I swallow hard. I wonder if these shadows are dark enough to hide me from God for the things I'm telling her tonight. "College Boy and I pick you up and place you across your own bed. You hang your head over the edge. And he's right there. He has a big, hard cock for you, princesa. Open wide."

Now Deanna and I are both breathing hard.

"He slides all the way into your mouth," I say, breathless. "I tell him to hold your neck because you like that. Suck him hard, Deanna. Give our guest all your attention."

She's quiet, panting softly.

"My turn." I hold the phone between my ear and shoulder and cradle my aching balls in my hand. With my other hand, I tighten my grip. I jack off right to the edge of release. My voice is a growl. "I look at your pussy. It's puffy and slick. Your pretty lips part and now I can see everything. Full bloom. Fucked wide open. I touch you. Tease you. Your pussy lips are swollen, gaping, beautiful. Your clit is swollen too. Aching. Poor little pussy. Ready to come."

"Angel," she whispers. "Please."

"I rub my cock over you. I fit the head inside you. I move back and forth, teasing you, feeling you stretch around me. I grab on to your hips and lean into you. I thrust deep. But you're ready for this. Prepped." I smile to myself. The muscles at the base of my dick twitch and flex. This orgasm is going to be a beast.

"Now it's my turn to fuck you. I fit you perfectly, don't I? Just right. Two men are thrusting into you. The bedsprings are breaking. How much dick can one woman take, princesa?" My brain struggles to pull the words out of the air. I'm so close. "College Boy can't hang. He's going to come. Where should we let him come?"

"In my mouth." Her whisper is ragged, rough.

"Lucky man. He lets go. He's shouting as he comes. He fills your mouth. Your throat. You swallow it down. Good girl."

I can barely get the words out. "I put my fingers on your little clit. I rub you, with my fingertips, just like you like. And now you explode with a dick in your mouth and a dick in your pussy. Your whole body seizes up like you've been hit by lightning. Do you feel it, princesa?"

"Yes, yes, yes. Fuck, I'm coming."

"Yes, Deanna. Come for me."

Her gasp is sharp, like she's touched fire. Then she lets out a deep, aching moan that grabs me by the balls. I jack off hard, my grip merciless. My whole body freezes for a split second, one breath away from ecstasy.

"Oh, God. Angel," she whispers.

And I fall over the edge.

The orgasm is so hard, I feel like I'm squeezing the life out of my own body. Long streams of hot come shoot out of my cock onto the dirt. It's fucking biblical.

I feel filthy. Wild.

Alive.

FOURTEEN
ANGEL

I TAKE off my sweatshirt and clean myself off. I pull up my pants and sit back down on the chair. For a long time, I look out at the shadows of the garden and listen to Deanna's soft breathing. The night air is sharp on my bare skin. It licks away my sweat. I sit still, content in the darkness.

"You should go inside," she says at last. "Get warm."

I grunt. That's all I can handle right now.

"Angel?"

I grunt again.

"Can I ask you a question?"

Deanna and her questions. I smile. "Sure."

"Is what you talked about tonight...something you have actually done in bed?"

My brain is jumbled, but I consider carefully what I'm going to say next. I want to be honest with her but I don't want to scare her away. The balance feels precarious, but I won't lie to her. "Yes, a long time ago," I say. "When I was living in that house in Salinas, our trainer had us abstain from all sexual activity for three weeks before fights. That's a lot to ask a bunch of guys in their twenties. After the fights, we needed to blow off a lot of steam. And there were always girls around who wanted to have fun."

She's quiet.

"What's wrong?" I ask.

"I liked the fantasy you came up with for me. I really, really liked it," she says. "But I don't think I could ever do anything like that in real life. And if that's what you like, that's not...I can't..."

I sit up straight. "Listen to me. I would never ask you to do anything you didn't want to do. Never. Those were wild times, but I don't miss them. I'm not nostalgic for them. What turns me on now is turning you on. In fantasy and in real life. That's how I get off. Knowing you're into it. If you're not, I'm not. Simple as that." My mind is getting clearer. A breeze weaves through the branches of the tree, rustling the leaves.

"I think it's sad that I'm older than you but you have more experience than I do."

I snort. "More experience doing what? Being a jackass? No. You have more experience than I do. In doing things that matter. That means something. Don't downplay that."

She's quiet again.

"Is there anything else that's bothering you?"

"I guess there's something I've been wondering," she says.

"Ask. I'll tell you."

"After everything that happened to you, you seemed to have a good life in Salinas."

"I did, in a lot of ways. Friends, a house, a stable job, boxing. Sure."

"So why come down here to LA? And why stay?"

"To help my brothers with the brewery," I say automatically, almost as if I believe it.

"But that's not all," she says.

I pause. "You could tell, couldn't you?"

"Something didn't add up. That's their dream, their business. They still don't treat you like an equal, even three years later."

I wince. It's harsh to hear out loud.

"You're intelligent," she continues. "You read people well. I bet you have a hundred new ideas for the brewery. They just can't see you for who you are and what you can contribute."

"Maybe. But they don't need new ideas right now. They need to stay alive."

"I've never run a business. I don't know what it requires," she says. "From the outside looking in, it seems that new ideas are how businesses are staying alive right now. Outdoor seating. The limited-run beers at the brewery. That kind of thing." She pauses. "But why else are you here, Angel?"

I take a deep breath and rub the back of my neck with my hand. "So, this is something my brothers don't know about me."

"Okay," she says cautiously.

"When I was in Salinas, I wasn't just into boxing." I take a deep breath. "I was in an underground fighting club."

"A what?" She sounds perplexed. "A fight club? Like the movie?"

"Yes and no," I say. "Yes to the secret part. No to all that... um, anarchy stuff."

"So was it illegal?"

"Technically, yes. But everyone who is there wants to be there. Everyone is training to be fighters. There are referees, rules, a ring. It's not just sucker punches behind the 7-Eleven, I swear."

"Okay," she says again, drawing out the second syllable like she's trying to stretch her mind around the idea.

"My friends at the boxing gym got me into it. The matches were held all over the place. Warehouses, private gyms. Even people's backyards and garages. I attended a few events, both private fights and spectator matches. Then I started to fight in them too."

"Were you...good?"

"I won some, lost some. I wasn't a superstar or anything." I try to boil it down for her. "If you're an amateur trying to make a name for yourself, there aren't a lot of places you can go to really fight. If you have no money, no sponsor, no one to vouch for you, then you will have no venue. The fight club gave us all a chance."

"Was there money involved?"

"For the fighters? Rarely. Once I was invited to fight in a spectator match in Tijuana. It was basically human cockfighting. I won $500, but I got my jaw busted really bad. I lost a molar. That match cost me fifteen hundred dollars in dental repair. So I even though I won the prize money, I ended up in the red." I add quickly, "But money is not really the point."

"If money is not the point," she says, "why not just fight in a gym?"

"Gyms have rules. You sign contracts to be there, and they're liable for you. They allow you to spar, but you can't really go full UFC. You can't make guys bleed, you can't go ham. The instructors and trainers won't allow that. So fighters go at it at sixty, maybe seventy percent of their full potential."

"And you didn't like that. You wanted to knock some heads."

"No. That's not it. I enjoy training. I trained for years. I'm not in the ring for fucked-up reasons. I don't want to kill anyone. I don't have unresolved anger. I fight to know who I am. Right before I stepped into a fight club ring for the first time, I was nervous. I was scared. But that's the moment I realized I didn't want to live the rest of my life without knowing what real combat felt like."

She makes a small sound of disgust. "This sounds like a big

alpha-male thing."

"That's part of it, sure. Some guys at our fight club had a beef they wanted to work out in the ring. But most of us were there to educate ourselves about fighting, about our capabilities. And there were all kinds of people there. Semiprofessional fighters on their way up. But also farmworkers. Students. Liquor store clerks like me. Security guards, law enforcement, mail carriers. We all had this one curiosity in common."

A cold wind blows. My body temperature is dropping. I shiver, trying to gear up to tell her a bigger, uglier truth. "I attended more events. Then I became friends with the founders. They liked that I knew everyone in town, so they hired me. I began promoting fights for them. I did that for about a year, and our underground events got bigger and bigger. The founders wanted me to branch out. I held fights in Castroville, Watsonville, Gilroy. We were careful not to get caught or raided. But it wasn't until they asked me to handle a fight in Monterey that things went upside down."

"What do you mean?"

Telling the story puts a bitter taste in the back of my throat. "It was a daytime meet-up, fairly low-key. Another backyard fight, this time in a quiet suburban neighborhood. We sent out the usual invitations to the local gyms, to our usual contacts. Everything was on the down-low, as usual. But a high-schooler at one of the gyms posted it on his social media. His friends told their friends. We got this enormous turnout. Our bouncer was able to keep most of the random people out. But I guess some hopped a fence."

"Then what?"

"The fight went on for a couple hours. A few matches, nothing out of the ordinary. Meanwhile, these kids from the high school are drinking beer and getting more and more wasted."

"You weren't much older than them at the time."

"No. I wasn't. But they were kids from the wealthy part of town. We had lived such different lives, we might as well have been from different planets." I shudder, thinking about how things went wrong that night. "It was getting dark. We were about to start the last match when a scuffle broke out in the audience, which was unusual."

"Unusual?"

"Think about it. A big group of dudes who know how to fight? No one's going to start something in the crowd unless they're ignorant or they have a death wish. We saved all of our fighting for the ring."

"So what happened?"

"A group of high school girls got into it. Cheating boyfriend or some shit. One of the girls hit another girl in the head with a beer can. Busted her face open. Her friends panicked and called the cops. When they arrived, everyone just ran. Scattered, like roaches. It was a shitshow. I had been to maybe a hundred events by then, but I had never seen anything like this."

"Did you talk to the cops and explain what happened?"

"I had been in and out of camps and juvenile halls. I was nineteen by then. If I got arrested and charged, I would be tried as an adult. So no—I didn't talk to the cops. I ran, and one of my homeboys gave me a ride back home to Salinas."

The wind blows again, this time harder. I rub my arms in the cold.

"I went to bed and pretended nothing had happened," I continue. "But when I woke up, it was all over the news. The police chief in Monterey was on every local news channel talking about the dangers of illegal fight clubs. How they are a cancer on society. How they harbor criminals, gang members and illegal aliens. Turns out, the girl who had gotten hurt was the daughter of a city council member, and her mother was furious that her daughter had gotten hurt. She was out for blood. Then things got much worse."

Deanna doesn't say anything. She's listening carefully. I can feel her unspoken disapproval over the phone, but I don't know how to spin this without lying to her. So I keep telling her the truth.

"A friend from the fight club called me. He was a police officer, a probationer. He could have gotten in a lot of trouble for telling me this. He said the police were looking for me. There was a warrant out for my arrest. He told me they were going to make an example of me, that the community was angry. He told me I needed to leave. I was scared—I had done everything I could to build a good, productive life in Salinas. But now that was gone. Dead and buried."

The old sadness sinks me for a minute. It sits like a smooth, heavy stone in my chest. I've had to start over so many times in my life—what's the point? There's always another goodbye, another "the end" just around the corner.

"Angel?" Deanna asks. "Are you okay?"

I clear my throat. "I packed a bag, smashed my phone and left. I didn't say goodbye to my boss. I didn't say goodbye to my trainer. I bought a bus ticket to Los Angeles and never looked back. That was three years ago now."

"Did you ever find out what happened?"

"No. I never saw anything else online about it. I lost contact with my friends from that time. They had no way to reach me. And I didn't have the heart to call any of them." I pause. "I've never told anyone this story. Aren't you supposed to feel lighter after confessing something?"

"Do you?"

"No. I feel like the world is heavier than before." The police helicopter circles nearer, then passes overhead with a deafening roar. When it's gone I say, "I can't go back. Not with an outstanding warrant for my arrest." I pause. "You know, it's strange."

"What?"

"My grandfather was in and out of jail. So was my father. Both of my brothers have been in prison. They all did scary, shady shit for their gang. I grew up far away. I never joined a gang, even when the protection of a gang would have made my life much, much easier. And yet, here I am. It's like, you can't fight who you are inside, no matter how hard you try."

Deanna says, "You know that's not true, right?"

"But I'm proof it's true." I stand up and stretch. I pick up my sweatshirt and the folding chair and walk quietly to the back porch. The grass rustles softly under my feet. "I'm walking proof that it's true."

"Have you heard of generational trauma?" she says. "It's the idea that the traumatic experiences of the older generations led them to develop negative coping mechanisms or defensive mechanisms that affected how they raised us. That affected how we see the world. How we behave."

"Look at that," I say. "My shithead father left me something, after all."

"I'm serious."

"My counselors taught me all about generational trauma, Deanna," I say. "I had hours and hours of therapy and anger management when I was a juvenile delinquent. I've sat in a lot of circles talking about my feelings only to get my ass beat in the showers thirty minutes later. So forgive me if I don't really like it when people try to shrink me."

"I'm not trying to shrink you," she says gently, and I immediately feel bad for accusing her of it.

I put the chair down in its place. There's a shed behind the house. I quietly open the doors and throw my sweatshirt into the washing machine there. "What do you think about everything I've just told you?"

She's quiet. I wait. I close the washing machine and the shed doors as quietly as I can. It must be two in the morning. I need to get some sleep if I'm going to be halfway functional for work tomorrow.

"Let me sit with this for a while," she says at last. "It's a lot to take in."

"Fair enough." I try to sound casual, but I am scared this might be the end for us. We both know I am no good for her.

"I have an idea," she says, "but I don't know what you'll think of it."

"What?"

"Do you go to fight clubs down here? In Los Angeles?"

"Sometimes. I know a few events."

"Can you take me? I want to see it in person."

"If you didn't like watching boxing on TV, you're really not going to like the fights."

"Probably not," she says, "but I want to understand where you're coming from, Angel. I want to understand what you're all about."

I don't know what to say. No one has ever said this to me. Her words go straight to the stone in my chest and hit it, hard, like a hammer.

"Are you sure?" I ask.

"Sure, I'm sure."

"Then I'll find the next event," I say. "We'll go together."

"Okay. Good." She yawns. "You need to get to sleep, Angel Rosas. Go. Go mimis."

I haven't been told to "go mimis" since I was a little kid. It's nighty-night in Spanish. I am glad she can't see the goofy smile on my face. "Good night, princesa."

"Good night."

FIFTEEN

DEANNA

I SPEND Saturday and Sunday looking for job openings, preparing my resume and Frankenstein-ing together some possible interview outfits from the office clothes in my closet that still fit me. There aren't many. Ro gleefully offers to accompany me shopping. We make a date to hit the outlets on Black Friday, followed by runs to the usual suspects, Ross and TJ Maxx.

Social workers can't really fuck with Neiman Marcus. Especially if they're on the verge of being unemployed.

The evenings belong to Angel and me. He brings me food from the brewery. When I tell him I don't cook, he insists on making me blueberry protein pancakes with real maple syrup for dinner, one of the things he used to make for himself when he lived in that house in Salinas. They're wholesome and tasty, the perfect fuel for our nighttime activities.

I have never been in a sexual relationship with a big, horny man.

He picks me up. He throws me around. He fucks me against walls, against the door, on the floor, on my kitchen counter (with a side of real maple syrup), against the bathroom sink, in the bathtub, and, for fun, against my window at night with all the lights turned off. And the bed—we spend hours in bed. I show him how my vibrator works. He uses it to make me come so hard I don't just see stars. I see galaxies.

On Monday night, Angel arrives at my apartment late, after he's trained at his gym. This week, his sparring partner turned out and did the work. After Angel takes a hot shower, I make him an ice pack for his jaw.

"You look like hell," I say.

"Just a chin check. You should see the other guy." His smile is crooked from the swelling. "Not a scratch. It's like he didn't even fight tonight."

"I guess your pretty face just makes a good target."

"Very funny," he says. "Why don't you bring your pretty face over here for a minute?"

Adrenalin withdrawal from sparring? Maybe. Angel comes three times that night. Me? I lose count.

On Tuesday after work, I give Ro the rundown. I'm helping her pack up her latest painting to send to Santa Barbara. It's that island, dreamy and lonesome. It's gorgeous.

"I love this journey for you," Ro says, securing the canvas in its special carton.

"There's a fight club tonight," I tell her. "He's taking me. I'm going to see what it's all about."

"It sounds beastly. Are you nervous?"

"A little. He told me what to expect. It helps to keep in mind that everyone who's fighting wants to be there."

"Consent—that's good. I approve."

"But I'm nervous about the blood and gore. I don't want to see anyone get seriously hurt."

"I couldn't." She looks at me sideways. "I know it's very early days, and of course you don't have to answer this if you don't want to, but I'm curious. Do you think this is just a little bit of fun for you two, or do you think there's something more there?"

I stop to consider her question. I wasn't looking for a relationship when Angel and I slept together three years ago. I wasn't looking for a relationship a week ago when I tumbled out of that mobile clinic into his arms. But I know myself. Whenever he sends me another awkward text, or whenever I hear him walking up the stairs to my apartment, or whenever I hold him as he falls asleep, I can't keep my heart in check. And I begin imagining what it would be like to be together. Really together, as boyfriend and girlfriend.

"He's still really young. He's still finding his way," I say, making excuses.

"He's not that young. And you seem to be finding your way too. Maybe you could make that journey together." Ro picks up her tape gun and punctuates her next sentences with loud rips of tape. "You know that I'm a big proponent of no-strings hooking up." Rip. "It's my elixir of choice." Rip, rip. "But make sure you and your gentleman caller are on the same page, okay?"

I sigh, clearly not eager to broach this topic with Angel. "Yes, Aphrodite. Okay."

She puts down the tape gun. "I just love you, Deedee, that's all. I don't want to see my girl get stung. You don't deserve that."

There's that word again—deserve. But I give my sweet friend a hug. "Thank you. I love you too."

After I drop Ro's painting off at FedEx, I drive to the brewery to pick up Angel. He's standing in the parking lot wearing dark jeans, new kicks, a gold chain and a new Crowns and Hops sweatshirt. He's got a fresh haircut, which contrasts surprisingly well with his lightly bruised face and the cut above his eye that's starting to fade.

My heart skips a beat. I can't believe I am sleeping with this ridiculously handsome man.

"Hey, beautiful." He opens my door. "Let me drive tonight."

As I get out, he grabs me and slaps my ass. "Look at you," he whispers in my ear. "What is someone as beautiful as you doing with a lowlife like me?"

When he kisses my neck, I shiver with pleasure. "Using you for sex, obviously."

"Obviously." He smiles.

He gets into the driver's seat and stops at a gas station before he gets on the freeway. He buys me a full tank. Gas is astronomically expensive right now, even for my little car.

"You didn't have to do that," I say.

"I did," he says. "We're going to Lawndale."

"Where?"

Angel navigates three freeways in weekday rush-hour traffic. We chat and listen to music until we reach a modest suburban neighborhood on the other side of the 405. Airplanes crisscross the sky overhead.

"We're not far from LAX," Angel says. "I don't usually attend fights out here unless I have a ride. It takes too long to get here by bus and the Green Line after work."

At a stoplight, I contemplate this. Angel doesn't have a car. He doesn't have days off. He doesn't have his own place. He's almost eight years younger than me. Ro's words haunt me—what if Angel and I really aren't on the same page?

We drive down Hawthorne Blvd. and turn onto a residential street. We find a parking space and walk, hand-in-hand, to a plain-looking two-story house in the middle of the block. Behind a tall wooden gate, I see lights and the top of a pop-up tent.

We put on our masks, and Angel leads me inside. We walk down a dark, narrow walkway to the backyard. There's a large crowd of people standing three deep around a boxing ring illuminated by a bright spotlight. Some people are filming on their phones. Inside the ring are two young men. They are barefoot with mouth guards, shorts and these strange fingerless gloves. They are little guys, lightning fast, kicking the shit out of each other. Suddenly they're on the ground, each trying to get the other in a hold. The crowd is screaming.

"Break the arm! Break the arm! Break the arm!" someone shouts.

One of the fighters grabs the other's arm and holds him down with both legs. The fighter caught in the hold tries to get free but the twist looks agonizing, like the other guy is going to pull his arm right out of its socket. Two seconds later, he taps out.

My stomach fizzes and cramps at the sight. I should've brought some Tums.

"Winner by submission," Angel says to me. "Come on, let's check in."

There's an enormous man sitting on a stool next to an open garage where people are selling tacos, Bud Light and T-shirts that say *Barrio Beefs*. He greets Angel with a handshake and a one-armed hug. Angel introduces him as Chuckles.

"Hello, nice to meet you," Chuckles says politely. He has a kind voice. "Vaccination record?"

At first, I think he's joking. But Angel takes out his wallet and shows Chuckles the card. I pull up the record on my phone. Chuckles examines both records carefully and nods.

"You two are good. Thank you. Enjoy yourselves."

I'm incredulous. "It's an illegal underground fight and they check vaccination records?" I ask as we walk to the far side of the yard.

"Chuckles and his brother Dee have their own landscaping company. They founded Barrio Beefs as a way to let off steam during the lockdown," Angel explains. "But they live with their grandmother. She has cancer. They just want to be extra cautious when it comes to her."

There must be a puzzled expression on my face.

"I told you, there are rules." Angel smiles. "Referees, judges, security. There are lots of rules."

"But what makes this illegal if there are so many rules?"

"Money. The state athletic commission requires a license to operate a fight like this. The license requires something like fifty, sixty grand in liquid assets and a ringside physician. Chuckles and Dee can't afford those things. So they're operating underground. Chuckles told me they got a cease-and-desist letter from the commission in September. They decided to ignore it."

"What? Won't they get in trouble? Won't they get fined or something?"

"They're hoping to fly under the radar for a few months more before they either quit or find some partners."

"That seems...sketchy."

"A little sketchy," Angel says, "but not everything illegal is bad. And not everything legal is good. Life is more complicated than that."

We post up near a gate that opens to an alley.

"Here?" I ask.

"In case we need to make a quick exit," he says.

Angel tells me there are eight matches tonight, five rounds each. We watch the next three fights, all MMA with kickboxing, holds and grappling. They're fast and brutal, just like the first fight, but all three of them are determined by judges and points rather than a knockout or another submission.

The next match begins. This time two boxers enter the ring. They're wearing shoes and big boxing gloves. One guy is a small, heavy Mexican guy. The other one is a tall, fit Black kid. They look really mismatched. They touch gloves and the bell dings. The shouting and yelling begin again, this time in two languages. Everyone's eyes are on the fighters. They exchange a few jabs.

"They're getting a feel for each other," Angel tells me. "The younger guy is a southpaw. The older guy's named Tenoch. I know him. Works in construction."

"Bodywork! Bodywork!" somebody yells. The young guy releases a flurry of jabs, and the sharp sound of gloves making contact with human flesh makes me ill. I put a hand on my stomach. It's cramping up.

"Are you okay?" Angel asks quietly.

"I'm okay." I'm not going to wuss out tonight. "That kid has way longer arms than Tenoch."

"It's an advantage. But that old man doesn't go down easily. Watch."

At the end of the fourth round, after they've been banging away at each other for what feels like a million years, Tenoch finally gets the kid on the ropes. The spectators roar back to life.

"Get him with the left jab! Left straight! There you go! Throw that straight!"

A woman watching the fight next to me tells her friend, "This is a slugfest."

The kid covers his face and finds an opening. He slips out and fakes left, but Tenoch throws a vicious uppercut that connects with the kid's head.

I hear the crack echo inside my skull, just like it did when my ex-boyfriend hit me.

The crowd gasps as the young man hits the mat and stays there. He doesn't move.

The ref, the trainers, Chuckles and his brother Dee climb into the ring. They huddle around the kid. I can't see what's happening, but the young man is still not moving. The crowd is quiet. Tenoch has left the ring. He's on the sidelines, watching, just like everyone else.

"Angel?" I say quietly. "Is this...normal? Is he going to be okay?"

"It happens every now and then," Angel says.

We wait. The collective anxiety of the crowd makes my stomach cramp up hard. I want to vomit. As the seconds pass, I find myself getting angrier and angrier with myself that I'm here. I didn't want to see this young man get brutalized. But it's an underground fight club. Why did I want to come here? What did I expect to see?

The men huddling around the kid are talking in quiet tones.

"Is he breathing? They need to call an ambulance," I say to Angel. "He could have a traumatic brain injury."

Angel takes my hand. "They know what to do, Deanna. It's okay."

A relative of the young man—his brother or his cousin—climbs into the ring, kneels down next to him and says something. The young man slowly sits up, but his eyes are glassy and dazed. The men help him to his feet and escort him out of the ring to a waiting folding chair and a bottle of water. Everyone claps in relief and respect.

"Winner, by knockout," says the announcer, holding up a battered Tenoch's gloved hand. The crowd goes wild. But I can taste the bile coming up, bitter and hot. I concentrate hard on keeping it down.

"I can't do this," I tell Angel. "Let's go."

I DRIVE US HOME. There's no traffic on the freeway. Angel sees that we're not heading to Koreatown, but he doesn't say anything about it.

"Are all the fights like that?" I ask, after I've gotten reasonable control of my emotions.

"More or less." Angel's watching my face, which makes me nervous. I know he's good at reading people and extremely good at reading me.

"God, why didn't they just call the ambulance?"

"Lots of reasons." He pauses. "I think you can guess what they are."

How do I convey to him the physical disgust I felt watching that kid go down? "It made me sick to watch that. Literally sick to my stomach."

"I was afraid you wouldn't like it. It's hard to watch, especially in person. It's not for everyone."

"That kid was what, nineteen, twenty? We watched his brains get scrambled in his skull. If that happened in any other sport, they'd stop everything. A paramedic team would carry him out on a stretcher. But at this event? They give him a folding chair and a pat on the back. It's barbaric."

"He's a fighter, Deanna."

"What is that supposed to mean?" I can hear my voice getting louder. "That he doesn't deserve medical care?"

"No. It means that we understand the risks involved when we volunteer to do something like this. I was his age when I started. He's not too young to understand what could happen."

I turn my anger on him. "Do you take other people down like that? Do you give them concussions and brain damage?"

"No, I haven't done that. Technical knockouts only, where the other fighter is too dazed or has another injury that prevents them from continuing the fight. But no, I've never won a fight by knockout."

"Have you ever lost a fight by knockout?"

"Yeah, but it wasn't in a ring," he says.

I'm quiet as that sinks in.

"That's why it's important to me to know how to fight," he

says. "So that I'll know how to handle other people's aggression. So that kind of thing never happens to me again."

Everything Angel has told me is reasonable, including this very valid reason for becoming a fighter. But I'm so conflicted, and I can't explain why. After all, what did I expect? I asked him to take me to some fights. He took me. So why? Why am I so angry?

Is it because it was easier to see him as a different person before I saw what he could do? A regular guy with a regular job instead of an abused runaway who grew up to be someone who unleashes hell on other people like the fighters I saw today?

Is it because as much as I think I'm open-minded about people with different backgrounds from mine, I'm actually not? Angel and I did not grow up in the same world. Do I really accept the values he had to form while growing up? Or have I only accepted them on the surface?

"How do you do something like that to another person?" I ask.

"It's what they expect of me when they sign up to fight me."

"No, that's not what I meant," I say, frustrated. "I mean, how do you mentally prepare to do something like that to another person?"

He thinks about my question, softly tapping his knee with his fist. "I turn off my brain," he says at last. "I don't think about who the other guy is. To be honest, I don't want to know anything about him. Some fighters are good at psyching their opponents out, making eye contact, playing mind games. I do best when I don't look in their eyes at all. To me, they're just a sack of meat. An obstacle between me and the end of my fight."

"A sack of meat?" I don't try to hide the disgust in my voice. "How could you possibly think that the human being right in front of you, with a family, with people who love him or even rely on him, is just a sack of meat?"

We exit the freeway and wait at another red light.

"That's the only way I can think of them," Angel says. "Otherwise I couldn't do it."

I blink. Every cell in my body recoiled at the sound of that kid getting punched in the head. A nerve under my left eye twitches—the exact place where Efren hit me.

Is that memory the real reason I am so angry right now?

I drive past the brewery and take Angel to Sal and Vanessa's house. I park in front.

"Deanna," Angel says, "we don't ever have to go again. I'm sorry. I should've prepared you better for what you'd see."

I lean into my anger and confusion. I need more reassurance from him. But what? "Help me understand. Why are these fights so important to you?"

"I told you why."

"You could fight at your boxing gym. You could spar. Why do you have to go so hard?"

He sighs. "To be honest, I don't. But these kinds of clubs, these kinds of fights—these are my people. We bond over the high of getting into that ring and giving it everything we've got." He sits still for a moment, as if he has something more to say.

"What?" I ask.

"I fought in an underground match a couple days before we met at the mobile clinic. Someone set up a ring in a driveway in El Sereno. My trainer at Hollenbeck thought I should do it," he says. "My opponent threw some bombs, some massive hits. But in the end, I jabbed the hell out of him and won by decision. I'm not going to lie to you. It felt great. It felt amazing." A tiny muscle in his jaw flexes. "Like I said, you don't ever have to attend a fight again. But this community feels like home to me. I don't think I can give it up. I won't."

I want him to say, "If it upsets you, I'm out. I'm done. Anything for you, Deanna." But that is obviously wishful thinking. And I refuse to give him an ultimatum. Right now, I don't feel strong enough or foolish enough to ask him to choose between underground fighting and our very new relationship.

"I'm tired, and I don't feel well," I say. "How about we hit the pause button and continue this another time?"

He nods. "That's a good idea."

I unlock the car doors and turn on the dome light.

"So where should I meet you tomorrow?" he asks quietly. "For Thanksgiving?"

"What?" I wasn't even thinking about it. I look him in the eye. "You...still want to go?"

"I do," he says. "I said I would go. And if you're going, I want to go."

I examine his face in the light from my dashboard. His swelling and bruising have gone down. The cut over his eye is only visible up close.

"I'll pick you up here at 9:30 tomorrow," I say. "My mother requested everyone wear 'something presentable.' I'll leave that up to your interpretation."

Angel touches my hair and sweeps it gently off my face. He looks sad that we've had this argument and that we haven't resolved it. Our first disagreement, and it won't be settled tonight. Not a good feeling.

"Okay," he says. "Get some rest, princesa. I'll see you tomorrow morning."

SIXTEEN

ANGEL

IN THE MORNING, I get up to do my roadwork. After a three-mile run, I do wind sprints in the park. I start by standing next to one tree. Then I sprint to a second tree on the opposite side of the park. I recover by jogging back to the first tree. Sprint again. Jog back. I do this six times until the muscles in my legs are burning. Then I do it one more time, just for the joy of making myself hurt.

Sweating like a motherfucker, I walk back to the house and enter through the back door. I take a shower, put on some sweats, and wander into the kitchen for some food. It's seven in the morning. Vanessa is up, sitting at the kitchen table with her coffee and her laptop.

"Happy día del pavo," I say to her.

"Oh, hey," she says. "Happy Thanksgiving. I thought you were at Deanna's for the night."

"She had some stuff to take care of," I say, neglecting to add that the stuff she had to take care of was sorting through her complicated feelings about me. "I hope you're not working," I say, eying her computer. "You need a day off."

"No, I'm not working," she says. "I'm just reading the

latest update to the covid policy at Muñeca's school. It's changing all the time. It's hard to keep up." She closes her laptop. "Chinita will be up soon to start cooking. We'll miss you today, but I know there will be lots of leftovers. Muñeca wants to try making the pie. She's been talking about it for two days. Carmen is going to show her while I play with the babies."

Vanessa does a little dance in her chair. She loves our niece and tiny nephew, and they love their tía Vane right back.

I pour myself a cup of coffee with two spoonfuls of Sugar in the Raw. "Vanessa, I was hoping to ask you for a favor."

"Sure, what's up?"

Once I break down my problem for Vanessa, she's equal parts overjoyed and annoyed at me. Overjoyed, because makeovers make her extraordinarily happy. Annoyed, because I haven't given her enough time. Chattering and excited, she grabs my arm and drags me upstairs away from my hot cup of coffee sitting on the kitchen table.

In their bedroom, Sal is sound asleep. Vanessa opens the curtains and the whole room fills with sunshine.

"Hrmph," says my brother.

"Don't mind us," Vanessa says. "It's a fashion emergency!"

He turns over and puts the pillow over his head.

Vanessa opens their closet. Ninety percent of it is her stuff. Sal's stuff is shoved flat against one side.

"'Presentable'? Is that all she said about what you should wear?" Vanessa asks.

"That's all."

"Deanna's parents own Casa Delgado Furniture, right?" She narrows her eyes at me. "Those are classy people, Angel." She studies me up and down. "You look like you're the same height as your brother, but not as beefy." Then she takes her phone out of her pocket and scrolls to the weather. "Hmm.

We're looking at a high of seventy-two. You're going to be outside the whole time? Shaded patio, I bet."

I had no idea this much data went into choosing the right outfit. "Have you ever considered a career in betting?" I ask her.

Under the covers, Sal snorts. Vanessa ignores us. Using her arm as a sort of crowbar, she pushes her dresses across the closet and yanks out two garment bags, a pair of pants hanging on a velvet hanger, and a dress shirt still in its dry-cleaning bag.

"This is what we've got to work with. It's the stuff Sal wears to trade shows and weddings. Take everything into the bathroom and try it on. Then we'll see what works best."

Before I know it, I am being scrutinized by a whole audience in their pajamas, posted up on Sal and Vanessa's bed. Sal sits with his arms crossed and his hair standing straight up. Muñeca yawns in *Coco* pajamas. Chinita lounges in a purple velour tracksuit that says VERY NICE on the back. Even the wiener dog sits on Chinita's lap, staring at me, completely unimpressed.

"I don't like the black suit," Muñeca says. "You look like a security guard. Like at the museum."

"Will they be taking pictures?" Vanessa asks. "Blue photographs better than black."

"That shirt is too big," Sal says. "It looks like a lawyer brought it to you for your court hearing."

"Turn around again, m'ijo. Let's see how those pants fit you in the back," Chinita says, petting the unimpressed wiener dog.

In the end, we—well, they—decide on a blueish suit with a black knit polo shirt. Vanessa won't let me wear any of Sal's dress shirts because they're way too baggy and I might have to take off the jacket if it gets warm.

"He looks much better in short sleeves anyway," insists Chinita.

"But what about the tattoos? I don't know how Deanna's family will feel about those," Vanessa says.

"As long as Deanna likes them, what her family thinks won't matter," Chinita says with a chuckle.

The shoes fit fine. Sal keeps them polished and dust-bagged because he's a neat freak, which for once works in my favor—good when he lends me clothes, bad when he makes me clean the pilot system a third time because I didn't do it to his liking.

Once I'm dressed, I take a quick covid test in the bathroom.

As I wait for the results on the front porch, Muñeca checks my hands. "I'll give you a manicure, Tío Angel." She brings out her Hello Kitty nail file and gives me the once-over.

When she's done, I show my hands to her for inspection. "Good?"

She nods. "Yes. You're supposed to give me a tip now, like Sal does."

"But I don't have any money." I look at her and shrug. "Uh, how about this kind of tip? 'Stay in school.'"

She rolls her eyes. "Is your test ready?" She looks at it on the patio table. "Negative, Tío Angel."

We high-five. She skips back inside and the screen door bangs behind her.

When Deanna pulls up in front of the house and gets out of the car, I get to my feet. I've never seen a more beautiful woman in my life. She is wearing a dress, a coat and a pair of tall suede boots that set my imagination on fire. She's wearing big gold hoop earrings that make her look like a badass and red lipstick I want to kiss right off her face.

"Hi there," she says. Her smile is tentative. I'm betting she's been thinking about our discussion on her way here. I push down the flash of self-doubt I feel before it highjacks my A-game.

"You're fucking gorgeous," I say quietly as she leans in to kiss my cheek.

"We're going to be late for mass," she whispers. She gives me a little hip check, but I pull her in for a proper kiss. When I open my eyes again, I see myself reflected in her glasses—in spite of myself, I'm smiling. Dreamy-eyed. I look completely, foolishly in love.

Love?

Where did that word come from?

"Negative test?" she asks.

"What?" I blink.

"Your covid test? Was it negative?"

"Negative. Yes."

"Me too." She looks up into my eyes. "Thank you for coming with me."

"Thank you for inviting me."

I load two twelve-packs of cold chelas into the trunk of her car. We take a short drive to a residential street near the hospital. The houses here are enormous and old. Some of them have been given a superficial makeover—the house-flipper special, a cheap paint job and a wooden fence with horizontal boards. Some of the houses look like they haven't seen new paint since the Great Depression, while others have been stuccoed and subdivided with their lawns paved over for tenant parking. A very few of them on the block look like they have been lived in and cared for for many years. Deanna parks in front of one of these, a large, beautiful house partially hidden from the street by a thick hedge.

"I thought we were going to a church," I say.

"No, it's online. We're having mass in my parents' living room."

I'd be lying if I said I wasn't nervous. I have never met the parents of a girl I was sleeping with. I've never had a fancy

Thanksgiving dinner at someone's nice-ass house. I haven't been to a proper mass since my grandmother died. I don't know too much about table manners—trying not to be a cochino is my main goal, but if there's more than one fork involved, I'm assed out.

Deanna turns off the engine. "Call my mom and dad Mr. and Mrs. Delgado until they tell you otherwise. My oldest brother is Gabriel, and his fiancée is Rayleigh. The twins are Diego and Mateo. Diego's girlfriend is Cecily and Mateo's girl-friend is"—she snaps her fingers softly, trying to remember —"Jennifer. Or Jessica? Shit. We'll have to listen for that name. He hasn't been dating her long. And my little sister is Marisa and her date is Enzo."

My head is spinning with names. "Wait. Elmo?"

"Enzo, not Elmo." She checks her makeup in the rearview mirror, picks her phone up from the dashboard and glances at the time. "Fuck, we're late. Come on!"

Holding hands again, we rush up the concrete walkway, up the steps, over the porch and through a big, beautiful wooden door.

Inside, the house looks like a cross between an art museum and a really fancy El Torito restaurant. I hear the sound of a church organ. Deanna pulls me into the living room, where a widescreen TV is mounted on the wall showing a livestream from Our Lady of the Angels Cathedral. Standing at attention in front of the TV are twelve wooden chairs and ten extremely well-dressed, good-looking people.

Deanna walks over to a small, pretty, serious woman and gives her a kiss on the cheek. "Hi, Mom. Sorry we're late."

Frowning, her mother gives us both a quick once-over. "They've already started," she says quietly. She gestures to two chairs in the back row. "Those are your places."

Obediently, Deanna nods, and I follow her to our spot.

On the screen, I see the inside of the big cathedral down-town. People are only sitting in one section. The rest of the church is empty. Everyone is masked. A cantor finishes the entrance song as the priest and his entourage take their places at the altar.

The rituals of the mass are familiar to me. The church was my grandmother's refuge during her long, stormy life. She took me with her to mass twice, sometimes three times a week. She made regular requests for the congregation to bless me, to pray for me, as if my soul were caught forever in a battle between good and evil and I needed divine intervention to choose the right path. I was always embarrassed when the priest read my name aloud over the microphone.

This mass lasts a long time. I stay as still as I can, stewing in my own nervousness, studying my surroundings. The wooden floors of the house are polished like mirrors. Every piece of furniture is beautiful. There are huge, jungle-looking plants in big baskets all over the house. The walls are painted turquoise or blood red. Big vases of sunflowers in colorful Mexican jars are everywhere. Each jar contains exactly seven flowers, arranged carefully.

Next to me, Deanna is sitting straight up. Her back is not touching the back of the chair. I look at the backs of her siblings. They are all sitting the same way. In the front row, her dad is beginning to slouch. Her mother leans over, whispers something to him, and he too sits up straight.

Mrs. Delgado runs a tight ship. Definitely the shot-caller of this house.

When the mass is finished at last, I bring the beer from Deanna's car into the kitchen. Then we walk through the dining room into a big, beautiful backyard. There's a clay tile patio and more jungle-looking plants. A long, fancy table is set with hand-painted dishes and glasses with blue rims. There are lounge chairs and outdoor couches, a fire pit, even a small Spanish-style fountain to drown out the sounds of the city all around us. Deanna hands me a fancy drink with berries, slices of apple and a cinnamon stick. Is that glitter?

"This house is amazing," I tell her quietly. "I always wanted to live like a drug lord."

She gives me a little smile. "Shh."

"Everyone, time for a toast!" says Mrs. Delgado. She's tied on a mandil like the kind my grandmother used to wear for work, but this one is embroidered and lacy. It's more of a decoration than an apron. "All of you! Gather around."

Obediently, her children and their partners gather around.

"First of all, what you're drinking is a Thanksgiving margarita. It's agave and apple cider. It's paleo and gluten-free, with no added sugar, so drink up."

I don't like how she nods and looks specifically at Deanna when she says *paleo* and *gluten-free*.

"Second of all, your father and I"—Mr. Delgado stands behind his wife with a grin pasted on his face—"feel so lucky and blessed to have our children here at home again. It has been a long, long time since we've gathered together. I'm truly grateful for this moment." She tears up a little bit and dabs at the corners of her eyes with the palms of her hands. "Excuse me. I'm a bit emotional."

"Aw, it's okay, Angie," says one of Deanna's brothers' girlfriends. She gives a sympathetic smile. I'm going to go out on a limb and say this one is Rayleigh.

"Raise your glass," Mrs. Delgado says.

"To better days ahead!" says Mr. Delgado. "¡Salud!"

"¡Salud!" we say.

We clink glasses. I take a drink. Guácala—it's awful.

"Delicious," says Rayleigh. "I want this recipe, Angie."

Deanna leans over and whispers, "Come with me." She

takes my arm and leads me over to where her parents are standing by the back door. I take a deep breath.

"Mom, Dad, this is Angel Rosas," Deanna says.

I shake their hands. "Thank you for inviting me to Thanksgiving today, Mr. and Mrs. Delgado."

"Good to meet you, Angel," Deanna's dad says.

"Mucho gusto, señor," I say. "Your home is really beautiful."

He gives me an easygoing nod, but I feel Deanna's mother's laser-beam eyes burning two holes into my cheek.

"Angel makes beer with his brothers," Deanna says.

"That's nice," she says icily. "I'm not a fan of beer, but I know some people who like it very much."

She rubs her husband's belly with a wink that feels more cruel than playful. I want to tell her to let a hardworking man enjoy his cheves, but even I know that would be a foolish thing to do.

Reading my face, Deanna takes my arm. "Come on. Let me introduce you to my sister."

Before we escape, her mother says, "When you're finished, come help me bring out the food, Deanna."

"Yes, Mom."

On the other side of the patio, there's a young woman with an asymmetrical haircut and round wire glasses like Boner's standing next to a dude wearing a suit and white sneakers. They are about my age.

"This is my sister, Marisa, and her date, Enzo," Deanna says. "Guys, this is my friend Angel. He works at Eastside Brewery."

"Hi," they say in unison.

Deanna says, "I have to help my mom in the kitchen with the food. I'll be back in a minute." Then she disappears.

I flash back to my juvenile hall days. I feel like a fish in a new dayroom, trying to get the bead on who's safe to talk to and who's going to steal my juice.

"I've been to Eastside Brewery," says Enzo. "That's a cool place."

"Thanks," I say. "It's my family's brewery."

"Do you make the beer?" Marisa asks.

"No, that's my older brother. I mop the floor," I joke.

They don't laugh.

"Deanna mentioned you're in pre-law school," I say, hoping to warm them up.

"There's no such thing as 'pre-law school.'" Marisa sips her drink and frowns a little. She puts it down on a nearby table behind one of the vases of sunflowers.

"We're psych majors," Enzo says. "I'm an English minor. Marisa's minoring in criminal justice. We'll be applying to law schools soon."

"That's cool. Where do you want to go?" I ask, because that seems like something college-y people enjoy talking about.

They both laugh, but quietly, to themselves, like an inside joke.

"We're not sure yet," Enzo says.

I wait for more, but they don't say anything else. They just stand there looking at a plant.

"What is this?" Enzo asks. "It's so...beautiful."

"Bougainvillea," says Marisa.

That's when I realize it—they're baked as fuck.

I take a sip of the shitty margarita, a little jealous.

"Let's chat with the kids, Rayleigh!" Deanna's oldest brother—Gabriel?—comes over with his fiancée, who is giggling. Her drink is almost gone.

Standing there, I notice something. Deanna looks like their father, with dark skin and wavy black hair, while all her other siblings look like their mother, who has brown hair and very light skin.

Gabriel introduces himself. "Gabe." We shake hands, and his grip is extra strong for no reason.

"Angel Rosas."

"He mops floors at Eastside Brewery," says Marisa.

"Bruh, I love that place! Love it!"

Gabriel goes on and on about how money, investment and new businesses have transformed the neighborhood for the better. Conveniently, he doesn't talk about the impossible rent increases, the new evictions or the rising homelessness. He asks me how business is at the brewery, but I get the feeling he doesn't really want to know. So I drag out Vanessa's favorite saying once again. "Luckily, people haven't given up drinking beer."

He laughs. "Good one."

Happy to focus on himself again, Gabriel goes on and on about his latest adventures in cryptocurrency. I zone out a little bit, coming back to earth to nod and give him the occasional "No way, really?" Soon Gabriel's voice gets dry from talking too much.

"Get me one of those beers, babe," he says to Rayleigh, who pats his shoulder and dutifully goes to fetch him one from the kitchen. As she leaves, I catch a glimpse of her engagement ring. It's a giant rock. And I think it might as well be the size of Saturn. I could never afford something like that.

"Food's ready!" calls Deanna. "Everybody come sit down."

We take our seats. Mrs. Delgado says a long prayer for Thanksgiving. Silently, I pray to God to speed this day along.

SEVENTEEN
ANGEL

THE FOOD IS BAD. The turkey is dry. The mashed cauliflower is undercooked. The kale salad has crunchy grains of dirt in it.

"This is delicious, Angie. So good, and so healthy," Rayleigh says.

"Buen provecho," says Mrs. Delgado, beaming.

As Deanna's mother watches me, I take a big bite and disassociate, pretending I'm eating turkey in mole sauce and honey-sweet camotes enmielados back at Sal and Vanessa's.

We all work through the meal. I wash down the taste with an Eastside Pride, poured into a proper beer glass. Fancy. Deanna's mom makes a point to ask everyone a question about their lives to keep the conversation flowing. However, when it's time for her to ask Deanna or me a question, she goes silent and concentrates on her turkey jerky instead.

Everyone notices. Marisa picks up the slack. "How's work, Deanna? I had a unit on reentry programs in my reading a few weeks ago. I thought it was interesting."

Deanna talks about the employment classes she gives her clients over Zoom. She talks about finding placement for some of her clients in a photovoltaic program at the local trade college. "Solar panels," she says proudly. "If people don't feel safe having formerly incarcerated people work inside their house, maybe they'll feel safer having them work on the roof."

Gabriel snorts. "'Formerly incarcerated'? Is that what the woke army is calling ex-cons now?"

"No," Deanna says calmly, "that's what they're called in a professional environment."

"I wish you would find a better job," Mrs. Delgado says. "All of that education. All of that college. And what do you end up doing? Working with criminals."

"And getting paid peanuts to do it," says Gabriel.

"But Deanna's trying to change the world," says Marisa. "Not everybody is motivated by money."

"Did you learn that in school?" Gabriel says to Marisa. "Because you wouldn't be sitting in that lecture hall without Mom and Dad writing a big fat check to your university every few months."

I'm about to say something, but Deanna puts her hand on my knee and gives her head a tiny shake. Annoyed, I take another long drink of beer instead.

"Gabriel, don't talk about things like that," says Mrs. Delgado. "It's not polite."

"What, money? Right, sorry." Gabriel takes a big bite of turkey. Talking with his mouth full, he gestures with his fork, pointing it at us every now and then as if accusing us of a crime. "Polite middle-class people never talk about money. Only rich people and poor people talk about money, but no one in between is allowed to. But why shouldn't we? Dad came from nothing. He worked hard for what we have. We're the next generation. It's our responsibility to keep it going."

Rayleigh nods. "That's true. Your family should be very, very proud of its accomplishments in this country."

I look at Deanna. She's staring daggers at her brother Gabriel. "But Dad didn't come from nothing," she says. "Dad inherited the business from Mr. Wyman."

"After years and years of faithful service," Mrs. Delgado says sharply.

"Mr. Wyman was the owner of the furniture store before my father," Deanna explains to me. "His family were Jews from Russia. They came here before World War II and opened the furniture store back when Cesar Chavez Ave. was called Brooklyn Ave. There was a huge working-class Jewish community here back then."

I learned this when I asked Vanessa's grandmother about the big building on Breed Street. She told me it had been a synagogue.

"Mr. Wyman didn't have any children," Deanna continues. "When he died, he left the business to his most senior employee, my father. As the neighborhood evolved, my dad changed the name of the business from Wyman's Furniture to Casa Delgado. He started importing handmade pieces and textiles from Mexico. He added the workshop in the back. He hired local cabinetmakers and upholsterers. That's when he started selling custom furniture." She points her fork right back at Gabriel. "He did build a successful business. One we should be proud of. But stop telling yourself the lie that he started from nothing. He didn't."

I'm so proud of her. She held her own. I realize that's something I admire about her—she won't be pushed around. Not by anyone. Not by me.

At the head of the table, Mr. Delgado is quiet, resigned to sit back in his chair and watch his children argue about their family story.

"Deanna," says Mrs. Delgado with a sly smile. "Maybe you

should become a history professor. You certainly are good at giving long lectures."

Gabriel and Rayleigh laugh.

Deanna sighs. "That's a good idea, Mom," she says. "Maybe I will."

Under the table, I put my hand on Deanna's.

"Let's change the subject, shall we?" Mrs. Delgado says. "Diego, tell us all about your internship in Asturias. We missed you so much this summer."

We listen as Deanna's other brother talks about the month he spent working at a university hospital in Spain. Then he and Cecily went backpacking until school started again. From their adventures, I realize how different these people's lives are from mine, and to some extent, to Deanna's too. We live on the same planet but we live in two different worlds.

"Did you go to the sidrerías?" asks Gabriel, who has apparently traveled all over Europe. He makes eye contact with me and decides I must have no idea what he's talking about. "Cider bars. That region of Spain, Asturias, is famous for its apple cider," he explains, speaking slowly, as if I were a small child. He picks up his glass and tips it sideways. He holds his other hand high and mimics pouring liquid into his glass from a great distance. "They pour your cider like this. And they stare at you. They don't spill a drop. Until you tell them that's enough. The pour can be five, ten, fifteen Euros depending on how long you let them pour."

I know Gabriel's type. Mouthy. Big talker. Easy to throw off balance, easy to subdue. "Really?" I exaggerate my East LA accent a little, just for fun. "There's a place in Tijuana where the bartender will pour tequila straight into your mouth for three dollars. For five dollars, he'll wipe your face off too."

Mr. Delgado laughs so hard we all jump. He's been silent

this whole time. When they see him laughing, Deanna's siblings join in too.

Smiling politely, I stare Gabriel down. He's not laughing. I've made my point.

Of course, Mrs. Delgado sees the exchange between us. She stands up. "Deanna, Marisa, help me clear the table. Mateo, could you move some of these chairs to the grass so everyone has a place to sit? Let's have our dessert in the sunshine."

We all sit on some of the nicest patio furniture I've ever seen in my life. Now that they're sober, Marisa and Enzo are fun to talk to. They tell me about how they met on campus at a meeting for student activists. The meeting organizers required everyone to wear a nametag and they reached for the Sharpie marker at the same time.

"It was annoyance at first sight," says Marisa.

"We've been annoyed with each other ever since," says Enzo.

It's warm in the sun. I'm sitting next to Deanna. We're quietly touching hands. That small connection makes me feel calmer, and I think it has a similar effect on her too.

"Hace calor," I whisper to her. I stand up, take off my jacket and hang it carefully on the back of the chair. A few feet away, Rayleigh is staring at my arms with her mouth open.

Gabriel notices. "Babe."

She doesn't answer.

"Babe, can you get me another beer?" he says, annoyed.

"What?" She blinks and turns to him. "Oh. Yeah, sure."

I sit back down and put my arm around Deanna's shoulders. I give Gabriel a little gangster nod. He frowns.

Deanna's father sits down next to us. "Hello, m'ija. Angel."

He's a big guy, with wavy salt-and-pepper hair. He's wearing a fly guayabera shirt. He pulls a cigar from his pocket and starts to cut it.

Mrs. Delgado is holding a tray of pumpkin cheesecakes that are dairy-, sugar-, and gluten-free. Under her breath, she tells Mr. Delgado, "Not here. That smoke is disgusting."

He looks at me and raises his eyebrows. "I don't want to smoke alone. You want one of these?"

"Sure."

"Come with me."

Deanna and I exchange glances. She nods at me. I follow Mr. Delgado to an ivy-covered wall at the back edge of his property. He opens a heavy wooden door and I follow him through. Now we're standing in a fenced gravel lot adjacent to the alley behind the house. There are trash cans, a tool shed, and a pile of extra lumber. There's also a big, battered pickup truck with a shell on it. On the back window of the truck, there's a faded Tomateros de Culiacán sticker featuring a big tomato holding a baseball bat.

In Spanish, he tells me, "My wife doesn't like my truck. She won't let me park it in the driveway or in front of the house. But this is the truck that built our business. So I'll never get rid of it. That would be disloyal."

He holds the cigar up so I can see it.

"Have you smoked one of these before?"

"No, sir."

"Okay." He cuts the top of one cigar and lights it with a torch lighter. He's methodical and careful. I notice his hands, like mine, are kind of destroyed, with big knuckles and calluses. He puffs on the cigar gently and hands it to me.

"There you go. From the Dominican Republic. Very fine," he says. "Hold a small amount of smoke in your mouth. Don't inhale. You can blow a little out of your nose too. It's about taste. Don't let it go out. Maybe once a minute give it a little puff."

I do what he says.

"There," he says. "You got it. Don't let the end get too red, and you'll be okay."

He lights one for himself. We smoke quietly for a minute or two.

"She's right, you know—Deanna. I was very lucky," he says. "I had a boss who saw something in me. Who took the time to teach me and listened to what I had to say. You need mentors like that in order to make your way in the world, don't you think?"

I nod. My old Cambodian boss and my first boxing trainer—they were my first mentors.

"Always look for mentors, Angel. If you find yourself in a situation without a mentor, change your situation." He puffs gently.

I immediately think about my relationship with my brothers at the brewery. They are too stressed and overextended to be mentors to me. I understand that now.

"Mr. Delgado," I say. "Can I ask you a question about your business?"

"Of course."

"How are you surviving the pandemic?"

"Well," he says. "We're doing a few things."

He chops it up with me. "Some things you do take years to come to fruition. At the dining table today, you were sitting on equipal chairs. They're made of wood and pig leather, very distinctive looking. Over the last few years, Gabriel built relationships with popular interior designers all over Southern California. He showed them the chairs. He talked them up. The designers started to use the chairs with their wealthy clients. The clients did photoshoots on social media and for different websites. We started to get phone calls. Right now, the equipal chairs are a huge part of our business."

"When restaurants opened again, they were scrambling to

build outdoor seating areas. We are local. We can deliver everything fast—tables, chairs, umbrellas, stools—custom-built if needed. We outfitted dozens of restaurants in the two weeks after the restaurants were opened again."

He takes another puff. "Then we realized the newest residents in our neighborhood were all affluent, young families. Most of them were able to work from home during the lockdown. So we pushed luxury outdoor furniture. We put it outside on the sidewalk. Tables, chairs, outdoor lounges, patio umbrellas, canopies. As much as we could. And it sold."

Mr. Delgado leans against his old truck. I know how much a truck means to its owner so I don't do the same.

"But something was starting to bother me," he says.

"What's that?"

"We were catering only to the wealthiest residents of the area. I remember this neighborhood before gentrification. It was tough. Working-class. I don't only want to sell luxury items. That disconnects us from the people around us. I was eating a hot dog at Costco when the idea hit me."

I smile. "A hot dog?"

"It hit me like a bolt of lightning—loss leaders. How could I use loss leaders to feel connected with my community? I started to think of products both wealthy and working-class families need during a pandemic. We started to stock those items at a loss. Futons and folding beds. Affordable office chairs. TV trays. Student desks. We also added small things. Handmade jewelry from Mexico. Scarves. Very small luxuries that everyday people could afford. We sent coupons to the local neighborhoods. We gave teacher discounts. Healthcare worker discounts."

"Did it work?"

"Slowly but surely. Soon more and more locals came to the store. The low-income families got the furniture they needed at a price they could afford. The high-income families were drawn into the store by the deals but ended up also buying fancy armoires and sectional couches. They balanced out our losses on the other items."

I am absorbing everything he's telling me.

"The last thing is customer service. When you buy something online, it arrives in a carton from who-knows-where. When you buy something from Casa Delgado, you're buying it from me, Alejandro Delgado, or my son, Gabe Delgado. Maybe you start buying from us regularly. Now you're not just a customer, you're a collector. We'll contact you directly when something from Mexico comes in, before we place it on the floor. And now I'm not just Alejandro, I'm your 'furniture guy.' See how it goes?"

I nod.

Then Deanna's dad demonstrates some of his salesmanship. "Do you have a patio at Eastside Brewery?" he asks.

"Some Astroturf and canopies."

He makes a face. "Tell me your budget and together we can build a paradise for your customers. The weather will be getting warmer. People will want to sit outside and drink. The nicer you make it, the more they will drink, don't you think?"

I can't tell him that the brewery is too much in the red to afford anything like that. Instead, I say, "That's a great idea. Let me discuss it with the family."

"I have some outdoor catalogs you can bring back to help them visualize the space—but wait, no." He clicks his tongue in annoyance. "They're at the furniture store. Here." He hands me his keys. "Deanna can take you. It's not far. You can take a look at some of the pieces in person."

"Are you sure?"

"Sure I'm sure," he says. "Take your time. It's all stocked up for Black Friday."

Very few people trust me with keys. I take them and put

them in my pocket.

He takes another puff and looks me in the eye. "Listen, Angel. I apologize for my family's behavior toward you today. Please don't judge them too harshly. They don't have the advantages you've had."

That confuses me completely. "Sir?"

"You have seen the world as it is. With the exception of Deanna," he says, "they have not."

I think carefully before responding. "I don't know your family well enough to agree with you," I say, "but I've seen how they treat Deanna."

He puffs quietly.

"Not everyone can do the work she does," I say. "She's smart and very tough."

Mr. Delgado smiles to himself, no doubt remembering countless times Deanna has stood up for herself. "That she is," he says.

My heart is beating hard. I'm approaching a line I shouldn't cross, but I have to speak my mind. "She would probably appreciate hearing that from you."

He stares at a pile of lumber near the garden wall. "My wife and I, we've always been hard on our kids. We only want what is best for them. But perhaps we have been unnecessarily hard on Deanna," he says. "Thank you for pointing that out."

Have I annoyed him? He's hard to read. I back off immediately, and we finish our smokes in silence. He shows me how to balance the cigar on an old ashtray and allow it to burn out on its own.

"That is called a 'dignified death,'" he says. "May we both have one—many, many years from now."

I shake his hand. "Thank you, Mr. Delgado. For the cigar and for the advice."

"Likewise, m'ijo. Call me Alex."

EIGHTEEN

DEANNA

HAPPY TO MAKE OUR ESCAPE, Angel and I drive to the furniture store. We park in the big, empty lot and walk together to the back door.

I hold my father's keys in my right hand. It's a massive key ring. He's got multiple door keys, truck keys, keys for the tool sheds behind the furniture store, keys for the dumpster padlocks. He has little arcane keys for the credenzas and the old rolltop desk he keeps in his office.

In my left hand, I hold my own keys. A key and fob for my car, two keys for my apartment, two keys for work. That's it. I balance the weight of my father's responsibilities against mine. Soon I'll have even fewer keys. And if I don't find a job soon, I won't have any keys left.

Angel helps me unlock the heavy back door of the furniture shop. I tap in the security code for the alarm. It's the year my oldest brother was born. The loud beeping stops.

This has never been a great part of town. Tagging crews and street artists hang out along the train tracks that run behind the old warehouses along this street. Crews of thieves break the locks on railcars and grab the cargo inside. In recent years, more homeless encampments have popped up under the nearby underpasses. My father has gotten his truck broken into a few times.

Angel pulls the metal door shut behind us until the security bar clicks. Then I hit the switches on the panel, and the store fills with light.

I haven't been inside the furniture store in a long time. You'd never know how beautiful this place is on the inside from how plain and unremarkable it looks on the outside.

In the daytime, skylights in the warehouse ceiling fill the dark building with sunlight. After sunset, three dozen chandeliers and pendant lights hanging from the rafters give the showroom a golden glow. Hammered copper, punched tin, wrought iron, antique glass, silvery mirrors, stars and teardrops and exploded crowns—as with almost everything in the store, the light fixtures are handmade by artisans my father knows in Mexico.

Angel follows me to the register. We pass living room sets, dining sets, sideboards and china cabinets stuffed with colorful Talavera pottery. The walls of the warehouse have been painted bright blue, yellow or brick red to highlight embroidered bedlinens, polished wood, bright paintings, wall sconces and decorated pillows. It's a Mexican IKEA, even though that's a comparison my father would abhor. "That stuff is massproduced garbage," he'd say. "I sell works of art."

I stub my toe on an enormous, medieval-looking leather rocking chair. Cursing, I notice the brand of the unfortunate cow, still visible on the seat.

Angel is walking closely behind me. "Are you okay?"

I frown. "Better than the cow."

I head behind the counter and through the French doors into the office. My dad seems to be able to navigate this room just fine, but to me, it's a cluttered, unholy mess. I begin to dig through the piles on the desk, searching for the catalogs. No luck. I yank open the overstuffed drawers and rifle through them. Nothing. I go through the piles and piles of junk mail from the post office. Nada.

My phone buzzes. It's my dad.

are you at the shop

I text back.

Yes.

the catalogs are here after all, but show him the patio furniture

I sigh.

Sure.

"What's wrong?" Angel asks.

"The catalogs are at the house," I say, "but he would like me to show you the patio furniture anyway."

"Okay."

He stalks around the front of the store, examining a display case of costume jewelry imported from Mexico. He looks so good in his dress clothes. It's petty, but I enjoyed watching people in my family sneak quick sideways glances at him. It made me feel strangely powerful to bring someone around who's so aggressively good-looking, he throws everyone else off balance a little bit. Including me.

He stops by the music player. "How do you turn this on?"

"Let me see." I sit down at my father's desk. I remove a stack of invoices from the keyboard and start up the old desktop. "Gabe set up the music in the store," I explain. "He once told me he goes into the office on the sly to change the songs depending on who's shopping. He claimed he could make people buy things using only the influence of music. 'Gen X, I turn on the Buena Vista Social Club. Millennials, I turn on Chicano Batman,' he told me. 'Boomers? Gipsy Kings. Every time.'"

"Does it work?" Angel asks.

"I didn't think so," I say. "But then he turned on 'Bamboleo' and proceeded to sell a sofa, a love seat, an armchair and two embroidered cushions to an older white lady wearing the most fabulous Lucite jewelry I have ever seen. I told him that she was going to buy that stuff anyway. He told me to believe whatever I wanted, but that he was right."

"He's a good salesman, then."

"We've never gotten along," I say. "But he's a genius at selling furniture. I'll give him that."

I scroll through the playlists and settle on Caetano Veloso, the Brazilian singer whose music always makes me feel like I'm relaxing on a beautiful sandy beach. The sound system in the store is surprisingly good. I turn the music down a little, then try to lean back in my dad's creaky chair. It's old and uncomfortable.

On the other side of the front desk, Angel says, "Come with me."

I get up and follow him to a deep sofa in the rear of the store. It's upholstered in a luxurious caramel-colored leather. I glance at the price tag and see that it costs more than three months' rent on my apartment.

Angel takes my hands and pulls me down with him. Together we sink into the cool, buttery softness. I sigh. Rich people's asses get all the good stuff. It's not fair.

I curl up next to Angel, and he wraps his arms around me. I rest my head on his shoulder. Together, we listen to the gentle bossa nova riffs. He strokes my hair slowly, and I lose myself in the guitar strings, the lazy sway of the music and the almost-whispered words I can't completely understand.

Maybe it was the bad cocktails, or having to play it cool against the hours-long passive-aggressive attacks of my family. Maybe it's my impending unemployment, or maybe it's this pinche pandemic that pivots and whirls around us like an opponent we can't seem to outsmart. Maybe it's the fact that I stayed up a little bit too late last night, nursing my upset stomach and wondering whether I could really be with an inherently violent man who doesn't think twice about beating his opponents to a pulp in the ring.

I am exhausted.

Angel kisses my forehead. Despite my unanswered questions, I lean against him and allow myself to enjoy this closeness.

"Descansemos," he says softly. "Descansemos, princesa."

I BLINK.

Angel's sitting on the sofa next to me. His long legs are kicked out in front of him, and his arms are folded. His chin is down and his cheek rests slightly on his shoulder. Music is still playing softly over the sound system. The doors of the store are still locked tight.

I check my phone.

I—we?—have been asleep in the furniture store for almost two hours.

I make a move to wake him up, but I pause when I realize he's sound asleep. His breaths are deep and slow. So I take this opportunity to stare at him as long as I want.

Next to his older brothers, Angel is narrower and less bulky. Even so, the broad muscles of his arms strain against the sleeves of his polo shirt. In sleep, the harder angles of his face are softer. And those long, long eyelashes? There's no hiding he's young. Still very young.

Who was I at twenty-four? Raw. Cocky, even. I dove headfirst into everything—school, work, play, love, sex—always believing that the world owed me back as hard as I gave. When it didn't meet my expectations, I'd lose my temper or retreat, hiding away with my pain. Again and again.

But Angel is not me. He's lived a very different life and survived things I can't imagine surviving. His experiences seem to have made him stronger, as if the scar tissue were a kind of armor that no one can dent.

That makes me wonder—is he testing his armor when he steps into the ring?

I reach out and touch his shoulder. His skin is warm against my fingers, even through his shirt.

"Angel," I say quietly.

His eyes open, dark and glassy. He blinks once. When he recognizes me, he smiles so sweetly my heart goes liquid in my chest.

"Hey," I say.

He sits up and unfolds his arms. He rubs his eyes with the heels of his hands and yawns. "Oh, man. I was out."

"We both were."

"I can't remember the last time I had a nap that good. This couch is magic." He stretches, then wraps his arms around me again and pulls me onto his lap. "You're magic."

I straddle him and cup the back of his head with my hands as he looks up at me.

"Angel?" I say.

"Yes?"

"I was thinking about our conversation last night."

He goes still and waits for me to say more.

"I wasn't prepared for what I'd see, but that's on me, not you." I run my fingers over his smooth neck. The edges of his beard are sharp. He shaved this morning. "You warned me to be ready, and I wasn't."

"Why do you think your reaction was so strong?" he asks.

"I guess I'm just not used to seeing violence like that. I'm lucky that—for the most part—I haven't had to face it."

He frowns. "What do you mean, 'for the most part'?"

I pause. Should I tell him? Compared to what Angel's been through, Efren's single punch seems like nothing. But then again, as my clients have taught me, a stressful experience is a stressful experience. And talking about it might help Angel and me find a path out of this disagreement.

"Okay, so." I take a breath. "My ex—he wasn't a good guy."

"Meaning?" Angel narrows his eyes.

"He hit me. One time, when he was drunk. That was the night we broke up."

Angel's mouth twitches.

"I haven't seen him since," I continue, "but I still remember what it felt like. And I think that's what my body was processing when I watched the fights last night. That's why I felt so sick." Before Angel can say anything, I quickly add, "But of course I understand these are two very different situations. That was abuse, and this is not. Knowing how to fight—I can understand how that was a necessity for you. It's how you survived. How you continue to survive, I imagine."

Angel ignores my attempt to steer the conversation away from my past. "Princesa," he says quietly. "I'm so sorry that happened to you."

"It's fine."

"No." He looks so deeply into my eyes, I have nowhere to hide. "It's shitty."

We're quiet. After a long time, I touch the newest cut on his face. His fight was days ago. It's almost invisible now. "Anyhow, that's what I was thinking about last night. My own history. My own baggage."

He tightens his hold on me. I feel warm and safe, as if the vitality of his body is flowing into me, giving me strength.

"Do you think I would ever hit you?" he asks quietly.

I study his face. "No. Never."

"Good. I would rather die than lay a hand on you. Never forget that, Deanna."

I take his big, rough hands and hold them. I know in my bones he is telling me the truth. I'm not afraid of him.

"Do what you need to do," I say. "I won't watch you fight, and I won't attend those fights again. But like I said before, I would never make you choose between me and something you love." Ugh, what an awkward choice of words. I cringe at myself. In a quick and desperate attempt to recover, I say, "Kiss me, Angel Rosas." I lean in.

"Wait," he says.

I panic. "What?"

"I have cigar breath," he says.

I sniff his breath. "Not really. You're okay."

"You sure?"

"I'd tell you if you were gross."

"Okay. Thanks."

I lean in for my kiss but he stops short.

"Thank you for sharing all this with me," he says. "I don't ever want to do anything that will upset you like that again. It's important to me to protect you. Your body, your mind and your heart. All of you. Do you understand?"

"Yes," I say. "I understand."

We kiss at last, but just when it's getting good, he stops again.

"What's wrong?" I ask.

"The kinds of things I want to do to you right now?" he says, considering every word. "I need more room to maneuver. I think I need a proper bed. A big one."

I smile. "Where should we go?"

He looks past me into the showroom. "See that king-sized bed on the opposite wall?"

Still in his lap, I turn around. "Yes."

"I'll race you there."

"Seriously?"

"Ready?" he says, his eyes twinkling.

"What?"

"Set?"

"Wait, what?" I wiggle off his lap.

"Go!" he shouts.

I make a run for it. Laughing, Angel chases me through the store and tackles me sideways on the enormous four-poster bed. I'm giggling uncontrollably. A few tiny down feathers from the duvet fly into the air like snowflakes.

Angel holds me close. He kisses my temple, my cheek, my chin. Then he lands his beautiful mouth on mine and kisses me until I have no idea where I am or what I'm doing here.

I open my eyes as he kisses my neck. The walls next to the bed are turquoise blue, and the sheets and duvet are bright white. There's an embroidered tapestry hanging on the wall. The picture is of a house on the beach. The house is covered in vines and bright red flowers, just like the ones in the photo Angel texted me a few days ago.

"Have you ever gotten it on in the furniture store?" Angel whispers in my ear. I adore how he pivots from tender to playful to horny in seconds.

"No," I say, "because I'm not a pervert."

"Well, it's your lucky day. Because I am."

He stands up. Eyes on me, he strips off his shirt and unbuckles his belt. He takes off his shoes and socks. As he slowly takes off his pants and boxer briefs, he smiles and bites his lip. That's when I see it—his big, beautiful cock, dark and hard and ready to go.

"Your turn," he says. "Get naked, girl."

He kisses me again and takes off my coat and dress. He holds me against his hot, rigid chest and unhooks my bra. As he stares at my breasts, he puts me on my back and hooks his fingers around my panties. He pulls them down. They get caught around my boots. I begin to unzip them but he stops me.

"No. On," he says. "I want those on."

Carefully, he untangles my panties and throws them on the floor. He runs his hands over the shafts of my boots.

"I have been fantasizing about fucking you in these all day long."

He holds up my left leg high in the air. I stare as he closes his eyes and kisses the leather edge of my boot, then trails kisses up the inside of my thigh. His cock jerks. The tip brushes my bare skin. It's wet.

Hang on.

A leather kink? Angel?

Very interesting.

He looks up at me. "I'm going to be between your legs for a long time," he says, smiling that wicked smile. "So let's make you more comfortable."

He builds a nest of pillows on the bed, picks me up, and drops me in it. More tiny feathers float down from the sky. He puts pillows under my ass, tipping my hips up high. Happy with his work, he kisses my mouth again and whispers, "At least two."

"What do you mean?"

"You'll see."

At this angle, I am completely vulnerable and open to him. A week ago, being this intimate with anyone would have been unthinkable. But now? He makes me feel safe and wanted. And I want him to know every part of me.

He drops a single kiss on my pussy. I take a deep, sharp breath.

"Que rico," he whispers. "Ya estás mojadita."

With one hand, he begins stroking me, turning me on with his perfect, gentle touch. With his other hand, he strokes the shaft of one of my boots, back and forth, achingly slowly. I'm hypnotized by the effect he's having on my body. Soon, I'm lost in a spiral of arousal.

"So good," I whisper.

The crisp sheets are cold against my skin. I can smell the furniture polish, the leather, and the dark wood of the furniture all around us. And I can hear Angel touching me. I can hear his soft, even breathing. When I look at him, his eyes are half-closed as he stares at me, as captivated by me as I am by him. And all of my senses are heightened, as if my body wants to take in as much of this moment as possible.

He pushes my knees apart gently and lies down between my legs. I am already close when his tongue finds my sweet spot. But instead of bringing me home, he teases me, licking me with the barest touch. How can a man who is basically a giant column of muscle be so gentle with me in bed? I grab fistfuls of the duvet in frustration.

"Please," I say. "Right there. I'm so close."

"I know."

He keeps doing what he's doing. I'm frozen, completely under his spell. Very slowly, he speeds up, then adds more and more pressure. Again, he brings me to the verge of coming.

Again, he backs off and looks at me with an innocent expression on his annoyingly handsome face.

"What are you doing to me?" I say, breathless.

"You've never edged?" he asks.

"No."

"You have now."

I narrow my eyes at him. "How dare you."

He chuckles like the villain he is. Then he proceeds to bring me right back to the edge of my orgasm. I am nearly sobbing. Then he does it twice more.

"Angel, please," I beg.

He's openly laughing at me.

"No seas cabrón," I say, frustrated.

"I like it when you speak Spanish," he says. "You should speak it more."

He licks his hand like a fucking porn star and jacks himself off until he's fully erect. I am so turned on that a draft from a window will set me off. But Angel leans forward and kisses me hard and long on the mouth. I close my eyes. I can taste myself on his lips, and something dark and primal ignites in my brain. Without breaking our kiss, he grabs my hands and pins them above me on the mattress. Then he shifts his hips and with one hard thrust, impales me on his thick cock.

We both let out a long, melancholy moan.

Still kissing me, he moves against me. The angle is so deep, I feel like I've never been truly fucked until now. This feels so good, warm tears spill out of the corners of my eyes. Gently, Angel takes off my glasses and places them on a small table next to the bed. Then he kisses away my tears.

He purses his lips and looks into my eyes.

"Salty," he whispers.

I run my fingers through his messy hair and hold him close to me. He rocks his hips back and forth slowly, almost soothingly, while his cock stretches me to my limit. I'm caught between Heaven and Hell—the soft white bed beneath me, and above me, an actual demon, so lusty and so beautiful he takes my breath away.

"Angel," I say.

He holds himself up on his arms and looks down at me. And so help me God, I want to be here, locked in this moment, forever.

Deanna. Get a grip.

"Angel," I say again.

"What?"

"I'm going to come," I whisper between my clenched teeth.

His gaze goes dark and thirsty. As he begins to thrust fast and hard, the muscles of his torso go rigid. I hold on to his hard, sweat-slick biceps and pull myself deeper onto his cock.

"Yes, Deanna," he says. "Yes."

My orgasm breaks free at last. My pussy clenches around him, and I feel unbelievably full, as if my body wasn't built to take this much dick. Nails digging into his skin, I am whimpering and cursing at him in two languages. But Angel keeps going, drawing out the biggest orgasm I've ever had in my life.

"You're not breathing," he says. "Breathe. Take a deep breath. Right now."

I will myself to do it. As soon as my lungs fill with cool air, another contraction seizes me, and another. The oxygen prolongs my climax, and I ride it for a long, long time until at last, it begins to subside.

But Angel is not interested in stopping.

He kisses me again, and I hear a growl deep in his chest. He pulls out of me quickly, then flips me over until I'm on all fours. He tucks the pile of pillows under my hips and knocks me down from my hands to my elbows. Now my ass is high in the air.

"Yes," he hisses, stroking my ass. "Fuck, yes."

He gets behind me and spreads my legs wide with his knee. He runs his hands up and down my back and grabs my ass cheeks in his big hands before letting them go and bringing his palms down with a sharp smack. The momentary pain lights up my nervous system and sends blood right back to my buzzing clit.

Without saying anything else, Angel puts his hand on the base of my spine. With his other hand, he guides his dick into my dripping, twitching pussy.

He grabs my hips and thrusts hard. Again. And again. Until the sound of his fucking me from behind is steady like a drumbeat, like a heartbeat. He's so strong. I arch my back and rest my forehead against the mattress, listening to the creaking of the heavy oak bed frame, feeling my body melting again into his.

With a groan, he leans back and changes his angle. He reaches around my hip and slides his hand between my body and the pillows. With the pad of his finger, he strokes my clit in time with his deep, rhythmic thrusts.

"Oh, God," I whisper.

And suddenly I'm coming again, screaming into the bedding, my body fucked so completely that arousal is running hot and wet down the insides of my thighs. Angel, joyful, spanks my ass again so hard that I flinch and clench around him. He hisses and carefully pulls out, still rigid as the limb on a fucking tree.

"Two," he says, grinning. "Just like I said."

NINETEEN
ANGEL

WHEN I GET up from the bed, I can't feel my feet. Now I'm standing. Wait. Am I standing? I might be flying. My blood is running hot and cold. I feel lightheaded, like I do when I've been working with too many industrial cleaners in a poorly ventilated area.

I know one thing, though. I can't look at Deanna.

If I do, I will come.

There's no explanation for why I haven't come yet except we've had more sex in the last week than I have in the last three years.

I want to think it's my steel will and Jedi-like control over my body, but no. It's not. It's luck, and the fact that we've been fucking and fucking and fucking. My recently celibate body is completely confused.

Deanna sits up in the middle of the bed and stretches her arms over her head. Her silky black hair tumbles over her shoulders and hangs down, barely hiding her big, beautiful breasts. The strands tease her brown nipples and...

And...

No, Angel. Look somewhere else. Right now.

She says something to me.

"Huh?"

"I said, 'Stand against the bedpost.'"

My dick, dripping with her, jerks to attention at the sound of her stern voice.

"Here?" I lean against one of the tall, carved wooden bedposts. I try smirking, like a jackass, as if I have any control over this situation at all.

"Yes." She climbs out of bed, puts her glasses back on and walks over to where my pants lie on the ground. She's still wearing those boots, and I can't help staring at her. Naked, her whole body blushing from two orgasms, in tall leather boots that she kept on just for me. It's almost too much for my brain to process.

I'm lost in another world when I hear the clink of a buckle.

"What are you doing?" I ask.

"Something I have a feeling you'll like," she says.

She slips the leather belt from its loops. Looking at me, she gives it a little snap.

And that—that sound—does something to me.

I blink, confused.

"How do you feel about this?" she asks.

She snaps the belt again. A chill runs down my spine, but somehow, my dick gets harder. I narrow my eyes at her and try to describe how I'm feeling.

"I really like that it's in your hands," I say, "but...I have a complicated history with belts."

Understanding dawns on her. Her expression grows softer and she lowers the belt. "I'm sorry. I wasn't thinking," she says. "We don't have to play with this."

I reach forward and cup her cheek with my hand. She has such a beautiful face. There's a faint crease between her chin and her bottom lip that makes her look like she is always pouting, always on the verge of not getting something she wants.

"No," I say. "I want to play. But you'll have to help me." I pause. "You'll have to help me feel a different way about belts. Can you?" Very softly, I kiss her lower lip.

"Should we set some boundaries?" she asks in a quiet voice.

"Sure." I study her face for a moment before I study the belt closely. It's soft leather with a chrome buckle. Nothing out of the ordinary. Nothing scary unless I give it the power to frighten me. "Don't hit me with the buckle end," I say.

She strokes my arm gently. "No. I won't."

"Don't hit my legs or my back."

"I won't," she says. "And please, if you want me to stop, just say stop."

"Got it." I think for a moment and hand the belt back to her. When she takes it, I realize that I trust her completely. I'm not afraid.

"I guess that's it," I say. "All systems go."

I lean back against the bedpost. The carved wood is cold against my spine. Deanna stands closer to me. Her nipples brush my chest. She straddles one of my legs and I can feel the soft suede of her boots against my skin. I shiver. My dick jerks against her and she gently, carefully wraps her free hand around my shaft.

Staring into my eyes, she holds me in a tight, unmoving grip. With her other hand, she holds the belt. It's folded in half. Gently, she touches my throat with the bent loop. The leather is cool and smooth against my hot skin. I swallow hard, surprised at my body's reaction to its touch.

She watches my face as she runs the edge of the looped belt down the center of my chest. The leather barely scrapes my skin, but everywhere it touches me, I get goosebumps. My heart is racing.

"Angel Rosas," she says softly, "I think you might have a thing for leather."

She lets go of my dick and holds the belt in both hands. She tucks a loop into the buckle and makes a quick cuff. "Hands behind your head," she says. "I'm going to tie you to the bedpost. Is that okay?"

My brain is not working well enough to explain to her how into this I am. But I manage to say, "Yes."

I lean against the post and put my hands behind my head. She climbs onto the bed, slips the belt over my hands and tightens the cuff around my wrists. I don't know what kind of bondage lessons she's taken because when I pull at the belt, I'm legit cuffed to the bedpost. I can't wiggle my way out. And when I realize this, my dick stands straight up. A drop of precome falls on the oriental rug at my feet.

She climbs out of bed and stands a few feet in front of me to examine what she's done. Her eyes linger on my face, my shoulders, my chest, my abs, and my achingly hard cock. She tips her head to one side, then the other. With the barest touch, she runs her hands up and down my torso, lingering on the sensitive points of my nipples and very lightly scratching my skin with her nails.

"I can't believe you're real," she says.

"I'm real," I say. "Real horny."

"I'm serious," she says. "I can't believe you're real. Like in a few moments, my alarm will go off and I'll wake up in my apartment the day of my booster shot and none of this will have happened."

"I didn't think I'd see you again either, princesa," I say. "But if this is not real, then how about we ride this as far as it goes?"

"What do you mean?"

Maybe I should have thought this through. But being tied

naked to a bed with a leather belt is doing funny things to my brain. "I mean, I don't want this to end. Be with me."

"What?"

"Let me be your boyfriend."

Her mouth opens. "Are you serious?"

"I am." I lick my lips, trying to make the words form properly. "I don't have anything to give you. I have nothing to offer you. And we're so different. But I want to be your boyfriend, Deanna."

She leans forward and kisses me deeply. I flick my tongue against hers just before she pulls away. Then she looks me in my eyes and says, "I want you thinking clearly when you ask me that question. So pretend you didn't ask it, and ask me again when I'm done with you, okay?"

"What do you mean?"

That's when she drops to her knees in front of me. With both hands, she gently holds the shaft of my cock. Looking up at me, she runs her pretty pink tongue across the tip of my dick before popping the head between her soft, full lips. She sucks on me like a piece of ripe fruit, then licks up and down my dick with flicks of her wicked, teasing tongue. Holding me steady, she does this again and again, taking me deeper each time. She begins using her hands, gently stroking my shaft up and down while using her sweet, sucking mouth to jack off the head of my cock.

"Deanna," I warn her.

She looks up at me with dark, seductive eyes and teases me with her tongue. She kisses the very tip of my dick and smiles.

Traviesa—my beautiful brat.

She doesn't break eye contact with me while she jacks off my dick in her soft, gentle fist. She goes faster and faster while sucking the head of my cock like a lollipop. I'm pulling hard against the belt, but the loop doesn't give way. I can hear the leather straining. My back arches and my hips buck against her.

Still, she doesn't stop.

She works me faster with her hand. Smiling, she opens her mouth so I can see the purple head of my dick cradled against her pillowy pink tongue. Every lick feels better and better. I'm clenching up hard, trying to keep from coming, but the sight of her is too hot. I can't hold back.

The contractions start at the base of my dick.

"Deanna," I say again, the barest whisper.

She speeds up her hands and opens her mouth wider. The pleasure is unimaginable. Every muscle in my body tightens. The leather of the belt creaks and cracks. I slam the buckle against the wood.

My orgasm is so strong, the first spurt lands on her glasses. We both gasp in surprise, but she laughs and keeps going, working me faster and faster. Hot come shoots out of me, hard and fast, pooling in her mouth and dripping over her lips, dark pink and white. Barely coherent, I see a montage of sexual images in my head. I imagine what it will feel like when I can fuck Deanna without a condom. I imagine what it will look like to come in her pussy until it's dripping out, just like this.

I'm drowning. Deanna licks down every drop of my orgasm. I'm captivated watching her. I want to touch her so badly. I want to stroke her face and hair and hold her close. But I'm still lashed to the bed. She's still completely in control.

When I'm done, I can barely stand up. She releases me, stands up, and smiles. She takes off her messy glasses and places them on a table. Then she unzips her boots and takes them off too. There's an imprint of the zipper going up the inside of her leg. I fight the urge to lick the lines away with my tongue.

After some concentration, she wiggles the belt loose and I'm able to slip my hands out. I rub my wrists and slowly lower my arms. Dazed, I stretch and climb back into bed with Deanna. We curl up under the luxurious covers and hold each other close. I bury my face in her hair and breathe deep. She smells like herself, shampoo and fresh peaches. She smells like me, like my sweat and my come. Right now, I feel so free with her that the rest of the world feels small. In this moment, this is the only universe that matters.

For a long, long time, we lie on our sides, face to face. She strokes my cheek and beard. Her touch is so gentle, my heart aches.

"I never thanked you for coming with me today," she says quietly. "I know my family is a lot to take. I guess I just didn't feel strong enough to face them alone this year. I apologize for dragging you with me."

"That was nothing," I say. "I thought it would go worse, to be honest. Like maybe your brothers would throw me out into the street or your parents would call the cops on me."

"Well, by those standards, today was a raging success."

"It was." I tuck a lock of beautiful dark hair behind her ear. "Listen to me, Deanna. I know you have probably done a lot of work to separate yourself from your family's beliefs about you. But from the little I saw today, I want to remind you that you're much more than what they see. You're much more than what they think they know about you."

She watches my mouth as I speak, but she says nothing.

"I haven't known you long," I say, "but I'm proud of you and the work you do. I think you're incredible."

I feel her drawing close to me. She wraps her arms around my chest and tucks her head under my chin. We tangle our legs together under the covers. Have there ever been two people in the history of the world who fit together better than Deanna and me? I doubt it. And the heavy emotional lifting we did today? She is amazing to me.

"Be my girlfriend," I say again. I kiss the top of her head. "Be with me."

"Have you thought this through?" she asks.

"Yes," I lie.

"But you've never had a girlfriend."

"No." I take her hand and kiss it softly.

"And it's been a long time for me," she says. "A very long time."

I stroke her hair.

"My ex is the reason I haven't dated. The real reason I never called you back. I was kind of a mess back then. I just didn't want to leave myself open to being blindsided. Or suffering for my loyalty. Never again." She pulls back and looks at me. In the soft glow of all the lamps, her eyes are enormous and dark, and I want to stare into them all night.

"I have nothing to give you. Not yet, at least. But I will never take anything from you. And I will never break your heart, Deanna, or take your loyalty for granted," I say. "Do you understand?"

"Yes."

"Please. Be with me."

She looks into my eyes. I lean forward and kiss her, soft and deep. I taste my own come on her lips. I've never tasted it before —I feel strange. Kinky. She does this to me—makes me want to learn about myself. She makes me want to know everything there is to know.

"Okay," she says at last. She kisses my lips again. "I'll be your girlfriend, Angel."

DECEMBER PASSES like a dream I don't want to end.

Deanna works the last few weeks at her job and goes on a couple job interviews. I work the same hours and exercise at the boxing gym. But every night, I find my way back to her doorstep. She welcomes me inside. We share a meal. We talk. We make love until late at night and fall asleep in each other's arms under a pile of blankets and pillows. The cold gray world outside can't touch us.

Deanna wants to know all about me. I tell her stories of growing up in Salinas, not all of them bleak. I talk about hiding out in the library after school, sitting on a blue bean bag and reading everything I could in the children's section until my grandma came to pick me up. I finished all the books on cowboys, sports and space travel. I read *The Guinness Book of World Records* three times, back to back. And then I started on *The Baby-Sitters Club*. I read all of those too.

"They were really good," I tell her. "Are you serious? You never read them?"

"No," she says, smiling. "I never did."

"Poor you," I say.

Bundled up together, we watch more old movies—*Rocky, Goodfellas* and *La Bamba*, which makes me kind of emotional. Between Ritchie Valens and Selena, I'm really bummed out.

"Can we please watch a movie about our people that doesn't end in tragedy?" I say.

Deanna's neighbor Ro takes us to her dispensary. We watch *Up in Smoke* all together before heading out, late at night, to a Korean diner a block away. We order chili-red tofu soup in stone bowls. The soup is hot—hot like a fucking volcano. I burn my mouth, but I can't stop eating. It's so good. We gorge ourselves and find a private room at a nearby karaoke parlor. We dance around while Ro sings "Oops! I Did It Again" by Britney Spears. Deanna sings "El Chico Del Apartamento 512" by Selena, and I can't keep my eyes off her. When I sing "All my

Exes Live in Texas," I make them laugh so hard that tears run down their cheeks.

"Country?" Ro exclaims. "You?"

"Salinas," I say. "I'm country as a turnip green."

Together, we all head out into the night, dancing and singing, arm-in-arm, Deanna linking Ro and me.

"Isn't she great?" Ro asks me.

I kiss Deanna's cheek. "She is."

I only stop at Sal and Vanessa's house now and again to shower and do the laundry. Vanessa's daughter Muñeca catches me one night before I hop on the bus to K-town.

"Wait, Tío Angel." She gives me a candy cane. "Here. This is for you. Happy holidays."

"Thank you," I say. "That's nice."

"I don't really like them," she says. "The principal gave them to us. I don't really like her, either."

"Oh." I put it in my pocket. "Well. Thanks anyway."

She jumps on my back and wraps her arms around my neck. I lift her off her feet and shuffle out to the shed in the backyard.

Muñeca tightens her grip. "Will you bring your girlfriend to Christmas? Mom says if you don't, you're probably ashamed of us."

"What? I'm not ashamed of you guys. Well, maybe your tío Eddie. I'm pretty ashamed of him."

She giggles. "What is your girlfriend like?"

My girlfriend. I could listen to that word all day. "Deanna? She's very nice and very smart, like you. She has long hair like your mom, and she wears glasses."

"Do you kiss her a lot?"

"Yes. I kiss her a lot. Like, a lot-a lot."

I open the back door, and Chancla the elderly wiener dog prances out, her tummy two millimeters from dragging on the porch steps. Muñeca hops off, but when I bend down to take a load out of the dryer, she jumps on me for another piggyback ride. I just got off another ten-hour shift, but I hold back the groan and keep unloading my clothes.

"What did you get your girlfriend for Christmas?" Muñeca asks.

I freeze. "When is Christmas again?"

"In two days, Tío Angel! You didn't get your girlfriend a gift?" She gives my forehead a gentle smack. "Now you have to get her something ugly from the dollar store. She's going to know you forgot."

I carry my laundry basket and the little girl back inside to the living room and dump them both on the couch.

"Can I give her this candy cane for Christmas?" I ask, taking it out of my pocket.

Muñeca starts folding my clothes with me. "No! You have to get her something nice. Like diamonds or a Gucci bag like my mom wants. Sal says he's going to Santee Alley to get the bag for her, but she says it will be a fake Gucci. It will say Fucci."

"Okay, so let me review. Diamonds. Real Gucci stuff." I unwrap the candy cane and start eating it. "Here's the problem. I'm broke. I can't afford that stuff."

Muñeca holds up one of my T-shirts. It's holey. She makes a face. "How did you get a girlfriend anyway?"

Punked by a ten-year-old. Ouch. "With my personality, obviously."

She folds the T-shirt. "Well, maybe she won't notice that the bag you give her says Fucci."

TWENTY

DEANNA

OF COURSE the phone would ring at 4:55 p.m. on December 23, the Thursday before a long Christmas weekend.

Ingrid is standing by the front door of the office with one foot out.

"Don't answer it," she says.

I hesitate.

"Don't you dare," she says, gritting her teeth.

It rings one more time. I answer it.

"Fuckin' Deanna," Ingrid whispers. "I swear to God."

"Evergreen Vocational Services Center, Deanna Delgado speaking."

"Ms. Delgado, good evening, ma'am." The familiar voice on the end of the line is crisp like the crease on a uniform. He sounds like the kind of law enforcement officer for whom no holidays stand in the way of justice. "This is Humberto Gavilan with Parole. How are you today, ma'am?"

"Hello again. What can I help you with, Agent Gavilan?"

"If you don't mind, let me verify once again that you are indeed the caseworker for Arturo Aguilar. Is that correct?"

I swallow down a groan. "Yes, that's correct," I say, "I am—I was—his caseworker. Do you have any news to share with me on Art?"

"Yes. I have an update for you."

Reflexively, I brace myself for bad news again. Out comes my trusty legal pad and a pen for notes. "Okay, what's going on?"

Agent Gavilan explains that since Art walked out of his reentry facility in Lincoln Heights last month, investigators have recovered the broken GPS device, but the program manager at Art's facility hasn't seen him since. They had three pings from a cell phone tower not far from Hollenbeck Park, but that was weeks ago.

Impatient, I ask, "And recently? Anything new?"

"Well, Ms. Delgado, that's why I am calling you today. One of our undercover gang officers sighted Mr. Aguilar two days ago. He was on foot near Al & Bea's, heading east. He gave our officer the slip and hasn't been seen since. Since your office is nearby, I thought to call you once again to see if you have had any contact with Mr. Aguilar. Has he reached out to you at all?"

This is annoying. "He has not. No phone calls. No in-person contact. If I hear from him, as I said, I will contact you immediately. But I still have not heard a peep from Art."

"All right," Agent Gavilan says. "If he contacts you, as I said, it's very important that you contact me immediately. Bringing Mr. Aguilar in is one of our top priorities."

Am I being paranoid? Or does Agent Gavilan sound suspicious of me?

Weird.

Again, he spells out his name, gives me two phone numbers, and reminds me of his unit: Fugitive Apprehension Team.

"Got it," I say, putting down my pen. "Thank you, Agent."

"Thank you, Ms. Delgado. And happy holidays to you."

"Happy holidays."

At the door, Ingrid is looking at me with a bored face. "Aren't you glad you answered that?" she says in a monotone. "Aren't you so proud of yourself?"

We turn off all the lights and lock the door. Outside, the air is frigid. I zip up my coat as we walk back to our cars parked side-by-side. Since that weird incident after the pub, I've noticed that Ingrid always parks close and walks out with me. It's an unspoken kindness.

I have four more days to tie up all my loose ends at Evergreen before I leave. That means four more days of working with Ingrid. The thought makes me profoundly sad, and I can't even talk to her about my feelings because we never talk about our feelings. Even though I know we'll see each other, it won't be to engage in the daily battle we've been fighting together for the last ten years.

Her hair is caught in the zipper of her down jacket. She takes off one glove and picks out the strands with her fingers. "Ugh. The struggle," she whispers. "So where are you spending Christmas? With your family or with Little Sleepy's?" She laughs to herself. "What was his name? Payaso? Big Loco?"

"Angel," I say. "Call him Angel. And yes. I'm going over to his family's on Christmas Day. And you? Are you spending the weekend with your family again?"

"No," she says, frustrated. "I finally have to meet the parents. In Coronado. The whole family will be there."

"Look at you! I'm so proud of you."

"I know, I know," she says. "I had to get my sideburns waxed and everything."

We get into our cars.

"Merry Christmas. See you Monday," she says.

"Merry Christmas," I say. "Good luck in San Diego."

❧

THE SUN IS SHINING on Christmas Day.

Angel and I do our covid tests and get dressed together in my apartment. Funfetti and Meatball, freshly washed, are ready to party. Ro is in Palm Springs, lounging by the pool of one of her artist friends like the good pagan she is.

Before we leave, I sit next to Angel on the bed and give him his Christmas present.

"Um, this is not something I can give you in front of your family," I say.

Grinning, he slips the bow off the present and lifts the lid. The smell of leather fills the room. Inside the box is a brand-new black belt with silver hardware. At first glance, it's nothing special.

"You can wear it like a regular belt. But it's a hobble belt," I explain. "Here."

I show him how to weave the belt through its loops to form a pair of cuffs. I slip them over his wrists and buckle the belt snugly.

"Ankles. Wrists. Forearms. Knees. Wrist to ankle. Ankle to wrist," I say, kissing his neck. In the last month, we've discovered he doesn't like impact play, but he is hardwired for bondage.

He slips his cuffed hands over my head and pulls me close for a kiss. "Fuck. This is so hot. I like it a lot. Thank you, princesa."

We get distracted for a few minutes.

I unbuckle him. He replaces the belt he's wearing with his new one and we both look in the mirror. The hardware is totally hidden. No one would know it's more than just a nice everyday belt.

"It's a good metaphor for you," I say, pulling his jacket back to show off the leather and, inadvertently, the huge bulge in his pants. "My boyfriend. Walking around pretending to be a regular guy."

He beams at me. He likes it when I call him my boyfriend. So do I.

"Your turn," he says. "Reach into my pocket."

I reach into one of his pants pockets.

"Hmm. Better try the other one," he says.

I take my hand out, not-accidentally brushing his hard cock. In his other pocket, there's a small silver box. Nestled inside is a set of earrings. They're flowers, carved from red coral. Hanging at the end of each delicate flower is a tiny jade hummingbird.

Carefully, he lifts one earring out of the box. "I saw these in the furniture store. I went back the next day and bought them from your father. He gave me a Black Friday discount." He lifts an eyebrow. "Not a big one."

I stare as he holds a red blossom in the sunlight. It's beautiful.

"They're red trumpet flowers, like the vines growing behind the brewery," he says. "I know you've been worried about finding a job. I know you're worried about what's going to happen next. So when I looked up the flowers, I was reminded of you."

"Why?"

"Because these flowers have their own meaning. They mean 'a fresh start.' That's what you're experiencing right now, isn't it? A new beginning." His smile is tender. "You know the tattoo on the back of my right shoulder? The Aztec god?"

"Yes."

"Huitzilopochtli. The god of war and the sun. Sometimes he's depicted as a hummingbird." He taps the green hummingbird with the tip of his finger. "The Aztecs believed that warriors who died in battle were reincarnated as hummingbirds. So the hummingbird is a symbol of reincarnation." He looks into my eyes. "When I think about what you do, about your work, I see you as a warrior. You have the spirit of a warrior, Deanna. Never forget that."

WHEN WE ARRIVE, Angel's brothers are carrying folding tables out of the garage and placing them in the backyard under the big avocado tree. Chancla the wiener dog waddles down the porch steps, barking irately at Meatball and Funfetti. Even though they are much bigger and stronger than her, they take a few steps back as she comes at them, chest out.

Angel pets my dogs reassuringly as he unclips their leashes. "Don't be scared, guys," he says quietly to my dogs. "She acts all tough, but she's a sweetheart once you get to know her."

After some requisite butt sniffing, all three dogs take a lap together around the back garden, showing off their pee skills and wagging.

Angel hangs up the leashes and puts an arm around my shoulder. "See? Friends already."

A sassy older lady comes out of the house with a pile of plastic tablecloths. She's wearing red-striped leggings and a sweatshirt with two cartoon tamales on it that says, *'Tis the Season for Tamales.*

"Angelito, is this your girlfriend?" She climbs down the back porch steps. Her elf hat jingles with each step. She offers me an elbow bump. "Welcome! Welcome to our house. My God, you're so beautiful. Please, call me Chinita. I'm Vanessa's grandmother. We're so happy to meet you."

Angel and I are quickly pressed into service putting out folding chairs and spreading the tablecloths. Wearing a Santa hat, Eddie comes by to say hello and introduces me to Sal, who at first glance is larger and scarier than either Eddie or Angel. But when he shakes my hand, his eyes are kind and warm.

"Nice to meet you, Deanna," he says. "I'm glad you're joining us today. Welcome."

"Deanna was Eddie's caseworker back in the day," Angel adds.

"I'm so sorry," Sal says to me with a smile.

"Rude," Eddie says.

Chinita elbows me. "When the Rosas brothers stand all together like this, it's almost too much handsome, isn't it? Like looking at an eclipse or something."

Vanessa comes outside holding a baby, Eddie's new son, Max. Vanessa's daughter, Muñeca, follows her outside holding the hand of Eddie's young daughter, Julia. Julia spots her dad and runs right for him. Eddie scoops her up in his arms and twirls her around while she squeals with laughter.

I'm pretty good with names, but the Rosas family is a whirlwind.

Sympathetic, Angel puts an open beer bottle in my hand. I take a sip. Someone taps my shoulder. I turn. It's Juan Luis, the gentlemanly musician who played me a song with his friends in the garage the first night I visited here. He touches the brim of his Panama hat and sits down next to me.

Everyone is talking all at once, a wall of joyful chatter. English, Spanish, Spanglish. I can hear parties going on all over the neighborhood. Loud music. The smell of grilling meat. The sound of laughter rising over the block.

Like order from the chaos, food starts appearing on the table. Roast pork. Salted cod and stewed greens in mole sauce. Tamales of every variety, deviled eggs, a salad made with yellow apples and cream. Clay mugs of traditional Christmas punch bobbing with little orange fruits called tejocotes. It's a feast. The dogs post up under our chairs, ready to catch any scraps before they hit the ground.

This food looks so good, no one needs to be called to the

table. I remember that Eddie's wife is a chef—of course their spread would be amazing. Chinita says a quick, cheerful prayer, and we all lean in to eat.

Angel sits with his brothers. On my left side sits Eddie's wife, a tall, willowy woman with dark skin and long black hair. She has cheekbones like a runway model and a gentle but exhausted-looking expression.

"Hi, I'm Deanna," I say.

"Hi," she says softly. "Carmen. Nice to meet you." She stares at me for a moment. "I like your earrings."

"Thank you."

Vanessa gives Carmen baby Max. While we eat, Carmen covers up with a gauze blanket and feeds the baby. I can hear him nursing softly. The sound is sweetly intimate.

"Aren't you hungry?" I ask Carmen, looking at her empty plate.

She shakes her head and gives me a placid smile. "You go ahead."

To my right, Juan Luis is talking to Chinita in Spanish. She answers him in English. When he talks to her in English, she answers him in Spanish. They're having a mild argument about something funny. They're both hitting the ponche pretty hard.

Across the table, Eddie and Sal are having a heated discussion.

"Cut it out," Sal says.

"No pressure," Eddie is saying. "No pressure or anything, but you're only holding the future of Eastside Brewery in your hands when you walk into this meeting."

"Who is Sal meeting with?" Chinita asks Vanessa.

"King and Country. It's a privately held brewing company from Denver. They're interested in acquiring Eastside Brewery and developing us alongside the new brewpub locations they want to operate in Southern California." Vanessa takes a bite out of a deviled egg. "Sal has a big meeting with their investors in San Diego at the beer summit next month. We've been laying the groundwork for this deal for five, maybe six months. He's feeling the pressure, for sure."

"Are you sure you can do this? I mean, shouldn't we send a talker? A real wheeler-dealer?" Eddie says. "Let's face it. We all know who the closer is in this family."

"That's right," Vanessa says, cutting him off. "It's me. That's why I'll be there with him, Eduardo. To blast them with numbers and seal the deal. You need to stay down here with Carmen to look after the brewery while we're gone."

"What happens if they buy the brewery?" Muñeca asks.

Vanessa touches her cheek and smiles. "I like that you're paying attention. Well, they'll invest in our equipment, like a new canning line so we don't have to pay someone to can the beer for us. They'll give us money to hire more employees so maybe Sal and I can finally have a day off. And they'll help us distribute our beer to more stores, restaurants and bars. Doesn't that sound good?"

"Yes." Muñeca is a smart cookie. "But what do they get back? For all that money?"

Vanessa and Sal exchange glances.

"They get us," Vanessa says. "Our expertise. Our brand. We've been doing this alone for almost four years. It's hard. If King and Country takes over, we will finally have someone on our side. Some stability. Some backup. We will be able to take a breath."

"Then can you take my cousins and me to Disney World for my birthday?" Muñeca asks, cutting Julia's meat into tiny pieces.

"Hmm. Maybe not Disney World," says Vanessa. "But Disneyland? Yes. I think so."

Sunlight filters through the leaves of the avocado tree,

creating dancing shadows on the table. Next to me, Carmen pushes a few bites of salad around her plate and stares absently at the patterns on the tablecloth. The baby is asleep in her arms, his little rosebud mouth open, milk-drunk.

"Are you all right?" I ask quietly.

"I'm fine, thank you," she says. "Just a little tired. We all went to midnight mass last night. Then we started cooking early this morning." She pauses. "Isn't it funny? I used to cook six days a week, twelve hours a day. I ran one of the most prestigious kitchens in the city. And now I can't handle putting a pork loin in the oven."

"But you have your hands full." I study her face.

"That's true."

"Is he sleeping through the night yet?"

"He can sleep about three hours at a time now."

I pause. I think about the new mothers who would sometimes come into the employment agency with their babies. Some of them were distant, adrift. We were told to always look out for those. "Do you have anyone to help you right now?" I ask.

"Just Eddie," she says.

"Anyone else?"

She shakes her head.

I nod. Eddie's at the brewery every day with Angel. Which means Carmen is at home alone with her babies twelve hours a day.

"May I hold him?" I ask.

"Sure," she says. "He always sleeps soundly after he's eaten."

Carmen hands me her plump little baby. He's warm and soft and smells like a vanilla cupcake. He's wearing fuzzy reindeer pajamas. He wiggles and makes a sleepy noise but falls right back asleep as soon as I rest him against my chest.

Carmen pours herself a cup of ponche and takes a long drink. She unwraps a sweet pineapple tamal and slowly—so slowly—eats half of it.

"For you, Mommy." Julia brings Carmen a glittery bow from a present and kisses her cheek before chasing Muñeca, laughing, to the other end of the garden.

"It's hard sometimes," Carmen says to me when no one else is near enough to hear her.

"It looks hard," I reply.

She nods.

"But you're doing amazing in a very difficult situation," I say. "And your children look happy and very healthy."

She nods again.

I rock Carmen's little boy back and forth while she sits quietly, watching her daughter dance like a snowflake across the lawn. I kiss the top of Max's head.

Across the table, Angel is watching me. In the middle of the chatter and noise, he holds me in his gaze. A feeling, both familiar and new, rises in me. And now I know I'm in trouble, because my whole life, falling in love has only ever caused me trouble.

The sun goes down. Chatting, we drink more ponche and small glasses of rompope, the Mexican eggnog with a saint on the bottle. We put on warm coats. All three dogs huddle together under the table, drowsy and content. Chinita turns on the Christmas lights, illuminating the backyard. Carmen holds baby Max under the rainbow of lights and his eyes open wide with wonder.

Eddie walks out of the house holding a big cardboard box.

"Let's go," he says to Angel.

Angel gives me a quick kiss and stands up. "Time to light it up," he says. I'm confused. He follows Eddie to the front yard.

Sal comes out of the house with another cardboard box. "Can we please borrow your lighter?" he asks Chinita.

"Here they go," she says to me, rolling her eyes. She slips her hot pink lighter into Sal's back pocket. "Make sure to give it back."

"Thank you, Chinita," he says, kissing her cheek. He follows his brothers down the driveway out into the street.

Chinita picks up Chancla and whistles for Meatball and Funfetti, who follow her and Juan Luis into the garage. Before she closes the side door, Chinita says to me, "We'll keep your puppies safe in here with us. They won't like the noise."

I'm confused. "What do you mean?"

"You'll see."

"Can we go? Can we watch?" Muñeca asks Vanessa. Julia stands next to Muñeca, a tiny smiling shadow.

Vanessa considers it, but she's frowning. "Sal and your tíos, they always get a little rowdy. I don't know how safe it will be out there for little ones."

"I can look after them," I say. "We can watch from the front porch."

"Please, please, please," Muñeca begs.

"Pees, pees, pees," Julia echoes.

"How can I resist that?" Vanessa laughs. "Both of you, stay with your tía Deanna, okay? Don't leave the front porch."

Holding my hands, the little girls walk down the driveway with me. I park them on the top step of the front porch and stand on the lawn, watching Eddie gleefully pick out a fat tube from one of the cardboard boxes. Angel takes out what looks like a bath bomb wrapped in paper and unfurls a long fuse.

I squint. "Wait. Are those...illegal fireworks?" I ask.

"No comment," Angel says, waggling his eyebrows.

They place the tube in the middle of the street and drop in the mortar. Sal hands Angel the pink lighter. Angel lights the fuse and all three brothers jog back up the driveway, giggling like fourth graders. Muñeca puts her hands over Julia's ears, which I think is a bit excessive until a ridiculously large boom shakes the ground under my feet. Startled, I turn my gaze upward. After a pop and a fizzle, white sparks form a giant dandelion above my head. Golden glitter seems to rain down on me as the Rosas brothers hoot and holler and slap each other's backs. White smoke and the smells of sulfur and charcoal fill the air as neighbors come out to enjoy the show.

Next, Sal sets up a line of empty bottles from the brewery. The brothers fill them with projectile rockets.

"Point them away from the palm trees, Eddie." Sal pops open another beer and takes a drink, keeping the bottle theme. "Away," he repeats. "Not toward. We don't want a repeat performance of the world's largest tiki torch."

"That was fucking epic," Eddie says, and now I have to wonder, did they once set a palm tree on fire?

Again, Angel lights the rockets. They go off, whistling and screaming, their silver tails twisting in the dark sky.

The little girls clap and cheer.

"Pretty," says Julia.

On and on it goes until the street is littered with spent fireworks, scraps of tissue paper and charred cardboard tubes. The Rosas brothers are giddy and playful. Sal can't stop smiling, and Eddie and Angel stand with their arms around each other's shoulders, drinking and singing Katy Perry's "Firework." Clowns.

"Deanna!" Eddie calls. "Deanna!"

I'm snuggling the girls close to keep them warm. "What?" I call.

"Is this fool being good to you?" Eddie points the neck of his beer bottle at Angel. He's slurring a little bit. "Say no and I'll kick his ass. I'll do it. Swear to God."

Playfully, Angel shoves Eddie, who trips over his feet and lands ass-first on one of the empty cardboard boxes, crushing it and turning it into an accordion. The girls erupt in giggles. Sal helps Eddie up. They clink bottles.

"Salud," Sal says, patting Eddie's chest.

Angel sets up one more round of bottle rockets.

"Why do you make Angel light everything?" I ask.

Laughing, Sal says, "His record's clean. We don't need another strike."

On the car ride home, I sit in the passenger seat. Angel drives with one hand on the steering wheel and the other hand on the back of my neck, massaging me softly. Meatball and Funfetti are snoring loudly in the back seat.

"Did you have a good time?" he asks.

Mellow and happy, I say, "Yes."

"Good." He smiles.

We drive in contented silence for a while. I think about how different I feel right now compared to how I felt after spending Thanksgiving with my parents and siblings. It's night and day. The relaxed, open-hearted Rosas family is what I always hoped a family could be.

"Hey, listen," I say. "I need your help."

"What?"

"I wanted to talk to Eddie today about it, but I didn't think it was the right time," I say. "I'm not a psychologist, but I think Carmen has postpartum depression. She is struggling. She needs to talk to someone."

"What is postpartum depression?"

"It's a kind of depression women develop after having a baby. It can be very intense. I see mothers sometimes at my job who have it and receive treatment for it." I pause. "I know how you feel about mental health care. But it really can help some people, especially when they're having a hard time."

"Carmen has been through some other stuff," Angel says. "Not just the baby."

"What do you mean?"

"I mean her parents both passed away in the past year. From pneumonia and covid. It must have been early in her pregnancy. She couldn't even see them in person to say goodbye."

"Poor Carmen." I sigh. "She needs support, Angel. She needs it really badly."

Angel nods. "How can I help?"

"Tomorrow, tell Eddie what I've told you. Her doctor should meet with her to find out for sure. Tell Eddie to call me if he needs help finding resources for her. I know some people at the hospital who can help match her to a therapist or a support group."

"Okay," Angel says. "I'll do that."

I put my hand on his. "Thank you."

"Thank you," he says, "for looking out for my family."

TWENTY-ONE

DEANNA

I DO two more job interviews on Zoom and one follow-up in person. They all go well as far as interviews go, but no one wants to take the leap and hire me. On our last day in the office, after Tod throws us a depressing goodbye lunch at a fancy gastropub downtown, we come back to clear our desks and load our files into paper boxes. I label everything carefully, making sure the next person to get my caseload has everything they need to do right by my clients.

The moving company arrives that afternoon to begin shifting our shitty furniture to the main office. Most of it is dusty and held together by duct tape. Fresh beginnings. Onward and upward.

I put my photos of my dogs, my sad little cactus, my degree and my still-full jar of candy into another box. I leave two boxes of books and some of the training binders for the courses I've developed in my cubicle. They don't fit in my car. I'll have to come back after the New Year to get them, just before I drop my keys off at the main office for good.

I take home all of my personal office supplies. I resist the urge to steal tape and staples because I know the quality of these things is bad. I helped Ingrid make the office supply order.

"I need better tape," Ingrid once told me. "I need to get a better job with better tape to steal."

When her desk is all packed up, she gives me a fist bump.

"I guess I'll see you when I see you," she says.

Ingrid is not into displaying her emotions, so I follow her lead and pretend I'm not fucking sad at all. We get into our matching shitty Hondas and start our engines.

She waves. I roll down my window.

"Happy hour soon," she says. "Promise."

"I promise."

We pull out of the driveway and head our opposite ways.

When I arrive at the brewery, Angel and Eddie are standing outside the front door talking. They both look worried.

"What's going on?" I ask.

Angel kisses my cheek. "Muñeca just tested positive for covid. So did Sal and Vanessa. They're under quarantine now."

My whole body runs cold. "What? Are they okay?"

"Yes. Sal has a cough. Vanessa says she just has a headache. Muñeca has no symptoms. But they have to stay home, and they need some supplies."

"How's Chinita?"

"Negative," says Eddie. "Her doctor told her she should isolate from the family, so she's staying with Juan Luis."

"Vanessa told me to find a folding bed for her," says Angel.

"We can swing by the furniture store to get one," I say, "but it won't fit in my car."

Eddie gives Angel some keys and a credit card. "Take Big Bertha."

After picking up a folding bed from my dad at the furniture store, we drive the beat-up van down to the Target in nearby Commerce. On the way, I try to turn on the radio to distract

Angel, but the speakers are blown and all the music sounds like distorted farts. I turn it off. The van is full of funny sounds and clicks and bangs. It stops for a second at one of the intersections, but through the angry honking, Angel keeps his cool when he starts it again, as if this happens on the regular.

Vanessa texts Angel a long shopping list. As I help him fill the cart, he looks worried. "They think Muñeca got it from a playdate on Monday," he says. "One of the neighbor's kids caught it from her father who works at the supermarket. The new variant is really contagious, apparently."

"I've heard the same thing." I pause. "Is Eddie's family okay?"

"They're good. I'm good. All of the employees at the brewery tested negative too."

We get everything on the list, but Angel makes a detour into the toy section. I know he doesn't have a lot of money, so my heart aches when he browses the after-Christmas markdowns and picks out some craft kits and an art set for his niece. He buys these in a separate transaction, carefully counting the bills from his own wallet.

When we arrive at Sal and Vanessa's, it's just after dark. Chinita is sitting on the steps hugging her wiener dog close and smoking a cigarette. Juan Luis is sitting next to her in the pale glow of the porch light. When she sees Angel, Chinita stands up at once. She opens her mouth to say something, but nothing comes out. Instead, her face crumples. Angel wraps her in a big hug and rubs her back as she cries.

Juan Luis and I watch quietly.

"I don't want to be apart from them," she sobs quietly.

Angel kisses the top of her head and tells her, "Por favor, no se preocupe, señora. They're strong. They'll be fine. We'll look after them. And we have to keep you safe. Do you understand? That's the most important thing."

We take all of the supplies out of the van and stack them on the back porch. Coffee, oranges, bananas, loaves of bread, frozen pizzas, bags of spinach, paper towels, ibuprofen, toothpaste, Kleenex, toilet paper. Such everyday things.

"And you? Do you have everything you need?" Angel asks Chinita after she has wiped away her tears.

"More or less," Chinita says. "But I have to stay with this derelict in the garage. Can you imagine? A musician, up all hours of the night." She sighs. "And there's only one bed! What about my reputation?"

"I told you, you can have the bed," Juan Luis says to her in Spanish. "I'll sleep on the floor. I've slept on the floor many, many times. It's not difficult for me."

"Luckily, we have a solution for both of you." Angel unloads the folding bed from the van. "I'll put this inside the garage, and you can arm wrestle to decide who sleeps where."

When we're done unloading, we put on our masks and stand at the bottom of the steps. Angel texts Vanessa. After a few minutes, she comes outside with Sal and Muñeca. Vanessa is smiling at us, but I can see in her eyes that she is anxious. I am too. Covid has taken too many people in this community for us not to be anxious.

That's when Juan Luis begins playing a bouncing rhythm on his guitar, and his softly powerful voice rises in the dark.

It's a Vicente Fernández song, "Un Millón de Primaveras."

Chente.

I let the music enter my heart. The lyrics tell about a woman who is embarrassed by the singer who won't stop singing love songs about her. In response, he tells her not to worry. He will only sing about her for a million more springtimes and then that's it. After that, he won't bring it up anymore.

Next to me, Chinita takes my hand and gives it a squeeze.

❧

BACK AT MY APARTMENT, Angel helps me carry the boxes from my office upstairs. I take out the jar of candy and place it on the kitchen counter.

"What is that from?" Angel asks.

"I kept it on my desk for my clients when we used to meet face-to-face," I explain. "Every day, I hoped we would be able to meet in person again soon, so I kept the jar full, just in case." I look at the colorful Starbursts in the jar—red, yellow, pink, orange. I remember the candy garlands my college friends painstakingly made for me when I graduated early. If only I'd known that ten years later, I'd be disillusioned, unemployed and apparently unemployable. I would've told them not to bother.

"I guess that was all just wishful thinking," I say.

Angel's giving me a strange, faraway look, as if he's remembering something too.

"What?" I say.

"Nothing," he says. "Can I have one?"

"Take as many as you want."

He lifts the glass lid and removes a single pink Starburst. He unwraps it carefully and pops it into his mouth.

"Mmm," he says, chewing with great enjoyment. "Pink. That really is the best one. Believe the hype." He gathers me to him and holds me tight. When we kiss, his mouth tastes like strawberries, tart and candy-sweet.

Tonight, when we make love, something changes between us. In the first weeks of our relationship, we used sex to escape our problems. We used our bodies to get lost, to get high. But right now, we're sad. When I reach for him, I don't want escape. I want comfort, and I think he wants the same thing. Tonight, our bodies give us shelter. I find it in him, and I hope he can find it in me.

In the middle of the bed, Angel sits cross-legged. I'm in his lap, my legs wrapped around his waist. He is deep inside me and has been for a long time. I can smell my own soap on his skin and, faintly, the rubber of the condom he's wearing. These two scents tell me the truth. He's in my life now. A boyfriend. A lover.

We move slowly, each gentle roll of our hips creating friction and heat.

"Lean back," he whispers in my ear.

I put my hands on the mattress behind me and arch my back. Angel thrusts upward and digs deliciously at my G-spot with the head of his cock. I arch deeper. He leans forward and sucks gently on my nipple. We stare at each other as he teases me with the tip of his tongue. I groan. Quickly, he thrusts again, and I gasp, as if I were breathing pure arousal instead of air.

He releases my nipple and kisses me so long and so gently, I fall deep under his spell and lose the ability to form coherent thoughts. When he pulls away, he kisses each of my closed eyelids. When I open my eyes again, I study his beautiful, familiar face in the candlelight. I see his full lips, slightly parted. I see his dark, intelligent eyes.

But I see things I haven't seen before—the faint line down the center of his bottom lip. Scars, some hidden by his beard, some faint, some deeper, most likely from cuts he's sustained during boxing. A single tiny birthmark just under the corner of his left eye. It's so small, I think only someone who loves him very much would know about it.

Now I know about it.

We touch foreheads and move together, our bodies speaking their own private language. When I grip him tightly, he gasps.

"So," he says with a mischievous smile, "I've slept with lots of women."

"That's a funny thing to bring up." I squeeze him again. Hard.

"Ah, fuck." He groans and laughs softly.

"I hope you have a point," I say.

"Yes. I do. No one ever felt as amazing as you do, Deanna." He runs his hands through my hair. "I mean it. You are perfect. We were made to do this. You and me." He grips my hair and pulls my head back gently. He kisses my neck, feasting on the sweet spot under my jaw. The mild, steady pain from having my hair pulled heightens the exquisite pleasure he's giving me everywhere else. He does this for a long time, overloading my senses and making me feel the delicious tension between my power and his control, his power and my control.

Trembling, I shut my eyes tight. He thrusts hard, and when I moan, deep and hungry, he places his big hand around my throat.

"Abre tus ojos," he commands. His deep voice calls me back from the edge. When I open my eyes again, he's looking right at me. His own eyes are half-closed, and he's smiling like the devil, as if he knows how good he's making me feel right now.

"Estaba perdido, Deanna," he whispers against my neck. "I was alone. Lost. You found me."

"No," I say. My voice is rough. "We found each other."

With a glance, he asks me a question, and I nod. At once, he yanks my hair back and digs his fingers into the sides of my neck. The pain shoots through my brain like a bright bolt of lightning. I grab on to his thick, rigid shoulders and press my feet into the mattress. And now I ride him. I ride him as hard as he likes to ride me.

"Así," he says. "Así, princesa."

I fuck him. I fuck myself. With each thrust, I feel myself becoming more and more addicted to him. My body longs for this—for him.

Angel gives one loud, astonished shout, and for the first time, we explode at exactly the same time. Crushed in his grip, I come silently, pleasure filling every cell of my body. The climax rolls on and on, each intense surge popping off like fireworks in my brain.

He is right—we were made for this.

We were made for each other.

LATER, lying together in the dark, I ask him, "Are you okay?"

He takes so long to answer I think he's asleep. But at last he says, in a quiet voice, "No. I'm nervous." He takes a deep breath and lets it out slowly. "I want them to make a full recovery. I don't want to imagine a world where they don't."

"They're all young and healthy. Chances are they will be fine."

"My head knows that. But my heart is...less convinced." He's quiet. "Sal called me."

"What did he tell you?"

"He told me there's a problem. Their quarantine overlaps with the beer summit. I told him to meet with the King and Country team on Zoom. He said that's what they've been doing for the last six months. He told me he and Eddie decided they want me to go and represent Eastside Brewery and meet the founders in person in San Diego."

"What? That's great!" My heart flutters with pride for him.

"It's not great," he says.

I'm confused. "Why not?"

"I asked Sal to send Eddie, but Eddie can't leave Carmen alone with the kids right now. They agreed that no one else can do this but me. What do I know about any of this?" He sighs. "There's a lot of money on the line. I'm nervous as fuck. And

I'm annoyed with myself for being nervous, since my brothers have such big problems to face right now."

I reach for his hand under the covers. It's big and rough. The hand of a working man, a fighter. In the last few weeks, I've watched how he lives. How he cares for other people. How he loves.

"Okay. So. I've been thinking about something," I say.

"What?"

"The world is filled with good and evil," I say. "Angels and demons."

I stroke his palm, feeling his calluses, feeling his knuckles, hardened and swollen from impact.

"There are those of us who are neither angels nor demons, like me." I stroke the center of his palm. "And there are those of us, like you, who are both."

"What do you mean?"

"You've found a way to walk the line. You survived hell. You fought your way out. And you came out on the other side. You know what the journey requires."

He's quiet, thinking. "Psalm 91," he says after a long time. 'Porque él ordenará que sus ángeles te cuiden en todos tus caminos.'"

I translate slowly. "'For he will give his angels orders to protect you in all your ways.' How do you know that?"

"My grandmother liked it when I read her Bible aloud to her. When I moved to Salinas, she made me memorize parts of it. And she taught me to recite prayers by heart."

"Like 'Ángel de mi Guarda'?"

"Yes." He strokes the back of my hand with a gentle touch. "She loved me, in her own way. I loved her too. She always worried about what lay ahead for me. And after she died, her worst fears came true. I dropped out of school. I ended up on the street. I was fighting all the time. Fighting everybody, all the time—she hated that the most."

"Tienes un don," I say. "Fighting's your thing."

I can hear him laugh softly in the dark. "I guess it is my gift. Some gift."

"You know, not all angels live in Heaven," I say.

"No?"

"The ones who live on Earth—they stand guard. They fight." I bring his hand to my mouth and kiss it. "Right now, your brothers need you to fight."

He takes me in his arms and holds me close, keeping watch until I fall asleep.

MUÑECA LEAVES me a present on her back porch. It's a bag of blocks, some modeling clay, some bubbles, and washable markers in an enormous cardboard box.

"This box is huge," I say over the phone.

"Little kids love cardboard boxes. Put her inside with some markers," Muñeca says. "Mom used to do that to me when she wanted to watch her telenovela."

I smile. "Thank you for helping me out."

"You're welcome. Say hi to my cousins for me."

I wave at her through the window of her house. She blows me a kiss.

Taking advantage of my in-between-jobs state, I volunteered to help Carmen out twice a week while she meets with her therapist online. I watch Julia and Max for two hours—one hour so that Carmen can take a shower and catch her breath, and one hour for her appointment, which she does on a tablet in her bedroom. Once I get Julia set up with an activity, I spend a few minutes trying to figure out the baby carrier before I finally am able to strap on baby Max. Then I do a little light housework on the sly.

"Tía Deanna," Julia says from inside the box. She's coloring the cardboard walls—and herself—with a rainbow of markers. "How do bees get to school?"

I'm loading dishes into the dishwasher. "I don't know, Julia. How?"

"On a school buzz!" Giggles.

It's quiet for thirty seconds.

"Tía Deanna."

"Yes, Julia?"

"¿Qué le dice la mama pez al bebé pez?"

"I don't know. What did the mama fish say to the baby fish?"

"Nada." More giggles. A play on words—nada means *swim* and *nothing*. I have to hand it to her. Pretty sophisticated for a preschooler.

Together, Eddie and Angel finalize plans for a no-cover event at the brewery for New Year's Eve. They hire Juan Luis's trio and an all-female mariachi band for live music. Sal writes out a list of cellared beers to put on tap, including a special New Year's Eve beer he brewed with crushed grapes. It's called Nochevieja. It got such good reviews on a popular beer website that people are snatching up the twelve-packs as soon as Angel puts them out.

"Did your family do the twelve grapes tradition?" Angel asks me.

"Las doce uvas de la suerte? Totally," I said.

"What is it, exactly?"

"On New Year's Eve, as soon as the clock strikes midnight, everyone eats twelve green grapes as fast as they can."

"Why?"

"Each grape represents good luck for the coming year. One per month." I pause. "Although I guess all of that good luck wouldn't matter if you choked to death eating grapes at midnight. There was always that danger."

I get two more interviews, but those are not until the second week of January. Instead of sitting in my apartment and getting spun up over my fears of extended unemployment, I decide to go with Angel to the piñata district downtown to buy party supplies for the brewery. We get a balloon drop bag, hats, tiaras, funny glasses and party horns. Outside the wholesale warehouse, Angel buys a fruit cup from a street vendor, and we sit in Big Bertha sharing big pieces of watermelon and cucumber covered in lime juice, chamoy and chili powder. Soon we're sharing sweet and spicy kisses in the front seat. A passing lunch truck honks its horn while the crew shouts and whistles at us. Angel laughs and honks back.

"Oh my God." I cover my face. "You're so embarrassing."

He leans forward, takes my hands and kisses me so deeply I know I'll now have an inadvertent sexual reaction to Tajín for the rest of my life.

"I'm not embarrassed," he says. "Are you kidding? Look at you. I want everyone to know you're my girlfriend. I want the whole world to know."

That night at the brewery, we ring in the new year to a full house of patrons. Arriving on Juan Luis's arm, Chinita is dressed in a hot pink pantsuit and a rhinestone crown. At midnight, we stuff our mouths with grapes on FaceTime with Sal, Vanessa and Muñeca. In the middle of the noise and chaos, Eddie stands behind the bar on the phone with Carmen. He's beaming, clearly head over heels in love.

After closing, before heading home, Angel and I stop by Mom's for a well-deserved bowl of late-night pho. Her kids, all home from college on winter break, are with her at the shop. She introduces each of them, beaming with pride.

"Eat up now. You should always eat long noodles on New

Year's," Mom tells us. She puts on the glittery cardboard tiara and pops open the cold beer we brought her. "Cheers. Good luck to all of us."

ON MONDAY MORNING, Angel's alarm goes off early. It's a cold morning, and I have a hard time letting him go. Under the covers, he whispers to me, kisses me and touches me until I am aching for him. We make love very slowly, breaking in a long, lingering orgasm that feels better than any sweet dream.

He gets up, showers, has a cup of coffee and feeds the dogs. He kisses me again and tucks the blankets around me. I blink sleepily at him. He's carrying his backpack, a garment bag containing another borrowed suit, and a convention badge on a lanyard that says Salvador Rosas, Brewmaster, Eastside Brewery.

"All good?" I ask.

"I need to fill Vanessa's car with gas," he says, "but I should be in San Diego by nine. I'll be back this evening, not too late."

"A one-day trip is too hard. You should stay there overnight."

"No, I have to save some lana," he says, smiling. "I would rather spend the cash on my girlfriend instead." He kisses me on the forehead. "Rest now, okay?"

As he gets up, I reach out and hold his forearm. "Hey."

He looks at me. "What's up?"

"Good luck. You'll do great."

I pause—now?

Yes, it's time.

"I love you," I say.

He puts his things down and kneels by the bed like he's saying a prayer. He takes my hands and kisses me, again and again, with those ridiculously soft, full lips. And I see him, all at once, the man and the boy, the lover and the beloved.

"I wanted to say it, but I didn't want to say it first because you'd think I was a weirdo for saying it so soon," he says in one quick breath, laughing.

"Great, now I'm the weirdo," I say. "Thanks for nothing."

We kiss again.

And again.

"I love you too," he says.

After Angel leaves, I lounge in bed for another hour, snoozing and daydreaming about my boyfriend. I scroll through social media, liking and commenting on Ro's poolside antics and Ingrid, on her best behavior, posing for pictures with her boyfriend's family who looks like an ad for Polo Ralph Lauren before they started hiring models of color. I shower, get dressed and take a grumpy Meatball and Funfetti on an extra-long walk around the neighborhood. I pass a fancy coffeehouse but resist the urge to buy a mocha. I've got to be extra careful with my finances right now. I don't know how long it will be until I have a stable job again.

After rush hour passes, I hop in my car and drive to my old office one more time to pick up my final boxes. I make a mental note to find an extra cardboard box for craft time with Julia, who I'll see later today.

The employment center parking lot is empty, and the office is dark on what should be a very busy Monday morning. Feeling blue, I heave the lonely boxes into my car and lock the office door for the last time. When I get into my car again, there's a strange smell inside. Some mildew or something has gotten into the boxes over the weekend. I'll have to air them out somehow. I start the engine and put the car in reverse when I hear the voice of a man in the back seat behind me.

"Don't scream, Deanna. Please. Don't scream."

TWENTY-TWO

ANGEL

THIRTY FUCKING DOLLARS FOR PARKING?

Fine. Whatever.

I take the garment bag into the public restroom in the lobby and change from sweats and a T-shirt into a suit. I put Sal's badge on and look in the mirror. Not bad. I'm feeling pretty good about myself until I get to the exhibit hall and see that it's filled with dudes in jeans, fleece jackets and hiking shoes. No one else is wearing a suit. Not even the local asshat politician giving the keynote address.

My meeting with King and Country isn't for another two hours. I've never been to a conference of any kind so I take a look at the program and wander around. There are some panels, and I sit in on one about diversity in craft beer. There are a lot of empty seats. Even the speakers look like they'd rather be somewhere else. When I get up to leave, someone slaps me on the back and yells, "Sal!" It's one of the panelists, the Black owner of a new brewery in Inglewood.

I lower my mask real quick to show him my face. "Hey, man. Sal couldn't make it. I'm Angel, his brother. Here on the down-low."

"What? You fooled me!" He gives me a fist bump. "Nice to meet you. Jules Williams. Sal and I met at the Great American Beer Festival three or four years ago. I was on the judging panel for his entry. After he won the silver on his first go-round, I said to myself, I have to meet this guy. What was his beer called? Esperanza. The Mexican dark lager. Amazing. So amazing. I'll never forget it."

I know Sal is good at what he does, but I feel proud to see that other people know it too.

"There aren't a lot of newcomers from that time who've been able to make it through covid. Eastside Brewery is goals, I have to say."

"We're working hard to make it through," I say, fully aware Jules faces many of the same problems.

As if I know about these things, he starts to talk about forgivable loans, emergency grants and delayed payroll tax payments. Again, I feel way out of my depth. How do I tell him I mop the floors without telling him I mop the floors? I'm thinking about this as he goes on about how he's planning for different scenarios for his employees three, six and twelve months out. I don't even know what I'm doing tomorrow.

Together, we walk around the exhibit hall. There are booths for homebrewers and equipment vendors of every kind. Colleges with brewing and cicerone certification programs pass out recruitment materials. Craft breweries from all over California offer pours on a large covered patio outside. I'd enjoy all of this if I wasn't so scared of making a mistake or saying the wrong thing.

"So, I heard something in the rumor mill," Jules says, dropping his voice. "I'm not sure if it's true."

"What?"

"Are you meeting with King and Country today? Are y'all really thinking of selling?"

Sal and Vanessa gave me a script for the meeting which I practiced over and over during the car ride down. But they didn't give me a script for what to say if someone asked me about the meeting.

Before I can decide how to respond, Jules says, "It's a bold move. Unless your brother and his wife know something I don't know, I wouldn't trust King and Country as far as I could throw them."

Jules looks over his shoulder to make sure no one can hear him. "King and Country are a little suburban brewery in Denver. Brand new. You know who's backing them, right?"

I should. I don't.

"Back when he was at MaxBev, Bill McAuliffe did a number on Chanticleer Brewery in Austin," Jules says. "Now he's bankrolling King and Country as they buy up all the struggling little guys in SoCal that the big beverage companies don't want to invest in anymore. Trust. They're going to take over each brewery, push out the owners, and make their shitty beers there. It's McAuliffe's MO. Buy, leverage, corporatize, demoralize, rebrand. Erase the culture, the passion, the connection to the neighborhood—everything that makes the breweries great. Pull all of the value out of the businesses and plant something soulless in their place." Jules shrugs. "That's the McAuliffe playbook. It's made him a very rich man."

In their briefing, Sal and Vanessa told me none of this. They only stressed that I stay on message and make a good impression. That King and Country was throwing us a lifeline when no one else cared if we drowned.

Also, I just met this Jules dude. Why is he telling me all this? Is it true? If it is, does he have Eastside Brewery's best interests at heart, or is there something in it for him if this deal tanks? He strikes me as a genuine guy, but good liars can strike you as anything.

"Be careful," Jules says. "If you don't believe me, ask them what other acquisitions they're looking at in the region. And ask them if your family will retain the brands and the beers."

We stop by the Los Angeles chapter's beer tasting bar. Jules's crew is pouring three different beers and they need him.

"Good talk," I tell him, noncommittally. "It was good to meet you."

"Likewise. Tell Sal Jules says hello."

My meeting starts in ten minutes. I find a quiet spot in the hall and immediately call Sal. He doesn't pick up. He never picks up. I call Vanessa. She picks up right away, but I hear crying and yelling in the background.

"Is it done? Is the meeting finished?" she asks.

"No, not yet, but—"

"We can't put frosting on the cake yet because it's too hot," Vanessa says. "I told you we have to—"

With Vanessa, you have to make your point fast. "Vanessa, do you know anyone by the name of Jules Will—"

"Tía Carmen is so much better at this than you!" Muñeca cries, hysterical. "I hate this! I hate that you can't cook!"   .

Vanessa sighs. "That's not very kind, Brianna."

I know things are bad when Vanessa name-checks her kid.

"This is horrible! It looks horrible!"

"Sal is sleeping. Could you please keep it down? Now wait, don't touch that cake pan, it's still hot—"

I hear a wail that is half wolf, half sonic boom.

"Angel, I have to go," Vanessa says quickly. "Good luck, call me later."

Click.

Okay.

Five minutes before the meeting.

I get on the escalator up to the hotel lobby. I'm meeting with the King and Country team in the bar, naturally, over a beer.

There are so many people at this goddamn conference that the Wi-Fi is jammed and I can't google Bill McAuliffe. Shit, I can't even spell Bill McAuliffe even if I could google him.

I check the time.

Two minutes.

Jules's words still tumbling around in my head, I put my phone away and rush to the hotel bar. If he's wrong? This deal is a lifesaver for Eastside Brewery. If he's right? This deal is a trap that will erase us and what we do forever.

I remember what Deanna told me—I'm a fighter. But I am not the kind of boxer who plays mind games. I focus on what my opponent is doing, not on what he is thinking, and definitely not on what he wants me to think.

Best keep my hands up and get a feel for the fight.

I'm not signing any contracts today. But I am fighting for my family, today and every day.

It's time.

At first glance, the two middle-aged white men sitting at a corner table in the hotel bar look like everyone else here. But instead of fleece jackets, they're wearing bowling shirts embroidered with crowns and swords and the name *King and Country* in Old English font. Very gangster. I think they're in their fifties, with small beer bellies and faces red from spending time in the sun. Golf? Fishing? They look prosperous.

They stand up when I approach. "Salvador," says the shorter one. He's got a British accent of some kind. "It's so good to finally meet you in person and not over a computer screen. We've been looking forward to this for so long."

"Salvador couldn't make it today, unfortunately. He's under the weather. He sends his regrets." I say. "My name is Angel Rosas, Cellarperson and Production Assistant. I'm Sal's younger brother."

I see that they're disappointed. Out of courtesy, they introduce themselves.

"Luke Brendan."

"Dennis Roth."

I shake hands with them. They may dress the part, but from the handshake alone, I know these two men have never seen a day of manual labor.

"I've heard all good deals start with a glass of beer," I say. "Let me show you what Eastside Brewery has to offer right now."

Luke and Dennis humor me while I go to the bar and ask the server to bring six beer glasses. Annoyed, he does it anyway while I take my seat and open my backpack. There's a cooler bag inside and three cold bottles of Eastside Brewery's finest.

This part of the meeting is easy. I've worked the taproom enough times to pour beer flights in my sleep.

First, I crack open Trouble for Breakfast, a special limited edition IPA brewed with white grapefruit from our community garden.

Then I pour them Eastside Pride, Sal's first original recipe, made with the fragrant herb hoja santa. Nothing on the market tastes like this one.

Last, I pour them Esperanza. Of course—our best-in-show.

"Every beer tells a story," I say, "And that's the story of our family. Eastside Brewery is a product of the neighborhood. We have strong ties to our local community and our local markets. Our taproom and production facility have been in the family for more than three generations. We own the building. We own the land. And we believe we have the responsibility to create something that we can pass down to the next generations. Something they can be proud of too."

The beers have softened up Luke and Dennis a little, but I can feel how impatient they are to be talking to me.

Luke starts. "As Sal and Vanessa know, we've done quite a bit of due diligence on the company. The brand is very exciting to us, and our investors see lots of potential in Eastside Brewery. You and your family have obviously put a lot of blood, sweat and tears into developing this business. We'd like to help you get to the next level."

Dennis continues, "We started King and Country two years ago."

I pause. They're younger than Eastside Brewery? And they want to expand to the West Coast?

Dennis goes on about how he and Luke met at business school in England. He points to the logo on their bowling shirt. "Hence, the name. King and Country. Since then, we've worked together on different hotel and restaurant ventures around the world and created the kinds of relationships with private investors that allow us to do business on handshake deals alone."

"People want to work with us, Angel." Luke laughs. "They want a hand in everything we do because they know they'll make money on the deal. Lots of money."

Good for the investors. But good for the breweries?

I think about how much time Sal spends on his Excel sheets, tinkering, reformulating, reinventing until his beers are pristine. I think about how I walked in on Vanessa at her desk one night, crying because she couldn't figure out whether to furlough the taproom servers during lockdown or whether to lay them off so they could collect unemployment and have enough money to eat. I think about Carmen, working until she couldn't fit in the prep area because she was so pregnant. I think about Eddie, on the phone with Carmen behind the brewery during his breaks, sometimes singing lullabies to the babies when he thinks no one can hear him. He never got time off to spend with his kids when they were born. There no one else to do the work that needed to be done.

These men have no idea what we are really worth.

"Can I ask you a question? How much time do you spend at King and Country?" I ask.

They look at each other. "Not much these days, admittedly," says Luke.

"I'd say we serve in a consultancy capacity," adds Dennis, with a shrug.

"Does Bill McAuliffe serve in a consultancy capacity too?"

Luke clears his throat, not ready for that question. "Bill is a longtime friend of mine. He's invested with me before. He's been my mentor for going on twenty years now. He was on my board of directors for three separate companies. We've built a relationship over many, many years."

"Can I ask your honest opinion on something? I'm new to the beer world. Just between you and me, what is your opinion on Bill's involvement with Chanticleer in Austin?"

A total fake-out. I have no idea what I am talking about. But Luke takes another drink of Trouble in the Morning, I think, for courage. Dennis turns bright pink, like a little schoolboy sent to the front of the class.

Luke says, "Well, I'll tell you what Bill told me. What works for one company is not going to work for another company. MaxBev saw the potential in the brand, but Chanticleer's culture just didn't resonate with a massive corporation."

"Craft brewers can't do international distribution," Dennis adds. "MaxBev could, and they invested in production facilities, warehouses, more skilled crew, a ton of retail sites that took Chanticleer all over the US."

"But in the end, the cultural issues were just too strong. Chanticleer just couldn't integrate into the larger company, and when most of their upper management left, the remaining employees did too. It just wasn't sustainable." Luke tries to bring it home, but the ship is sinking. "But that's why King and

Country is so different. We can't provide giant facilities or dramatically increase your barrel production. But we've got that independent spirit. We can take your company in a direction that makes sense for craft beer. Keep the integrity of Eastside Brewery."

I stare at him and say nothing. With the same group of investors behind this deal, we both know what he's trying to spin is bullshit.

I make a mental note to buy Jules Williams a beer.

Time to end this.

"What other acquisitions are you looking at in the region?"

Dennis gets pinker. "We're open to a number of possible breweries in the area."

I nod. "If we work with you, will Eastside Brewery retain its brands and beers?"

"That is still on the table," says Luke.

"Listen, Angel," Dennis says.

I'm surprised he remembers my name.

"Just because we're a big company doesn't mean we're the bad guys here."

"What do you mean?" I say. "You're just a little suburban brewery in Denver with that independent spirit."

They're speechless for a second.

Technical KO.

"Please tell Sal to call us when he feels better. We're eager to continue this conversation," says Luke.

We shake hands again. They tell me to enjoy my time in San Diego. I tell them I already have.

PYRRHIC VICTORY.

Definition. A victory that comes at such a high cost that the ordeal negates the win.

I looked that one up when I was studying for my GED. I was living in the house in Salinas where the only quiet place to do my schoolwork was sitting on the roof. I learned the definition quickly because I had already experienced many, many pyrrhic victories in my life, both in and out of the ring.

I find Jules Williams again. I buy him a beer, like I promised myself I would. Luckily, beer is free at this conference. He tells me not to be upset, that Sal will, probably after a long, long time, appreciate what I've done here today.

"Sal has dodged bullets before," I say.

"He's also been shot," Jules says, which proves to me that he and Sal really are good friends, because Sal doesn't share that fun tidbit of information with everyone.

I'm way past tipsy when Jules shoves me into an Uber. We ride through the crowded Gaslamp District. Girls catcall us through the open car windows.

"Where are we going?" I ask.

"A local brewery," Jules says. "There's a private event for the conference. Just beer people."

"I'm not really a beer person."

Jules laughs. "Good one."

"I'm drunk, Jules."

"It's a beer conference. It was inevitable."

This brewery is dark. There are so many people here. I see old-fashioned arcade games like Ms. Pac-Man and Galaga. There's pizza. Somebody gives me a slice of pizza. It's good. Someone gives me a beer. It's not bad.

An unspecified amount of time passes. I meet a lot of people —I think.

Now I'm in the bathroom taking a piss. I wash my hands. There used to be a mirror above the sink but it's been ripped off or something. Just four empty holes where the screws used to be. That's fine. I don't want to see my own face right now anyway.

Fuck me.

What have I done?

Even if King and Country are the devil incarnate, it was not my job to call them out. Sal and Vanessa wanted me to make nice. To give them our beer, make a good impression, shake hands and get the fuck out. And I couldn't even handle that, could I? I tanked this relationship for sure. They're probably tearing up the paperwork at this very moment, laughing about the uppity younger brother who shat in the punch bowl.

Fuck me.

This is bad.

Feeling desolate, I return to the bar and carefully put myself on an empty stool. I look around. Lots of people, but Jules is nowhere to be found. I need to sober up enough to head home tonight. I sit very still, trying to gather my thoughts as if I can will the alcohol out of my system.

Next to me, someone says in Spanish, "Dude. Are you okay?"

I turn to the guy. A paisa, about my age and height, but slim and clean cut. Like everyone else except me, he got the memo not to wear a suit. He's dressed in jeans and a Muhammad Ali T-shirt.

"I'm okay," I reply in Spanish. "Just one too many."

In perfect English, he orders me a glass of water from the bartender. In Spanish, to me, he says, "Here you go."

"Thank you." I take a drink. "Do you work in beer too?"

"Me? No. I'm merely a curious enthusiast."

I clock right away that he's not from around here. His Spanish is different—Mexico, born and raised. Educated too.

He squints at my badge. "Salvador?"

"Sal's my brother. My name is Angel. Eastside Brewery is my family's brewery." I take the badge off and put it in my pocket. "What's your name?"

"Carlos," says my new buddy.

"What do you do?"

"Not much," he says. "Study. That's it, for now."

"Are you studying abroad?"

"Something like that." He smiles, clearly enjoying his mysteriousness, and I decide not to press him. "But I do want to learn more about beer," he says. "I bet you know a lot. What can you teach me?"

I sneak a look at my phone. It's seven p.m.—early enough. I can drive home later when there are fewer cars on the 5.

The menu over the bar is a full board of craft beers, no doubt in honor of all the beer nerds descended on San Diego this weekend for the summit. It's an impressive selection. So I ask Carlos what I ask everyone who comes into the taproom for the first time.

"What do you like to drink?"

TWENTY-THREE

DEANNA

I FREEZE. I don't speak. I don't breathe. I don't turn around.

"Turn off the engine," says the man.

I turn the key, and the car goes still. My hands are shaking when I put them on the steering wheel where he can see them.

"I'm not going to hurt you," he says, "but I need you to stay in your seat and listen to me."

"Art," I say.

He pauses. "You remember me."

"Of course I do."

He takes a deep breath. I glance quickly at the rearview mirror, but he's seated at an angle where I can't see his face. My stomach cramps up painfully, but I don't make a sound.

"Listen to me," he says again.

"I'm listening."

"There's no one else who can help me. No one else I can trust."

I say nothing.

"My family is in trouble, Deanna. Big trouble, and I need to help them."

I remember what Agent Gavilan told me. I have to get more information. "What do you mean? Trouble how?"

"It's a long story."

"Tell me the story. That way I'll know how to help you."

"Please, I just need you to bring something to my mom."

"Your mom? Is she okay?"

"Yes, she's okay, but..." Art blows out a frustrated breath. "Just listen, okay?"

"Okay."

"My mom is the only one working in the family right now. She's nannying on the west side, and she supports my brothers who are still in high school. My dad doesn't send her anything for child support. Money is really tight so two months ago my brothers did something stupid to try to help her out."

"What do you mean by 'something stupid'? What did they do?"

"You've seen the news about all the trains getting jacked in El Sereno and Lincoln Heights, right?"

"Yes. I've seen the photos." People have been breaking the locks on cargo trains inbound from the harbor loaded with packages. The tracks are littered with discarded boxes and cartons after the thieves have taken everything they can sell for cash.

"My brothers struck gold. A carton of guns bound for Tennessee. Brand new. Worth thousands and thousands of dollars on the street. And these fools tried to fence them without informing the local Hillside Locos."

My heart sinks. "The gang who controls the rail yards."

"Yes."

"Oh, no. Oh, God," I say. Art's gang, East Side Hollenbeck, and the Hillside Locos are at war.

"HSL took the guns. And now they're demanding a tax on the guns from our family, out of respect."

"What?"

"A payment. Or they will take out my brothers and my mother." Art's voice catches in his throat. "Deanna—my whole family. All of them."

"We have to go to the cops," I say. "They can put you in protective custody. They can help you and your family, and we can get those guns off the street."

"The guns are long gone," Art says. "And the cops can't help us. Not with this. Even ESHB has washed their hands of us. Deanna, we're on our own. I'm desperate."

"What are you going to do?" I ask.

"I already did what I was going to do."

He drops a black plastic bag in the passenger seat, the kind that liquor stores give you to hide your purchases. It lands with a thump.

"There's twelve thousand dollars cash in there."

My stomach twists violently. I taste acid in my mouth. "What the fuck, Art?"

"It's clean money. I would never dirty your hands. Not after what you've done for me."

I dread the answer to my next question. "How did you get it?"

He's quiet.

"Tell me," I say.

"I brought two families over the border," he says.

He's a pollero. A smuggler. The work is difficult, illegal and extremely dangerous.

"That is human trafficking. I can't help you with this," I say. "I can't."

"The people are safe, Deanna," Art says quickly. "They are safe with their relatives. Two families, both with young children. I brought them here by myself. No one was hurt. I swear to God. I swear on my life."

"You are putting me in an impossible situation."

"I know. I know. And I'm sorry. I can't trust anyone with this amount of money but you. I can't risk the cops seeing me go to the house, and I can't let my family see me like this. Please." His voice breaks. "The address is written on a piece of paper inside the bag. Give it directly to my mother. She's a good woman. She worked so hard to raise us. She doesn't deserve any of this."

I wait a moment while he gathers himself.

"You were the one calling me with that unknown number. And that was you in the parking lot that night, wasn't it?" I ask quietly. "You scared the shit out of me."

"I'm so sorry. I just wanted to talk to you before I went to Mexico." He sounds like a ghost talking to me beyond the grave. "I just wanted to tell you what I was doing. In case something happened to me. There would be at least one person who knew."

"You were scared."

"Fuck, I'm scared right now. I've been scared since I walked out of the transition house." He pauses. "I kept thinking to myself, if I can get this money to my mom, I don't care what happens to me. I don't care. As long as my mom and brothers are safe, they can toss me in the hole and throw away the key."

"There's no guarantee they'll be safe even if HSL gets this money, you know that, right?" I say.

"But this money is not for HSL," Art says.

I'm confused. "It's not?"

"No. No way," he says. "It's for my family. To get the hell out of Los Angeles. To start over somewhere far away. Somewhere safe."

I look in the rearview mirror one more time. I can see he's wearing a paper mask, but his face is dirty and his eyes are exhausted. I recognize the tattoos over his eyebrow. He's wearing a black beanie and baggy sweatshirt. He looks like he has aged twenty years in two months.

"What will you do now?" I ask.

"Disappear. If I'm lucky, maybe I'll see my family again. On this side or the next."

My voice catches in my throat. "I don't know what to say," I croak.

"You don't have to say anything else." His voice is soft. "Just close your eyes and count down from fifty."

I do it. But by the time I reach forty-five, he's gone.

My car is empty. I'm completely alone in the parking lot.

I unbuckle my seat belt and get out of the car. I walk around, swallowing down big gulps of cold air but this doesn't help. My heart is beating so fast I'm afraid it's going to burst. Dizzy, I put two hands on the hood, bend over and vomit violently on the pavement. Acid burns my throat. I heave again. Tears are running down my cheeks. I had no idea I was crying.

After a couple minutes, I get myself under control. I wipe my face with a spare sweatshirt from my trunk and drink some water from the bottles I keep in my car for emergencies. My hands are still shaking as I dig through my bag for my phone.

There are three people I could call right now.

Of course, Agent Gavilan of the Fugitive Apprehension Team.

Next, Ingrid. Who would probably tell me to hang up with her and call Agent Gavilan instead.

Third, Angel. Who would—well, I don't know what Angel would tell me to do, actually.

I stare at my screen. Then I look at the black plastic bag in the front seat of my car. Through the opening, I can see a piece of paper on top of the money. There, in Art's neat handwriting, is a very short message in two languages.

Ninfa Aguilar
1899B Chicago St.
Con todo mi amor
With all my love

Y

IN THE END, I make a decision.

I call no one.

The fewer people who know about this, the better.

I find the small house across the street from a large building site for a housing development. The construction noise is deafening, and there are cranes and piles of lumber and large pipes parked up and down the street. I find a space on the next block. Nervously, I stash the black plastic bag inside my own bag. I've never carried this much cash around with me before. I chew a couple more Tums, put on a mask, climb out of my car and say a prayer to God that I'm doing the right thing.

As I walk the block, I feel jittery and nauseous. In my paranoia, every parked car is an undercover cop car. Every construction worker across the street is an informant. Every passing car is filled with Hillside Locos watching everything I do.

Art's mother's house is old and tumbledown in contrast to the big new-looking apartment buildings surrounding it on all sides. It's been subdivided into four units. The grass is overgrown but there are lemon trees laden with fruit growing along the perimeter of the yard.

I walk down the shaded driveway and knock on the unit marked B. There's a dollar-store Christmas wreath hanging on the door and security bars on every window. When the front door opens, I see a small woman who looks far too young to be the mother of a grown man like Art. She puts on a mask.

"Buenas días," I say. "Estoy buscando a la señora de la casa, Ninfa Aguilar?"

She can hear my Americanized accent and responds in English, "I'm Ninfa Aguilar. How can I help you?"

"Ms. Aguilar, this is for you." I hold up the black plastic bag.

Cautiously, she takes the bag. But when she looks inside, her face turns pale.

"Oh my God," she says in English. "Oh my God."

"He wants you to start over," I say softly. "Somewhere safe."

"Is he okay? Did you talk to him?"

"He's okay. I mean, I think he's okay. He's thinking about you." I stumble over the words. We shouldn't have a conversation. "I really should go."

I turn to leave, but the woman grabs my arm. My nerves are fried, so when she does this, I jump back. I stumble, but she catches me. Before I realize what she's doing, she's holding me in a tight embrace.

"I don't know who you are, but God bless you for this," she says. "God bless you."

LATER, while I'm playing with Julia and baby Max, I get a phone call. I'm hoping it's Angel, but unfortunately, it is not. It is the Chicano Buzz Lightyear.

"Ms. Delgado, good afternoon, ma'am. This is Humberto Gavilan with Parole. How are you today, ma'am?"

"Hello again, Agent Gavilan."

"I tried calling your work phone number but it was disconnected. Is that correct? Are you still employed with"—he checks his notes—"Evergreen Vocational Services Center, Ms. Delgado?"

"No, Agent. I'm no longer with Evergreen. But how

resourceful of you to find my personal cell phone."

"It was publicly listed, ma'am. Not hard to find at all." He sounds quite proud of himself.

"How can I help you, Agent?"

"Well, Ms. Delgado, I'm calling once more to ask if you've had any contact with Arturo Aguilar. We have cause to believe he is still in the vicinity of your former office. Has he reached out to you at all?"

"No, I'm afraid he still has not reached out to me," I say, keeping my voice steady.

"No phone calls? No in-person contact?"

"No, nothing."

Agent Gavilan is writing something down. I hear the rustling of papers. "All right, Ms. Delgado. As before, if he contacts you, it's very important that you call me immediately."

"Is bringing Mr. Aguilar in still one of your top priorities?"

He pauses. "Among many top priorities, yes."

"Well, good luck to you and your team," I say.

He says nothing for a moment.

"No contact at all, correct?" he asks one more time.

I don't blink. "None, sir. No contact at all."

"Well, all right, then. You know the drill." Yet again, he spells out his name, gives me two phone numbers, and reminds me of his unit: Fugitive Apprehension Team.

"Got it," I say, pretending to write his number in the air. Julia makes a face at me.

"Thank you, Ms. Delgado. And happy new year to you."

"Happy new year to you too, Agent Gavilan."

I'M sound asleep when my phone rings. From the kitchen, Funfetti gives one curious woof. I squint at the time before I answer. It's four in the morning. Angel is still not home. I left him a voicemail before I went to bed. I figure he decided to stay overnight in San Diego, after all, which is good. I don't want him falling asleep on the road.

I answer the call. It's a recording. "You have a collect call from an inmate at San Diego Central Jail. This call and your telephone number will be recorded and monitored. To accept this call, say or dial five now."

I sit straight up in bed. "Five," I say.

"Deanna."

"What is happening?"

"First of all, please don't worry. I'm okay. Everything is okay. Nobody is hurt."

"Why are you calling me from jail?"

"I only have a few minutes, so I'll tell you everything I can before it cuts off, okay?" Angel says.

"Okay." I'm pacing the apartment before I realize I'm even out of bed.

"I got to the conference fine," Angel says. "I met with the King and Country founders, but it didn't go well. I met one of Sal's friends, and we went to a bar. I met another dude there named Carlos. We got to talking about beer and boxing. He started asking me about fight clubs, and I decided to bring him to the fights in San Diego."

"Angel, what the fuck?" I ask in disbelief. "Exactly how drunk were you?"

"By that time, sober. I told Carlos I have some friends in San Diego. I used to fight at their events."

"Who is this Carlos?" I ask.

"He's just some guy from Mexico. We got along really well. But here's the thing," he says, "the owner of the warehouse where the fights were being held called the police and had us all arrested."

"For what?"

"Trespassing."

I'm a law-abiding citizen. I never get in trouble. In one day, I've lied to the police and talked to my boyfriend in jail in another county. So I surprise myself when I say, "That doesn't sound so bad."

"No, it doesn't," he says, slowly. "But I'm still worried."

"Why?"

He says, "I'm worried about the thing we talked about."

I think about this for a moment. Then I remember—his outstanding warrant from the fight club in Monterey. The whole reason he had to leave Salinas. I stop myself from blurting it out and say instead, "Oh. Yeah. That."

"I'll know more tomorrow. You'll hear from me then."

"What do you want me to do until then?"

He sighs. He sounds so tired. "I'm sorry, princesa. I never wanted anything like this to happen."

"Just tell me what you need, baby," I say. "We'll work it out."

The recorded voice drops into our call. "You have sixty seconds remaining."

"I'll be okay in here," Angel says. "Tomorrow, go see Eddie at the brewery. He'll be there by eight. Tell him everything I told you, plus the thing we talked about. He doesn't know about any of it. We'll wait to talk to Sal and Vanessa until we know more." He pauses. His voice is tight and full of regret. "I don't want to worry them while they're still recovering."

"Is there anything else I can do to help you?"

"I want you to remember how much I love you," he says, "and I'm sorry."

"Take care of yourself," I say, even though I know he will. "I love—"

The call ends before I can finish the sentence.

TWENTY-FOUR

DEANNA

INGRID DOESN'T START work at the new office for another week. She agrees to meet me at the brewery in the morning if I buy her breakfast. I'm the one who's unemployed, but I agree to do it because I don't have the emotional strength to strongarm a hustler right now.

Eddie arrives at exactly eight. He looks tired, but his usual upbeat personality shines through.

"Late night?" he asks when he sees Ingrid and me standing by the back door. "Hair of the dog?"

"Not exactly," I say.

He lets us in, opens the security gates and makes a pot of coffee. We sit at the big table together in the bright morning sunshine, and I give Eddie and Ingrid the rundown. Their faces get more and more puzzled as I go on.

When I'm finished, Eddie says, "Angel never mentioned any of this fight-club garbage to us. We always thought he was sparring after hours at the boxing club with his trainer."

"He does that too. But he's part of a very large underground fight club community," I say. "He took me to the fights in Lawndale a few weeks ago. I had a hard time watching, but everyone there is serious. It's not just chaos. They're really well-planned, well-attended events."

"Is he any good?" Eddie asks.

"I haven't seen him fight yet. He says he was never a star, but he's fought all over the state. In Mexico too."

"I had no idea," Eddie says. "No idea at all. We work him so hard here, I didn't think he had any juice left at the end of the day to do anything like that."

"I've been wanting to talk to you about that," I say. "I know that you're having some staffing problems and that you need Angel to fill a lot of odd jobs here at the brewery right now. But I think you should include him in more than just maintenance and deliveries. I think he should be able to learn more about the business itself. He's really intelligent, Eddie. More than he lets on."

Eddie considers this for a moment before he says, "Here's the thing. The beer summit and the meeting with King and Country were his first test. And he ended up in jail. That's kind of a worst-case scenario."

My stomach cramps up again. "That didn't occur to me." I take out a bottle of Tums and put a few in my mouth. "I've been popping these nonstop since yesterday."

"That's not good." Ingrid gets up and heads to the kitchen. "May I?"

Eddie waves her through. "Help yourself."

"Eddie, do you think Angel is in real trouble?" I ask.

"It's all relative," Eddie says with a shrug. "Trespassing in and of itself is no big deal. But I don't know what his warrant is for. Everything depends on that..." He trails off and studies my face. "Sugar, are you okay? You're looking pale," he says. It's his old nickname for me, back from when I used to be his case-worker. Eddie regularly cleaned out the jar of candy on my desk back when we worked together.

"I'm okay," I say. "I just don't want Angel to have to stay in jail, and I don't want him to get sent back to Monterey. He told me to wait for his call, but I'm so nervous. I couldn't go back to sleep after the first time he called."

Ingrid comes out of the kitchen with a tray. There's bananas and milk in a bowl and a small plate of sliced watermelon. "Eat," she says in a voice as motherly as a scorpion. But I take a bite, and it makes me feel much better.

I'm about to take my dishes back into the kitchen when the back door of the brewery bangs open. Eddie jumps up to see who it is, since no other workers are scheduled to be here this early except for him and Angel.

And that's when I hear it.

Angel's laughter, loud and bright, coming from the kitchen.

I push past Eddie. Angel is standing by the back door in his undershirt and suit pants, looking rumpled and handsome like an actor at the end of an action movie. I run to him and he spins me around in his arms.

"Princesa," he whispers in my ear. "Oh, man. Am I glad to see you."

I hold on to him tightly, relieved that he's safe.

When we come up for air, I see that behind him is a young guy, about the same height as Angel and handsome in a preppy way. He takes off his expensive sunglasses, and Angel introduces him to all of us as Carlos Rodriguez, his new compa. They have bonded, apparently, over getting arrested and spending the night in jail.

"In the end, we were ticketed for trespassing," Angel says. "Carlos paid for both of us. I owe you, man."

"Not at all," Carlos says in Spanish. "My treat." He and Angel bump fists.

"And the other thing?" Eddie asks. "The warrant?"

"Well, I learned a lesson." Angel looks at me. "Don't listen to cops on probation."

"What do you mean?" I ask.

"I did have a warrant," Angel says. "A non-extradition warrant for Monterey County for disturbing the peace."

Eddie throws his head back and laughs.

"Misdemeanor," Angel says sheepishly. "Loud party."

"You dork," Eddie says. "You can't even break the law right."

"But what does that mean?" I ask again, lost.

"It means that nobody cares," Eddie explains. "A non-extradition warrant means San Diego doesn't have to send him back to Monterey. As long as he doesn't get arrested in Monterey, he doesn't have to worry about it. Plus, if he wants the warrant to go away for good, he could probably just pay a fine and do some community service. No jail time." He ruffles Angel's hair, then looks at all of us and shakes his head. "Okay, I have work to do. You criminal masterminds enjoy your meeting." He pauses. To Angel, he adds, "Oh, and think about what you're going to tell Sal and Vanessa about King and Country, because I'm not going to do it for you."

Angel nods, his smile fading a little bit.

Eddie heads to the office. Carlos looks around the kitchen and peeks through the handoff window into the taproom.

"Can you show me around?" he asks in English. "This place is cool."

I decide to tag along and take the tour. I learn that Eastside is a fifteen-barrel brewhouse with a taproom and that while he was still on parole, Sal attended college to receive his brewmaster certification. He's also gotten multiple national awards for his beers. Vanessa was an accountant in the food and wine industry, and Carmen was a top chef in the city. Her family owned this building for three generations—back then, it was a panadería, a Mexican bakery.

"What does Eddie bring to this operation, you may ask yourself?" Angel says loudly as we pass the office where Eddie's working. "Well, we made him a business card that says 'Get Shit Done Guy.' We pat him on the head every now and then. He likes that. Technically he's Eastside Brewery's production manager."

Eddie waves at us like the Queen of England.

"And what are you?" Carlos asks Angel.

"Cellarperson and production assistant." Angel points to all the tanks. "Basically, all this equipment owns me. I keep everything clean and flowing."

"He's really bad at it!" Eddie calls.

"I am," Angel says proudly. "Really bad. But I have heart. Lots of heart."

We join Ingrid at the big table. Tired of waiting for me, she's scarfing down a gigantic bowl of cold chicken tinga with tortillas and a spoon.

"What?" she says. "I was hungry."

Angel pours us one of Sal's new creations, an American wheat beer brewed with cucumber and watermelon. "We call this one SB946," Angel says, "after the state law that protects street vendors in California."

We clink glasses. It's beer o'clock.

"Tell me," Carlos says, "what is your vision for this business?"

"Sal and Vanessa can answer that question better than I can," Angel says.

"But I want to know what you think first," Carlos says. "What do you see when you look at this place in five, ten years?"

Angel sits back in his seat. He takes a deep breath and looks around the empty taproom. "I see people, to be honest. I see this as a place to gather, a place to celebrate. Events, parties, family milestones. The beer is not the heart of the company, but it's what brings people together. That's what we need right now, isn't it? Family? No—what's the right word?" He pauses. "Kinship."

Carlos listens closely. "Go on."

"My brothers and I, we were not beer people. We didn't grow up in any kind of brewing culture. But we grew up in this community. You can taste it in the food we sell. You can definitely taste it in the beer. If we had the resources to distribute this product more widely, we could share our story with the world." Across the table, Angel takes my hand and smiles. "This brewery has given my brothers and me a second chance. A job. A livelihood. I think it could be a harbor for other people too. People just like us who've had a hard time finding their place."

I watch as Carlos studies the remaining beer in his glass. He swirls it and drinks it down with a thoughtful look on his face. There's something strange about him. Like he's here, but he's not here at the same time. I don't know how to explain it.

He points at Angel. "You have the wrong job."

"What do you mean?"

"Brand ambassador." Carlos grins. "You said to me yesterday, 'Every beer tells a story.' You're the one who needs to tell the story of this brewery. The story of his family." He puts his beer glass down and suddenly slaps the table with the palm of his hand. We all sit back, surprised. "This is it," he says in Spanish. "This is it!" He stands up, makes two fists and punches the air with some kind of boxing combo.

We're confused.

"Carlos, what's up?" Angel asks.

"This is it," Carlos says a third time. Excited, he takes his phone out of his pocket and types in some notes. "I have to make some calls. When will your older brother and his wife be back?"

"If they test negative this week," Angel says, "they'll be back Monday. Why?"

"So can I come back on Monday? I want to meet them. I really, really, really want to meet them."

"Of course," Angel says.

"Good. Then I have a lot of work to do until then. Let me get the ball rolling," Carlos says in English. He pauses. "Is that the right saying? 'Get the ball rolling'? It's a weird one. Does it come from Indiana Jones or something?" He puts his phone back in his pocket. "Thank you, thank you. I can't tell you how happy I am to have met you all."

Without another word, Carlos walks to the front door of the taproom. Angel looks at me, puzzled, and runs over to open the door.

To my surprise, there's a black Town Car with tinted windows parked right in front. A large, special-forces-looking gentleman in a mask and a sharply tailored suit gets out of the passenger seat and opens the car door. On the sidewalk, Carlos gives Angel a big hug.

"Thank you for one of the most exciting nights of my life," he says in Spanish. "The beers, the fight club, the road trip. And now I can tell everyone I know that I've been to jail!"

Just as puzzled as I am, Angel says, "You're welcome."

"See you soon."

With a wave, Carlos climbs into the car. The giant man closes the door and gets back into the car before it speeds off. Angel comes back inside and sits down at the table very slowly.

"What just happened?" he asks.

"I have no idea," I say.

Ingrid finishes the last bites of her breakfast and wipes the red sauce off her face with a napkin. She shakes her head at us. "Really? You guys really don't know who that was?"

"At the jail, they checked him in as Carlos Rodriguez," Angel says.

"Should we know that name?" I ask.

"Mexicans—I mean, Mexican-Mexicans, from Mexico—use three names, right?" Ingrid says. "That weirdo was Carlos Colibrí Rodriguez."

Angel and I stare blankly at her.

"Colibrí? Nothing?" Ingrid raises her eyebrows. "Hans Colibrí?"

We're lost.

She throws up her hands. "Colibrí Tequila? Only the oldest producer of tequila in Mexico and a multinational corporation that owns spirits producers all over the world. Irish whiskey. Kentucky bourbon. Jamaican rum. One of his cousins lived in my building at USC. She was a total bitch. Tried to pay me to write one of her papers." She takes out her phone and taps in the name. "Here. Read, you losers."

I hold the phone while Angel and I read about the Colibrí family.

"Hans Colibrí Domingo," I say slowly, "businessman and chief executive officer of Colibrí Tequila."

"Carlos Colibrí Rodriguez," Angel reads. "Son of Hans Colibrí Domingo. Angel investor. Partner, Mayahuel Group."

We look at each other.

"Now scroll up," says Ingrid.

At the top of the Google search is an article about the wealthiest families in Mexico. I click on it and find the paragraph on the net worth of the Colibrí family.

"Eight billion dollars," Angel and I say in unison.

I hear Ingrid yelling at me as I drop her phone.

WHEN THE LUNCHTIME staff arrives at the brewery, I drive Angel and Eddie over to Sal and Vanessa's. Eddie sits shotgun with the passenger seat rolled all the way back. Angel is squished in the back seat. These two giant men have turned my Honda Fit into a lowrider, and I pull carefully into the street to avoid scraping the bottom of my car.

There's a little late-morning traffic. I peek in the rearview mirror. Angel's arms are folded and he's snoozing.

"He did good, Eddie," I say quietly. "You have to admit it."

"He did good by pure chance," Eddie says.

"No, not by pure chance. Do you even know who your brother is?" I turn up the defroster on my car. The Rosas brothers breathe a lot. "He's never been to an event like that, and he went in cold. He realized King and Country was a threat, not a savior. And he stood up for the brewery—for your family."

I glance at Eddie. Maybe because we once had a working relationship, he seems to listen to me in a way he doesn't listen to Angel. That needs to change.

"I am just an observer," I say, "but I think your business is made up of many parts. Sal and Vanessa are the brains. You and Carmen, you're the guts. You've all been so busy trying to keep the business alive in hellish conditions that you haven't had the chance to examine its true potential."

"True potential? For what?"

I think for a moment, but I realize it's not my place to answer that question. "I can't tell you what exactly," I say, tipping my head toward Angel in the back seat, "but he can. And he will."

There's some road construction ahead. I make my way through the bottleneck, careful not to knock down any cones or the worker in an orange vest holding a sign that says SLOW.

"I never thanked you for helping Carmen," Eddie says. "I knew she was struggling. She was sad for a little bit after Julia, and she kept telling me it was just like that. She was convinced her baby blues would fade away after a few weeks and she would be fine again. But with the loss of her parents, the isolation from the pandemic, I should have known it was more serious than..."

He trails off for a moment. I don't say anything.

"She's the light of my life, Deanna." His voice cracks. "I should have done more for her."

I take his big hand and give it a squeeze. It's rough, but not as battle worn as Angel's. "Hey," I say. "You're okay. I recognized signs I had seen before, that's all. And you're giving her the support she needs now."

Eddie squeezes my hand back as he gathers himself.

"I've spent lots of time with her and your beautiful children," I say. "You live in a house full of love. Some people only dream of what you've got."

In a brief moment of clarity, I realize that I'm talking about myself.

"You're a real one, Sugar," Eddie says.

I smile. "Thanks."

I stop in front of Sal and Vanessa's house. Eddie gets out and Angel wakes up with a stretch and a yawn.

"Ready?" I say.

He puts his arm around my shoulders as we walk up the driveway. "Let's do this."

Sal and Vanessa sit on the top steps of their back porch while the rest of us post up on folding chairs on the lawn. Muñeca runs in wild loops around us, talking a mile a minute but keeping her distance. "Sweetheart, can you please go play in the garden for a little bit?" Vanessa says. "We have to talk business."

"Ugh, fine."

"Thank you."

Frowning, Muñeca kicks her soccer ball to the back fence and runs after it.

"She's more than ready for this quarantine to be over," Vanessa says. "I don't blame her."

Always the serious eldest brother, Sal leans forward on his knees and focuses his sights on Angel. "So. What happened?"

I watch as Angel tells the story of what happened in San Diego. He starts off in a quiet, uncertain voice, answering Sal's questions with single-word answers. But as he continues sharing the details of his conversation with Jules Williams and the King and Country guys, he becomes more confident and animated. All of us listening to him can see it. He cares—deeply—about his family's business. He wants to see it succeed, and he has the skills to help it do so.

When he's finished, Sal and Vanessa exchange a long look, communicating something meaningful in that nonverbal way close partners can.

"Six months of work," Vanessa says to Angel, shaking her head.

"I'm so sorry, Vanessa," says Angel. "I fucked it all up."

"No," Sal says. "Don't be sorry."

"What I mean is, six months of work, and we didn't see what you saw in a single morning," Vanessa says. "We've been about the hustle for so long. King and Country knew we were desperate and afraid to lose the business. They wanted to capitalize on our fears."

"You did the right thing," Sal says to Angel. "I'm not going to lie to you. This sets us back. But signing with King and Country would've been catastrophic. You were looking out for us. Thank you."

I study Angel. He sits up straighter, but he has an uncomfortable look on his face, like he is not used to being recognized for anything good and isn't sure how to react.

Seeing the same thing I'm seeing, Eddie grins and says, "Now tell them about the guy you met at the bar."

Y

BACK AT MY APARTMENT, Angel takes a long, hot shower. We climb naked into bed with the intention of getting something started, but he's been awake for more than twenty-four hours. I hold him and stroke his damp hair as he falls asleep in my arms. Lying very still, I watch as the sunlight shifts and migrates across my apartment. When it finally hits the bed, the warmth makes me drowsy, and I fall asleep too.

I have wildly beautiful dreams. I dream of standing under an enormous tree with deep, gnarled roots. Its branches are covered with dark green leaves as big as my hands. Now I dream of walking across a bridge carved with angels. Below the bridge is a concrete river. The thin stream of silver running down its spine mirrors the gray sky above. In the near distance, just over the bridge, is a city of gold. But when I look more closely, I realize I'm not facing west toward downtown. I'm looking toward my community. I am looking east.

When I wake up, sunset has set the sky on fire. Everything in my apartment is orange, yellow and crimson.

And my Angel is with me.

Together, we wake up slowly. I take a deep breath. The bed doesn't smell like me, or him, but us—our bodies, mingled together. The sheets and blankets are tangled and twisted around us like a strange work of art we make together, in private.

He curls his big body around me. His face is close to mine. I can see where the bedsheets have pressed faint lines into his cheek. I can see the very tiny secret birthmark under his eye.

"I have something to tell you," I say.

Quietly, under the sheets, I tell him about Art. I tell him how scared I was, but how strangely calm I felt lying to Officer Gavilan. I tell him I was going to turn in Art up until the moment I saw the note he wrote to his mother inside the bag of money. Angel's body tenses up as he listens to me, but he says nothing until long after I'm finished.

"Do you feel like you did the right thing?" he asks at last.

In my mind, I go over what I did for the hundredth time since I walked away from Mrs. Aguilar's house, as I probably will go over it again and again, for the rest of my life.

"Yes," I say. "I think I did."

Angel says in Spanish, "Everyone deserves a chance to start over."

He doesn't say anything more. Instead, he drops a long line of kisses down the side of my neck and along my jaw. I wrap my arms around him and close my eyes. Under the covers, he begins to move. I feel the rigid leanness of his body. His smooth, warm skin. His cock, hard and thick and hot as a brand, pressing against the inside of my thigh.

When he kisses my lips, I flash back to the first time he kissed me in the street on that summer night more than three years ago. I was asleep then, and he woke me up—woke me up to my body. Woke me up to the possibility, however unlikely, that I might find true happiness in love with someone as beautiful—and as sweetly filthy—as Angel Rosas.

Locked in our kiss, I open my legs. I reach down and wrap my hand around him. Gently, I use him like a toy, pressing the already-slick head of his cock against my clit. I massage myself with him, soothing the never-ending ache that he has put in me.

He breaks our kiss enough to whisper against my lips, "I dream of you. I wake up, rock hard, with the taste of your pussy in my mouth." He kisses me again. "I need to taste you."

Quickly, he climbs out of bed, grabs my hips and pulls my ass to the edge of the mattress. He kneels down on the floor between my legs and gently runs his fingers over my slick, aching pussy. He studies my face as he touches me. In the red light from the windows, he looks like he is on fire.

"Princesa, I need you."

When he gives me the pure, potent pleasure of his tongue, I arch against the bed. While he licks me, he presses one long finger inside me and strokes my G-spot. As I listen to the steady, soft click of his tongue on my clit, I think, this isn't happening to me. Things like this don't happen to me. Lovers like him don't happen to me.

But then, with the knuckle of his ring finger, he strokes my ass, and I come so hard, I grab handfuls of the fitted sheet like the reins on a runaway horse and yank it right off the mattress.

He's laughing at me.

"I'm going to—ah—I'm going to get you," I say, gasping through my orgasm, completely at his mercy.

While I'm still trembling and gasping, Angel stands up. He reaches for the condoms in the nightstand, but I stop him.

"No. It's time," I whisper to him. "We don't have to use those."

"Are you sure?"

"Yes. I put it in my calendar after my appointment with the doctor. The pills are effective now." I smile. "All systems go."

He climbs back into bed, takes my hands and pins them to the mattress above my head. He kisses me for such a long time that my brain wanders in spiraling loops of pleasure. When I open my eyes at last, Angel is looking straight at me. His eyes are golden brown, molten in the sunlight. He lets go of my hands. There are red marks on my wrists from his grip. His perfect lips are full and swollen and even more beautiful than before.

"I have never done this," he says. "Not once."

"I think you'll like it," I say.

Eyes locked on his, I reach for his hips. He slides forward on his knees, takes his cock in his hand and rests the big, slick head in the tender opening of my pussy. The twinge of another orgasm ripples through me, and I groan, holding back.

I had no idea that love could be a fire you threw yourself into, every day, burning away the bullshit again and again until you were the strongest, cleanest version of yourself. A purification. An affirmation.

We are breathing hard. I reach up and run my hands over his shoulders, his chest and his pretty brown nipples. I run my middle finger down the deep crease dividing the cans in his ridiculous six-pack. I think, how could someone be so beautiful have such a beautiful spirit? And why is he here with me?

"Deanna, you are everything I've ever wanted," he says. "Smart, gorgeous, brave, strong, sexy." His deep voice hums in my blood. "I will love you as long as you let me."

"Then let's see about forever," I whisper.

Like a curtain lifting, his kind eyes turn fierce. He arches over me, all desire. And all at once, I see him, the survivor and the fighter. The lover and the storyteller.

The guardian.

Finally here—finally home.

TEN MONTHS LATER

EPILOGUE
ANGEL

YOU WANT A HERO.

Before the story ends, you should know—I'm not him.

I'm not your hero.

A hero is my brother Sal, who brought our family into the light. A hero is my brother Eddie, who broke our ties with the past so that we could move forward. They survived years of gangs, prison and unfathomable violence. The things they've seen will stay with them for the rest of their lives.

All I've done is walk down the road they built—a road that leads to the big, beautiful building in front of me.

It's early, just after dawn.

The brewery is closed. Deanna is sitting at a table on the new covered patio. She's wearing a red dress and the earrings I got her for Christmas last year. She's listening to Carmen, who's telling a story while braiding Julia's hair. Their laughter rises up and weaves through the hundreds of trumpet flowers blooming along the rafters.

As if she can feel me looking at her, Deanna makes eye contact with me and smiles.

Whenever she does that, she takes my breath away.

Everyone is here. My brothers, the kids. Vanessa, in high heels as usual, is walking around the tables holding Max's hands as he learns to walk. He's wearing a tiny suit and bowtie. Even Deanna's friend Ro is here, taking photos she'll use for paintings we've recently commissioned for the taproom.

We don't spend a lot of time together like this, my family. This year has been a busy one. Vanessa and Eddie are working together to handle the brewery renovation and expanded distribution. Sal and his new cellarperson and assistant brewers are adjusting to the brewery's larger capacity and production. There's a whole crew of new employees, including two full-time drivers and two more taproom servers.

The most important addition? We've hired a dozen trainees, all of them formerly incarcerated. They are the first cohort of Eastside Brewery's job-training program, a program conceived of and coordinated by Deanna Delgado.

In our many meetings together, Carlos, his partners and I brainstormed ways to integrate Eastside Brewery into the community. The job-training program was the main component, along with local events like game nights, school fundraisers, and yes—a karaoke night. Following Deanna's father's advice about loss leaders, I worked with Vanessa and Carmen to develop Worker Wednesdays with the idea that everyone deserves a night out. With special five-dollar beers, torta sliders, bacon-wrapped hot dogs and non-alcoholic Angel's Brew, the evening event draws families from the neighborhood. On Wednesday evenings, they listen to live music on the large kid-friendly patio furnished by none other than Casa Delgado, who offered us a discount—but not a big one.

One of my jobs as brand ambassador is to spread the word about Eastside Brewery. We'll never be a national brand, and we'll never run with the big dogs. But putting cans in the right hands is my goal. And after a few sit-downs, Chuckles, Dee and I brewed up something amazing. Barrio Beefs is now Eastside Brawlers, a fully licensed fight club sponsored by Eastside Beer with events scheduled all over the city. Our first fight is in January. I'm hyped.

With Deanna's support, I have found a way to stay active in the underground fight scene. The rush I feel bringing fighters together—this time legally—has overshadowed the rush I used to feel facing an opponent in the ring.

Fighting taught me the limits of my strength. But Deanna has taught me that once you find the work you were meant to do, there are no limits to what you can accomplish. Her sense of purpose inspired me to find my own. Now we fight together, side by side.

Muñeca dashes onto the patio from the parking lot.

"They're coming! They're coming!" she shouts.

Together, my family follows her out into the street. Around the corner, we can hear the procession before we can see it.

"¡Que viva Santa Cecilia! ¡Que viva!"

Santa Cecilia was a martyr, but her memory is a joyful one. She is the patron saint of musicians, especially mariachis, who hold a festival in her honor every year at Mariachi Plaza. And this year, we are all attending for a very special reason.

At the front of the procession, two women carry a painting of Santa Cecilia hung with garlands of fresh flowers. Behind them walk about a hundred mariachis of every kind, dressed in their most beautiful charro suits. The guitars, violins and brass are all polished and dazzling. Strings and trumpets soar. Guitars and guitarrones keep the rhythm of the song like a collective heartbeat. And above all, human voices rise above the streets in song.

The procession passes the brewery. In the middle of the

mass of people, I spot Juan Luis walking with the other guitar players. Dressed in his dove-gray charro suit, he is singing and smiling with his entire heart. Walking right next to him is Chinita in a matching dove-gray dress, with flowers in her hair and a bouquet in her hands. And, because she's Chinita, she's wearing bright hot pink lipstick.

Next to me, Sal puts his arm around Vanessa, who is dabbing at her eyes with a Kleenex.

"Look at them," Sal says quietly. "They look happy."

After the mass at Mariachi Plaza, we are going back to the church, where Juan Luis and Chinita will be married. Juan Luis insisted on attending the morning procession because he didn't want to miss a chance, as he put it, "to show off my beautiful bride."

Behind the musicians, we fall in with other members of the community who have joined in. Together, we walk through neighborhood streets to the plaza. Residents come out of their houses to watch and listen.

I'm a resident now too. Last month, Deanna and I moved out of her apartment in Koreatown into a small house not far from the brewery. For the first time in both our lives, we have good salaries and can start building a future instead of just surviving. For someone who had nothing for a long time, this kind of safety is strange and exhilarating.

Because I'm new to all this, Vanessa helped me set up a retirement account and a savings account. Last week, she also came with me to the jewelry district to make sure I didn't get ripped off.

The small velvet box is hidden in my pocket. It's soft and surprisingly heavy. I have a plan—during the wedding reception at the brewery, I'm going to ask Deanna for her opinion on a new merchandise shipment. When we're alone, I'll ask her to marry me.

My family and I walk in step. When we reach our destination, the procession joins the large group of mariachis already gathered in the plaza. Next to me, Deanna takes my hand. At that moment, the clouds break overhead, and bright morning sunlight falls on us like a benediction. The music swells and rises, sending a blessing to Heaven in return.

AN EASTSIDE BREWERY PLAYLIST

"The Town I Live In"—Thee Midniters
"One Time One Night"—Los Lobos
"Forever Mine"—The O'Jays
"Handful of Water"—Sofia Valdés
"Ojos Del Sol"—Y La Bamba
"Rayito de Luna"—Los Panchos
"You Don't Know Me"—Caetano Veloso
"Put Me In Jail"—Sunny & The Sunliners
"Andar Conmigo"—Julieta Venegas
"Devil or Angel"—The Clovers
"That's All"—Thee Midniters
"El Chico del Apartamento 512"—Selena
"Angel Baby"—Rosie and the Originals
"Nobody's Clown"—Los Yesterdays
"Oh My Angel"—Bertha Tillman
"Un Millón de Primaveras"—Vicente Fernández
"I'm So Proud"—The Impressions
"I Wish You Love"—Joe Bataan
"Tu Cabeza en Mi Hombro"—Enrique Guzmán

"When Somebody Loves You Back"—Teddy Pendergrass
"Las Golondrinas"—Mariachi Vargas De Tecalitlán
"Por Mujeres Como Tú"—Pepe Aguilar
"Saint Behind the Glass"—Los Lobos
"Always and Forever"—Heatwave

NOTE TO READERS

Up to one in six mothers and one in ten fathers experience perinatal mood and anxiety disorders including postpartum depression. You are not alone. Help is available. For support and resources, please talk to your physician. You can also contact Postpartum Support International at 1-800-944-4773 or visit their website at www.postpartum.net.

ACKNOWLEDGMENTS

To Jennifer Haymore, thank you helping me bring all the Rosas brothers home safe and sound. You are a miracle worker.

To Deidre Knight, I am so lucky to have you in my corner. Thank you as always for your encouragement and support.

To Oscar Ramirez, Cheryl Klein, Suleikha Snyder, Zenobia Neil, Berenice Escobedo, Fatima Djelmane Rodriguez, Jenny Nordbak and Vanessa Campos. Thank you for sharing your kindness, time and expertise with me. This book would not exist without you.

To Cinthya Cisneros, a true inspiration. Please visit her spot, La Cheve Bakery and Brews in Napa, California. I took this book's dedication from La Cheve's website: "A toast to those who watch us and smile down on us from Heaven."

A special shout-out to Elizabeth Kahn, who is very good at jumping out of cakes and cheering me up.

To Brent Hopkins, for believing in me when all I wanted to do was sob under the desk. My first reader, my compass and my heart. You are amazing.

To Jewish Family Service LA. Your postpartum support program was a vital resource for my family and me during the early days of this book. Thank you for all the work you do for our community.

To the staff and trainees at Homeboy Industries, my deepest respect and gratitude.

And most of all, to the readers, reviewers and amazing book people who have joined me on this long journey to the Eastside. The love you have shown this series over the years is unreal. Thank you, always and forever. ¡Salud! Cheers.

ABOUT THE AUTHOR

Mia Hopkins writes lush romances starring fun, sexy characters who love to get down and dirty. Her award-winning books have been featured by many publications including *The Washington Post*, *USA Today* and *Entertainment Weekly*. She lives in Los Angeles with her family.

For more information...
www.miahopkinsauthor.com

@miahopkinsxoxo

ALSO BY MIA HOPKINS

The Eastside Brewery series

Thirsty

Trashed

Tanked

The Cowboy Cocktail series

Cowboy Valentine

Cowboy Resurrection

Cowboy Player

Cowboy Karma

Cowboy Rising

The Kings of California series

Deep Down

Hollywood Honkytonk